T0171674

André Gide

LAFCADIO'S ADVENTURES

André Gide was born in Paris in 1869 and died there in 1951. He was awarded the Nobel Prize in Literature in 1947. His works include *The Immoralist, The Counterfeiters, Strait is the Gate,* the autobiography *If It Die . . . ,* and three volumes of *Journals.* He also wrote plays, essays, short stories, and books of travel.

INTERNATIONAL

BOOKS BY ANDRÉ GIDE
available from Vintage

Lafcadio's Adventures
The Immoralist
The Counterfeiters
If It Die . . .

LAFCADIO'S ADVENTURES

LAFCADIO'S ADVENTURES

A NOVEL

André Gide

Translated from the French by Dorothy Bussy

Vintage International

Vintage Books

A Division of Random House, Inc.

New York

VINTAGE INTERNATIONAL EDITION, MAY 2003

Copyright © 1925, 1928 and renewed in 1953, 1956 by Alfred A. Knopf, Inc.

All rights reserved under International and Pan-American Copyright
Conventions. Published in the United States by Vintage Books, a
division of Random House, Inc., New York. Originally published in a
French language edition as *Les Caves du Vatican* by Librairie Gallimard
in Paris in 1914. Copyright © 1914 by Librairie Gallimard. Originally
published in hardcover in the United States by Alfred A. Knopf,
a division of Random House, Inc., New York, in 1925.

Vintage is a registered trademark and Vintage International and
colophon are trademarks of Random House, Inc.

Cataloging-in-Publication Data is on file at the Library of Congress.

Vintage ISBN: 978-0-375-71338-5

www.vintagebooks.com

CONTENTS

LAFCADIO'S ADVENTURES

BOOK I: ANTHIME ARMAND-DUBOIS

*"Pour ma part, mon choix est fait. J'ai
opté pour l'athéisme social. Cet athéisme, je
l'ai exprimé depuis une quinzaine d'années,
dans une série d'ouvrages. . . ."*
—Georges Palante.
Chronique philosophique du Mercure de France
(December, 1912).

I

In 1890, during the pontificate of Leo XIII, Anthime
Armand-Dubois, unbeliever and freemason, visited Rome
in order to consult Dr. X, the celebrated specialist for
rheumatic complaints.

"What!" cried Julius de Baraglioul, his brother-in-
law. "Is it your body you are going to treat in Rome?
Pray Heaven you may realise when you get there that
your soul is in far worse case."

To which Armand-Dubois replied in a tone of excessive
commiseration:

"My poor dear fellow, just look at my shoulders."

Baraglioul was obliging; he raised his eyes and
glanced, in spite of himself, at his brother-in-law's
shoulders; they were quivering spasmodically as though
laughter, deep-seated and irrepressible, were heaving
them; and the sight of this huge half-crippled frame spending the last remnants of its physical strength in so absurd

9

a parody, was pitiable enough. Well, well! They had taken up their positions once and for all. Baraglioul's eloquence wouldn't change matters. Time perhaps? Or the secret influence of holy surroundings? . . . Julius merely said in an infinitely discouraged manner:

"Anthime, you grieve me." (The shoulders stopped quivering at once, for Anthime was fond of his brother-in-law.) "When I go to see you in Rome three years hence, at the time of the Jubilee, I trust I may find you amended!"

Veronica, at any rate, accompanied her husband in a very different frame of mind. She was as pious as her sister Marguerite and as Julius himself, and this long stay in Rome was the fulfilment of one of her dearest wishes. She was a disappointed, barren woman who filled her monotonous life with trivial, religious observances and, for lack of a child, devoted herself to nursing her spiritual aspirations. She no longer had much hope left, alas! of bringing her Anthime back to the fold. Many years had taught her the obstinacy of which that broad brow was capable, and the power of denial with which it was stamped. Father Flons had warned her:

"Madam," said he, "the most unyielding wills are the worst. You need hope for nothing but a miracle."

She had even ceased to mind much. They had no sooner settled in Rome than they arranged their private lives independently of each other—he on his side, she on hers; Veronica in the care of the household and in the pursuit of her devotions, Anthime in his scientific researches. In this way they lived beside each other, close to each other and just able to bear the contact by turning their backs to one another. Thanks to this there reigned a kind of harmony between them; a sort of semi-felicity settled down upon them; the virtue of each found its modest exercise in putting up with the faults of the other.

Their apartment, which they found by the help of an agency, combined, like most Italian houses, unlooked-for advantages with extraordinary inconveniences. It occupied the whole first floor of the Palazzo Forgetti, Via in Lucina, and had the benefit of a fair-sized terrace, where Veronica immediately set to work growing aspidistras—so difficult to grow in Paris apartments. But in order to reach this terrace one had to go through the orangery, which Anthime had immediately seized on for a laboratory, and through which it was agreed she should be allowed to pass at certain stated hours of the day.

Veronica would push open the door noiselessly and then, with her eyes on the ground, would slip furtively by, much as a convert might pass a wall covered with obscene graffiti; at the other end of the room, Anthime, stooping over some villainous operation or other, with his enormous back bulging out of the arm-chair on to which he had hooked his crutch, was a sight she scorned to behold! Anthime, on his side, pretended not to hear her. But as soon as she had passed out again, he would rise heavily from his chair, drag himself to the door, and, with tightened lips and an imperious thrust of his forefinger, would viciously snap to the latch.

This was the time when Beppo, the procurer, would come in at the other door to take his orders.

He was a little ragamuffin of twelve or thirteen years old, without either family or home. It was in front of the hotel in the Via Bocca di Leone, where the couple had stayed for a few days while they were looking for rooms, that Anthime had noticed him, soon after their arrival in Rome. Here Beppo used to attract the attention of passers-by with a grasshopper which lay cowering under a few blades of grass in a little cage made out of twisted rushes. Anthime paid six soldi for the insect and then in his broken Italian gave the boy to understand, as best he could, that he wanted some rats to be taken to the apartment in Via in Lucina, into which he was going to move the next day. Anything that crept or swam or crawled or flew served to experiment on. He was a worker in live flesh.

Beppo was a procurer born; he would have brought to market the eagle or the she-wolf from the Capitol. The profession pleased him—indulged him in his taste for thieving. He was given ten soldi a day; he helped besides in the house. Veronica at first looked on him with no favourable eye; but the moment she saw him crossing himself as he passed the image of the Madonna at the north corner of the house, she forgave him his rags and allowed him to carry water, coal and fire-wood into the kitchen; he used even to carry the basket for Veronica when she went to market—on Tuesdays and Fridays, the days when Caroline, the maid they had brought with them from Paris, was too busy at home.

Beppo disliked Veronica; but he took a fancy to the learned Anthime, who soon, instead of going laboriously down to the court-yard to take over his victims, allowed the boy to come up to his laboratory. There was an entrance to it direct from the terrace, which was connected with the court-yard by a back staircase. Anthime's heart beat quicker when he heard the light patter of the little bare feet on the tiles. But he would show no sign of it; nothing disturbed him in his work.

The boy used not to knock at the glass door: he scratched; and as Anthime remained bending over his table without answering, he would step forward three or four paces and in his fresh voice fling out a *"Permesso?"* which filled the room with azure. From his voice one would have taken him for an angel; in reality he was an under-executioner. What new victim was he bringing in the bag which he dropped on to the torture table? Anthime was often too much absorbed to open the bag at once; he threw a hasty glance at it; if he saw it stirring, he was satisfied: rats, mice, sparrows, frogs—all were welcome to this Moloch. Sometimes Beppo brought him nothing; but he came in all the same. He knew that Armand-Dubois was expecting him even empty-handed; and while the boy, standing silent beside the man of science, leaned forward to watch some abominable experiment, I wish I could certify that the man of science experienced no thrill of pleasure—no false god's vanity—at feeling the child's astonished look fall, in turn, with terror upon the animal, and with admiration upon himself.

Anthime's modest pretension, before going on to deal with human beings, was merely to reduce all the animal activities he had under observation, to what he termed "tropisms." Tropisms! The word was no sooner invented than nothing else was to be heard of; an entire category of psychologists would admit nothing in the world but tropisms. Tropisms! A sudden flood of light emanated from these syllables! Organic matter was obviously governed by the same involuntary impulses as those which turn the flower of the heliotrope to face the sun (a fact which is easily to be explained by a few simple laws of physics and thermochemistry). The order of the universe could at last be hailed as reassuringly benign. In all the motions of life, however surprising, a perfect obedience to the agent could be universally recognised.

With the purpose of wringing from the helpless animal the acknowledgment of its own simplicity, Anthime Armand-Dubois had just invented a complicated system of boxes—boxes with passages, boxes with trap-doors, boxes with labyrinths, boxes with compartments (some with food in them, some with nothing, some sprinkled with a sternutatory powder), boxes with doors of different shapes and colours—diabolical instruments, which a little later became the rage in Germany under the name of *Vexierkasten*, and were of the greatest use in helping the new school of psycho-physiologists to take another step forward in the path of unbelief. And in order to act severally on one or other of the animal's senses, on one or other portion of its brain, he blinded some, deafened others, emasculated, skinned or brained them, depriving them of one organ after another, which you would have sworn indispensable, but which the animal, for Anthime's better instruction, did without.

His paper on "Conditional Reflexes" had just revolutionised the University of Upsal; it had given rise to an acrimonious controversy, in which many of the most distinguished men of science had taken part. In the meantime fresh problems were crowding into Anthime's mind; leaving his colleagues to indulge in empty verbiage, he pressed forward his investigations in other directions, for he was bold enough to aim at storming God in His most secret strongholds.

He was not content with admitting in a general way that all activity entails expenditure, and that an animal expends simply by the exercise of its muscles or senses. After each expenditure, he asked himself: "How much?." And if the extenuated sufferer attempted to recuperate, Anthime, instead of feeding him, weighed him. To have added any further elements to the following experiment would have led to excessive complications: six rats which had been bound and kept without food, were placed on the scales every day; two of them were blind, two were one-eyed, and two could see, but the eyesight of the two latter was continually being strained by the turning of a little mechanical mill. After five days' fast, what did their respective loss of weight amount to? Every day at noon, Armand-Dubois filled in his specially prepared tables with a fresh row of triumphant figures.

II

The Jubilee was at hand. The Armand-Dubois were expecting the Baragliouls from day to day. The morning that the telegram came announcing their arrival for the same evening, Anthime went out to buy himself a neck-tie.

Anthime went out very little—as seldom as possible, because of his difficulty in getting about; Veronica used often to do his shopping for him, or the tradespeople would come themselves to take his orders from his own patterns. Anthime was past the age for worrying about

the fashion. But though he wanted his tie to be unobtrusive—a plain bow of black surah—still, he liked choos-
ing it himself. The ends of the dark brown satin spread
tie, which he had bought for the journey and worn during his stay at the hotel, were constantly coming out of
his waistcoat, which he always wore cut very low. This
tie had been replaced by a cream-coloured neckerchief,
fastened with a pin, on which he had had mounted a
large antique cameo of no particular value. Marguerite
de Baraglioul would certainly not consider this neckwear
dressy enough; it had been a great mistake to abandon
the little ready-made black bows he used habitually to
wear in Paris, and particularly foolish not to have kept
one as a pattern. What makes would they show him?
He would not settle on anything without having seen
the principal shirt-makers in the Corso and the Via dei
Condotti. For a man of fifty, loose ends were not staid
enough; yes, a plain bow made of dull black silk was
the thing. . . .

Lunch was not before one o'clock. Anthime came in
about twelve with his parcel, in time to weigh his animals.

Though he was not vain, Anthime felt he must try
on his tie before starting work. There was a broken bit
of looking-glass lying on the table, which he had used on
occasion for the purpose of provoking tropisms. He
propped it up against a cage and leant forward to look
at his own reflection.

Anthime wore his hair *en brosse;* it was still thick and
had once been red; at the present time it was of the grey-
ish yellow of worn silver-gilt; his whiskers, which were
cut short and high, had kept the same reddish tinge as
his stiff moustache. He passed the back of his hand over

his flat cheeks and under his square chin, and muttered: "Yes, yes, I'll shave after lunch."

He took the tie out of its envelope and placed it before him; unfastened his cameo pin and then took off his neckerchief. Round his powerful neck, he wore a collar of medium height with turned-down corners. And now, notwithstanding my desire to relate nothing but what is essential, I cannot pass over in silence Anthime Armand-Dubois' wen. For until I have learnt to distinguish more surely between the accidental and the necessary, what can I demand from my pen but the most rigorous fidelity? And, indeed, who could affirm that this wen had no share, no weight, in the decisions of what Anthime called his *free* thought? He was more willing to overlook his sciatica; but this paltry trifle was a thing for which he could not forgive Providence.

It had made its appearance, without his knowing how, shortly after his marriage; and at first it had been merely an inconsiderable wart, south-east of his left ear, just where the hair begins to grow; for a long time he was able to conceal this excrescence in the thickness of his hair, which he combed over it in a curl; Veronica herself had not noticed it, till once, in the course of a nocturnal caress, her hand had suddenly encountered it.

"Dear me!" she had exclaimed. "What have you got there?"

And, as though the swelling, once discovered, had no further reason for discretion, it grew in a few months to the size of an egg—a partridge's—a guinea-fowl's—and then a hen's. There it stopped, while his hair, as it grew scantier, exposed it more and more to view between its meagre strands. At forty-six years of age, Anthime

Armand-Dubois could have no further pretensions to good looks; he cut his hair close and adopted a style of collar of medium height, with a kind of recess in it, which hid and at the same time revealed the wen. But enough of Anthime's wen!

He put the tie round his neck. In the middle of the tie was a little metal slide, through which a fastening of tape was passed and then kept in place by a spring clip. An ingenious contrivance—but no sooner was the tape inserted into the slide than it came unsewn and the tie fell on to the operating-table. There was no help for it but to have recourse to Veronica. She came running at the summons.

"Just sew this thing on for me, will you?" said Anthime.

"Machine-made," she muttered, "rubbishy stuff!"

"It was certainly not sewn on very well."

Veronica used always to wear, stuck into the left breast of her morning gown, two needles, threaded one with white cotton, the other with black. Without troubling to sit down, she did her mending standing beside the glass door.

She was a stoutish woman, with marked features; as obstinate as himself, but pleasant on the whole and generally smiling, so that a trace of moustache had not hardened her face.

"She has her good points," thought Anthime, as he watched her plying her needle. "I might have married a flirt who would have deceived me, or a minx who would have deserted me, or a chatterbox who would have deaved me, or a goose who would have driven me mad, or a cross-patch like my sister-in-law."

"Thank you," he said, less grumpily than usual, as Veronica finished her work and departed.

With his new tie round his neck, Anthime engrossed himself in his work. No voice was raised; there was silence round him—silence in his heart. He had already weighed the blind rats. But what was this? The one-eyed rats were stationary. He went on to weigh the sound pair. Suddenly he started with such violence that his crutch rolled on the ground. Stupefaction! The sound rats . . . he weighed them over again—there was no denying it—since yesterday, the sound rats had *gained* in weight! A ray of light flashed into his mind.

"Veronica!"

He picked up his crutch and with a tremendous effort rushed to the door.

"Veronica!"

Once more she came running, anxious to oblige. Then, as he stood in the doorway, he asked solemnly:

"Who has been touching my rats?"

No answer. Slowly, articulating each word, as if Veronica had ceased to understand the language, he repeated:

"Someone has been feeding them while I was out. Was it you, may I ask?"

Picking up her courage, she turned towards him, almost aggressively:

"You were letting them die of hunger, poor creatures! I haven't interfered with your experiment in the least; I merely gave them . . ."

But at this he seized her by the sleeve and limping

back to the table, dragged her with him. There he pointed to his tables of records.

"Do you see these papers, Madam? For one fortnight I have been noting here my observations on these animals. My colleague Potier is expecting my notes to read to the Académie des Sciences at the sitting of May 17th next. To-day, April 15th, what am I to put down in this row of figures? What *can* I put down?"

And as she uttered not a word, he began scratching on the blank paper with the square end of his forefinger, as if it were a pen, and continued:

"On that day Madame Armand-Dubois, the investigator's wife, listening to the dictates of her tender heart, committed—what am I to call it?—the indiscretion—the blunder—the folly . . . ?"

"No! say I took pity on the poor creatures—victims of an insensate curiosity."

He drew himself up with dignity:

"If that is your attitude, you will understand, Madam, that I must beg you henceforth to use the back staircase when you go to look after your plants."

"Do you suppose it's any pleasure to me to come into your old hole?"

"Then, pray, for the future, refrain from coming into it."

And, in order to add emphasis to his words with the eloquence of gesture, he seized his records and tore them into little bits.

For a fortnight, he had said; in reality, his rats had been kept fasting for only four days. And his irritation, no doubt, worked itself off with this exaggeration of his grievance, for at table he was able to show an unruffled brow; he pushed equanimity even to the point of holding out to his spouse the right hand of reconciliation. For he was still more anxious than Veronica that the religious and proper Baragliouls should not be offered the spectacle of disagreements, which they would certainly lay to the door of Anthime's opinions.

At about five o'clock Veronica changed her morning gown for a black cloth coat and skirt and started for the station to meet Marguerite and Julius, who were due to arrive in Rome at six o'clock.

Anthime went to shave; he had consented to exchange his neckerchief for a black bow; that must be sufficient; he disliked ceremony and saw no reason why his sister-in-law's presence should make him forswear his alpaca coat, his white waistcoat, spotted with blue, his duck trousers and his comfortable black leather slippers without heels, which he used to wear even out of doors, and which were excusable because of his lameness.

He picked up the torn bits of paper, pieced them together, and carefully copied them out while he was waiting for the Baragliouls.

III

The Baragliouls (the *gl* is pronounced Italian fashion, as in *Broglie* [the duke of] and in *miglionnaire*) came originally from Parma. It was a Baraglioul (Alessandro) who, in 1514, married as his second wife Filippa Visconti, a few months after the annexation of the Duchy to the Papal States. Another Baraglioul (also Alessandro) distinguished himself at the battle of Lepanto, and was assassinated in 1589, in circumstances which still remain mysterious. It would be easy, though not very interesting, to trace the family fortunes up till 1807, the year in which France took over the Duchy of Parma and in which Robert de Baraglioul, Julius's grandfather, settled at Pau. In 1828 Charles X bestowed on him the title of Count—a title which was destined to be borne with honour by his third son (the two elder died in infancy), Juste-Agénor, whose keen intelligence and diplomatic talents shone with such brilliancy and carried off such triumphant successes in the ambassadorial career.

Juste-Agénor's second child, Julius, who since his marriage had lived a blameless life, had had several love affairs in his youth. But at any rate he could do himself this justice—he had never placed his affections beneath him. The fundamental distinction of his nature and that kind of moral elegance which was apparent in the slightest of his writings, had always prevented him from giving rein to his desires and from following a path down which his curiosity as a novelist would doubtless have urged him. His blood flowed calmly but not coldly, as many beautiful and aristocratic ladies might have testified. . . . And I should not have made any allusion to this fact, had not his early novels made it abundantly clear—to which, indeed, their remarkable success in the fashionable world was partly due. The high distinction of the public to which they appealed enabled one of them to appear in the *Correspondant* and two others in the *Revue des Deux Mondes*. And thus he found himself, almost without an effort and while he was still young, on the high road to the Academy. Already this destiny seemed marked out

for him by his fine presence, by the grave unction of his
look and by the pensive paleness of his brow.

Anthime professed great contempt for the advantages of
rank, fortune and looks—to Julius's not unnatural morti-
fication—but he appreciated a certain kindliness of disposition in Julius and a lack of skill in argument so great
that free thought was often able to carry off the victory.

At six o'clock Anthime heard his guests' carriage draw
up at the door. He went out to meet them on the landing. Julius came up first. In his hard felt hat and his
overcoat with silk *revers,* he would have seemed dressed
for visiting rather than for travelling, had it not been for
the plaid shawl he was carrying on his arm; the long
journey had not in the least tried him. Marguerite de
Baraglioul followed, leaning on her sister's arm; she, on
the other hand, was in a pitiable state; her bonnet and
chignon awry, she stumbled upstairs with her face half
hidden by her handkerchief, which she was holding
pressed up against it like a poultice.

As she drew near Anthime, "Marguerite has a bit of
coal dust in her eye," whispered Veronica.

Julie, their daughter, a charming little girl of nine years
old, and the maid, brought up the rear, in silent
consternation.

With a person like Marguerite, there was no question
of making light of the matter. Anthime suggested sending for an oculist; but Marguerite knew all about the
reputation of Italian saw-bones and wouldn't hear of such
a thing for the world. In a die-away voice she murmured:

"Some cold water! Just a little cold water! Oh!"

"Yes, my dear Marguerite," went on Anthime, "cold water may relieve you for the moment, by bringing down the inflammation, but it won't cure the evil." Then, turning to Julius: "Were you able to see what it was?"

"Not very well. As soon as the train stopped and I wanted to look in her eye, Marguerite got into such a state of nerves . . ."

"Don't say that, Julius. You were horribly clumsy. Instead of lifting my eyelid properly, you pulled my eyelashes so far back . . ."

"Shall I have a try?" said Anthime. "Perhaps I shall be able to manage better."

A facchino brought up the luggage, and Caroline lighted a lamp.

"Come, my dear," said Veronica, "you can't do the operation in the passage." And she led the Baraglioul to their room.

The Armand-Dubois' apartment was arranged round the four sides of an inner court-yard, on to which looked the windows of a corridor which ran from the entrance hall to the orangery. Into this corridor opened, first, the dining-room, then the drawing-room (an enormous badly furnished corner room, which the Armand-Dubois left unused), then two spare rooms, which had been arranged, the larger for the two Baraglioul and the smaller for Julie, and lastly the Armand-Dubois' bedroom. All these rooms communicated with each other on the inside. The kitchen and two servants' rooms were on the other side of the landing. . . .

"Please, don't all come crowding round," `moaned Marguerite. "Julius, can't you see after the luggage?"

Veronica made her sister sit down in an arm-chair and held the lamp while Anthime set about his examination.

"Yes, it's very much inflamed. Suppose you were to take off your bonnet?"

But Marguerite, fearing perhaps that in the disordered state of her hair certain artificial aids might become visible, declared she would take it off later; a plain bonnet with strings wouldn't prevent her from leaning her head back against the chair.

"So, you want me to remove the mote out of your eye before I take the beam out of my own," said Anthime, with a kind of snigger. "That seems to me very contrary to the teaching of Scripture."

"Oh, please don't make me regret accepting your kindness."

"I'll say no more. . . . With the corner of a clean handkerchief . . . I see it. . . . Good heavens! Don't be frightened! Look up! There it is!"

And Anthime, with the corner of the handkerchief, removed an infinitesimal speck of dust.

"Thank you! Thank you! I should like to be left alone now. I've a frightful headache."

While Marguerite was resting and Julius unpacking with the maid and Veronica looking after the dinner, Anthime took charge of Julie and led her off to his room. His niece, whom he had left as a tiny child, was hardly recognisable in this tall girl, whose smile had become grave as well as ingenuous. After a little, as he was holding her close to his knee, talking such childish trivialities as he hoped might please her, his eye was caught by a thin silver chain which the child was wearing round her neck. "Medallions!" his instinct told him. An indiscreet jerk of his big forefinger brought them into sight outside her bodice, and, hiding his morbid repugnance under a show of astonishment:

"What are these little things?" he asked.

Julie understood well enough that the question was not a serious one, but why should she take offence?

"What, uncle? Have you never seen any medallions before?"

"Not I, my dear," he lied; "they aren't exactly pretty pretty, but I suppose they're of some use?"

And as even the serenest piety is not inconsistent with innocent playfulness, the child pointed with her finger to a photograph of herself, which she had caught sight of propped up against the glass over the mantelpiece, and said:

"There's a picture of a little girl there, uncle, who isn't pretty pretty either. What use can it be to you?"

Surprised at finding a Christian capable of such pointed repartee and doubtless of such good sense too, Uncle Anthime was for a moment taken aback. But he really couldn't embark on a metaphysical argument with a little girl of nine years old. He smiled. The child made use of her advantage immediately, and, holding out her little sacred images:

"This," said she, "is my patron saint, St. Julia; and this, the Sacred Heart of Our . . ."

"And haven't you got one of God?" interrupted Anthime absurdly.

The child answered with perfect simplicity:

"No, people don't make any of God. But this is the prettiest—Our Lady of Lourdes. Aunt Fleurissoire gave it to me; she brought it back from Lourdes; I put it round my neck the day that Papa and Mamma offered me to the Virgin."

This was too much for Anthime. Without attempting for a moment to understand all the ineffable loveliness that such images call up—the month of May, the white and blue procession of children—he gave way to his crazy desire to blaspheme.

"So the Holy Virgin didn't want to have anything to do with you, since you are still with us?"

The child made no answer. Did she realise already that the best answer to certain impertinences is to say nothing? As a matter of fact, after this senseless question, it was not Julie, it was the unbeliever that blushed; and then, to hide this moment of confusion—this slight qualm which ever secretly accompanies impropriety—the uncle pressed a respectful and atoning kiss on his niece's candid brow.

"Why do you pretend to be so naughty, Uncle Anthime?"

The child was not to be deceived; at bottom, this impious man of science had a tender heart.

Then why this obstinate resistance?

At that moment Adèle opened the door.

"Madame is asking for Miss Julie."

Marguerite de Baraglioul, it seems, was afraid of her brother-in-law's influence and had no wish to leave her daughter alone with him for long. He ventured to say as much to her in a whisper a little later on, as the family were going in to dinner. But Marguerite, with an eye still slightly inflamed, glanced at Anthime:

"Afraid of you? My dear friend, Julie is more likely

to convert a dozen infidels like you than to be moved
a hair's breadth by any of your scoffs. No, no! Our
faith is not so easily shaken as that. But still, don't
forget that she is a child. She knows that in an age as
corrupt as this, and in a country as shamefully governed
as ours, nothing but blasphemy can be looked for.
Nevertheless, it's sad that her first experience of offence
should come from her uncle, whom we should so much
like her to respect."

IV

Would Anthime feel the calming effect of words so
temperate and so wise?

Yes; during the first two courses (the dinner, which
was good but plain, did not comprise more than three
dishes altogether) and as long as the talk meandered in
domestic fashion round about subjects that were not
contentious. Out of consideration for Marguerite's eye,
they first talked about eyesight and oculists (the Baragliouls pretended not to notice that Anthime's wen had
grown); then about Italian cooking—out of politeness
to Veronica—with allusions to the excellence of her
dinner; then Anthime enquired after the Fleurissoires,
whom the Baragliouls had recently been to see at Pau,
and after the Comtesse de Saint-Prix, Julius's sister, who
was in the habit of spending her holidays in that neighbourhood; and then after the Baragliouls' charming elder
daughter, whom they would have liked to bring with them
to Rome, but who could never be persuaded to leave her
work at the Hospital for Sick Children, in the Rue de
Sèvres, where she went every morning to tend the suffer-

ing little ones. Julius then broached the serious subject of the expropriation of Anthime's property: Anthime, when travelling as a young man for the first time in Egypt, had bought a piece of land, which, owing to its inconvenient situation, had hitherto been of very little value; but there had lately been some question of making the new Cairo-to-Heliopolis railway pass through it. There is no doubt that the Armand-Dubois' budget, which had suffered from risky speculations, was in great need of this windfall. Julius, however, before leaving Paris, had discussed the affair with Maniton, the consulting engineer of the projected line, and he advised his brother-in-law not to raise his hopes too high—for the whole thing might very well end in smoke. Anthime, for his part, made no mention of the fact that the Lodge, which always backs its friends, was looking after his interests.

Anthime spoke to Julius about his candidature to the Academy and his chances of getting in; he spoke with a smile, for he had very little belief in them; and Julius himself pretended to a calm and, as it were, resigned indifference. What was the use of saying that his sister, the Comtesse de Saint-Prix, had got Cardinal André up her sleeve, and in consequence the other fifteen immortals who always voted with him? Anthime then said a vague word or two of sketchy compliment about Julius's last novel, *On the Heights*. As a matter of fact he had thought it an extremely bad book; and Julius, who was not in the least deceived, hurriedly put himself in the right by saying:

"I was quite aware that you wouldn't like a book of that kind."

Anthime might have excused the book. But this allusion to his opinions touched him in a sore place; he began to protest that they never in the least influenced his judgment of works of art in general, or of his brother-in-law's novels in particular. Julius smiled condescendingly, and, in order to change the subject, enquired after his brother-in-law's sciatica, which he inadvertently called "lumbago." Ah! why had he not enquired instead about his scientific researches? Then it would have been a satisfaction to answer him. But his "lumbago"! It would be his wen next, most likely! But his brother-in-law, apparently, knew nothing about his scientific researches—he *chose* to know nothing about them. . . . Anthime was exasperated and his "lumbago" was hurting him. With a sneering laugh, he answered viciously:

"Am I better? Ha, ha, ha! You'd be very sorry to hear that I was!"

Julius was astonished and begged his brother-in-law to say why such uncharitable feelings should be imputed to him.

"Good heavens! You Catholics aren't above calling in a doctor when one of you falls ill; but when the patient gets well, it's no thanks to science—it's all because of the prayers you said while the doctor was looking after him. You would think it a gross impertinence if a man who didn't go to church got better."

"Would you rather remain ill than go to church?" said Marguerite, earnestly.

What made her poke *her* oar in? As a rule she never took part in conversations of general interest, and as soon as Julius opened his mouth, she would meekly efface herself. This was man's talk. Pooh! Why should he show her any consideration? He turned to her abruptly:

"My dear girl, kindly understand that if I knew that an instantaneous and certain cure lay to my hand, there— do you hear?—*there!*" (and he pointed wildly to the salt-cellar) "but that before taking it, I must beg the Principal" (this was his jocose name for the Supreme Being on the days when he was in a bad temper) "or beseech him to intervene—to upset for my sake the established order—the natural order—the venerable order of cause and effect, I wouldn't take his cure. I wouldn't! I should say to the Principal: 'Don't come bothering me with your miracle! I don't want it—at any price! I don't want it!' "

He stressed each word—each syllable. The loudness of his voice matched the fury of his temper. He was frightful.

"You wouldn't want it? Why not?" asked Julius, very calmly.

"Because it would force me to believe in God—who doesn't exist," he cried, banging his fist down on the table.

Marguerite and Veronica exchanged anxious glances, and then both looked towards Julie.

"I think it's time to go to bed, my darling," said her mother. "Make haste. We'll come and say good night to you when you're in bed."

The child, terrified by the dreadful words and diabolical appearance of her uncle, fled.

"If I am to be cured, I want to owe it to no one but myself. So there!"

"Then what about the doctor?" ventured Marguerite.

"I pay him for his visits. We are quits."

"Whilst gratitude to God," said Julius in his gravest, deepest voice, "would bind you. . . ."

"Yes, brother Julius, and that is why I don't pray."

"Others pray for you, my dear."

This remark came from Veronica, who up till now had said nothing. At the gentle sound of her well-known voice, Anthime started and completely lost all self-control. Contradictions and incoherences came jostling from his lips. "You have no right to pray for a person against his will, to ask for a favour for him without his leave. It's treachery! You haven't gained much by it, however. That's one comfort. It'll teach you what your prayers are worth. Much to be proud of, I'm sure! . . . But, after all, perhaps you didn't go on praying long enough."

"Don't be alarmed! I *am* going on," Veronica announced in the same gentle voice as before. And then, smiling quietly, as though she stood outside the range of his tempestuous anger, she went on to tell Marguerite that every evening, without missing a single one, she burnt two candles for Anthime and placed them beside the wayside figure of the Madonna standing at the north corner of the house—the same figure in front of which she had once caught Beppo crossing himself. There was a recess in the wall close by, into which the boy used to tuck himself, when he wanted to rest. Veronica could be sure of finding him there at the right time. She couldn't have managed by herself, as the shrine was too high up—out of the reach of passers-by. But Beppo (he was a slim lad now of about fifteen) by clinging to the stones and to a metal ring that was in the wall, scrambled up and was able to place two candles, already lighted and flaring, beside the holy image. . . . The conversation insensibly drifted away from Anthime—closed over him, so to speak, as the sisters went on to talk of the simple, touching piety of the common folk, who love most to honour the rudest statues. . . . Anthime was completely engulfed. What! not content with feeding his rats behind his back, Veronica must needs now burn candles for him! His own wife! And, moreover, mix Beppo up in all this idiotic tomfoolery. . . . Ha, ha! We'll soon see!

The blood rushed to Anthime's head; he choked; his temples drummed a tattoo. With a huge effort he rose, knocking down his chair behind him. He emptied a glass of water on to his napkin and mopped his forehead. Was he going to be ill? Veronica was all concern. He pushed her away brutally, made for the door and slammed it behind him; they heard his halting step, accompanied by the dull thud of his crutch, clatter down the passage.

This abrupt departure left them perplexed and saddened. For a few moments they remained silent.

"My poor dear!" said Marguerite at last. This incident served once again to illustrate the difference between the two sisters. Marguerite's soul was of that admirable stuff out of which God makes his martyrs. She was aware of it and with all her might yearned to suffer. Life unfortunately offered her little to complain of. Her lot overflowed with blessings, so that she was reduced to seeking occasions for her power of endurance, in the trifling vexations of daily life. She did her best to find thorns in the smoothest path and caught eagerly at anything that had the smallest resemblance to a bramble. It must be admitted that she was an adept in the art of managing to get herself slighted; but Julius seemed con-

tinually endeavouring to give her less and less scope for
exercising her virtues. Is it to be wondered at, then,
that her attitude towards him was always discontented
and complaining? How splendid her vocation would
have been with a husband like Anthime! She was vexed
to see her sister make so little of her opportunities.
Veronica, indeed, eluded every grievance; sarcasms and
jeers alike slipped off her smiling unruffled smoothness like
water off a duck's back. She had no doubt long ago
become reconciled to the solitude of her life; Anthime,
moreover, didn't really treat her badly—she didn't grudge
him speaking his mind. She explained that the reason
he spoke so loud was that he found it so difficult to move.
His temper would be less violent if his legs were more
active; and as Julius asked where he could have gone to,
"To the laboratory," she answered, and when Marguerite
added that perhaps it would be as well to go and see
whether he hadn't been taken ill after such a fit of anger,
she assured her it was better to let him get over it by
himself and not pay too much attention to his outburst.

"Let us finish dinner quietly," she concluded.

V

No! Uncle Anthime had not stayed in his laboratory.
He had passed rapidly through the room in which the
six rats were bringing their long-drawn sufferings to a
close. Why did he not linger on the terrace which lay
bathed in the glimmer of the western sky? Perhaps the
celestial radiance of the evening might have calmed his
rebel soul—inclined his . . . But no, he stopped his ears
to so wise a counsel. He went on, took the difficult wind-

ing stairs and reached the court-yard, which he crossed.
To us, who know what efforts each painful step cost him,
this crippled haste seems tragic. When shall we see him
show such savage energy in a good cause? Sometimes
a groan escaped his lips; his features were distorted.
Where would his impious rage lead him?

The Madonna, who stood in the corner niche, was
watching over the house and perhaps interceding for the
blasphemer himself. Grace and radiance—whose light
was borrowed from Heaven's own—streamed from her
outstretched hands upon the world below. This figure
of the Virgin was not one of those modern statues, made
out of Blafaphas' newly invented *Roman Plaster,* such as
the firm of Fleurissoire and Lévichon turn out by the
gross. In our eyes the very artlessness of the figure
makes it all the more expressive of the people's simple
piety—gives it an added beauty—an enhanced eloquence.
The colourless face, the gleaming hands, the blue cloak,
were lighted by a lantern, which hung some way in front
of the statue; a zinc roof projected over the niche and at
the same time sheltered the ex-votos, which were fixed to
the wall on each side of it. A little metal door, of which
the beadle of the parish kept the key, was within arm's
reach and protected the fastening of the cord to which
the lantern was attached. Two candles burnt day and
night before the statue. Fresh ones had been placed there
that afternoon by Veronica. At the sight of these candles
which were burning, he knew, for him, the unbeliever's
wrath blazed out afresh. Beppo, who was munching a
crust and a stalk or two of fennel in his hole in the wall,
came running to meet him. Without answering his
friendly greeting, Anthime seized him by the shoulder and,

bending down, whispered something in his ear. What could it have been to make the boy shudder? "No! No!" he protested. Anthime took out a five-lira note from his waistcoat pocket. Beppo grew indignant. . . . Later on he might steal perhaps—perhaps he might even kill—who knows with what sordid defilement poverty might not smirch his brow? But raise his hand against his protectress?—against the Virgin to whom every night he breathed out a last sigh before he slept, and whom, every morning when he woke, he greeted with his first smile? Anthime might try in turn entreaties, blows, bribes, threats; nothing would make him yield.

But don't let us exaggerate. It was not precisely the Virgin that was the object of Anthime's fury. It was more particularly Veronica's candles that enraged him. But Beppo's simple soul could make nothing of such distinctions; and, moreover, the candles had by now been consecrated; no one had the right to extinguish them.

Anthime, exasperated by this resistance, pushed the boy away. He would act alone. Setting his shoulder against the wall, he seized his crutch by the lower end and, swinging it backwards, hurled it with terrific violence into the air. The wooden missile rebounded from the inside wall of the niche and fell noisily to the ground, bringing with it some fragment or other of broken plaster. He picked up his crutch and stepped back to look at the niche. . . . Hell and fury! The two candles were still burning! But what was this? The statue's right hand had disappeared and in its place there was nothing to be seen but a piece of black iron rod.

For a moment he gazed with disillusioned eyes at the

melancholy result of his handiwork. That it should end
in such a ludicrous assault! . . .

Fie! Oh, fie! He turned to look for Beppo; the boy
had vanished. Darkness was closing in; Anthime was
alone; but what was this he caught sight of, lying on the
pavement?—The fragment which he had brought down
with his crutch; he picked it up—it was a little plaster
hand, which with a shrug of his shoulders he slipped into
his waistcoat pocket.

Shame on his brow and rage in his heart, the iconoclast
went up again to his laboratory; he wanted to work but
the abominable effort he had just made had shattered him.
He had no heart for anything but sleep. He would certainly not say good night to anyone before he went to
bed. And yet, just as he was entering his room, a sound
of voices stopped him. The door of the next room was
open and he stole into the darkness of the passage.

Little Julie in her night-gown, like some tiny familiar
angel, was kneeling on her bed; at the head of the bed,
full in the light of the lamp, Veronica and Marguerite
were both on their knees; a little further off, Julius, with
one hand on his heart and the other covering his eyes, was
standing in an attitude at once devout and manly; they
were listening to the child's prayers. The deep silence
in which the scene was wrapped brought back to Anthime's recollection a certain tranquil, golden evening on
the banks of the Nile. Like the blue smoke that had
risen that evening into the pureness of the sky, the little
girl's innocent prayer rose straight to Heaven.

Her prayers were no doubt drawing to a close; the
child had gone through all the usual formula, and was

praying now in her own words, out of the fullness of her heart; she prayed for the little orphans, for the sick, for the poor, for sister Genevieve, for Aunt Veronica, for Papa, for dear Mamma's eye to be well soon. . . . As he listened, Anthime's heart grew sore within him; from the threshold of the door where he was standing, he called out in a voice that was meant to be ironical, and loud enough to be heard at the other end of the room:

"And is God not to be asked anything for Uncle Anthime?"

And then, to everyone's astonishment, the child, in an extraordinarily steady voice, went on:

"And please, dear God, forgive Uncle Anthime his sins."

These words struck home to the very depths of the atheist's heart.

VI

That night Anthime had a dream. There was a knock at his bedroom door—not the door into the passage, nor the door into the next room; the knock was at another door, which he had not noticed in his waking hours and which led straight into the street. That was why he was frightened, and at first, instead of answering, lay low. There was a faint light which made the smallest objects in the room visible—a sort of dim effulgence, such as a night-light gives—but there was no night-light. As he was trying to make out where this light could come from, there was a second knock.

"What do you want?" he cried in a trembling voice.

At the third knock, he fell into a kind of daze; an extraordinary feeling of yielding—in which every trace of

fear was swallowed up—paralysed him. (He called it afterwards a tender resignation.) He suddenly felt both
that he was incapable of resistance and that the door was
going to open. It opened noiselessly and for a moment
he saw nothing but a dark alcove, which at first was
empty, but in which, as he gazed, there appeared, as in a
shrine, the figure of the Holy Virgin. At first he took
the small white form for his little niece Julie, dressed as
he had just seen her, with her bare feet showing below her
night-gown; but a second later he recognised her whom he
had insulted; I mean that her appearance was the same as
the wayside statue's; he could even make out the injury
to her right arm; and yet the pale face was still more
beautiful, still more smiling than before. Without seeming to walk exactly, she came gliding towards him, and
when she was close up against his bedside:

"Dost thou think, thou who hast hurt me," she asked,
"that I have need of my hand to cure thee?" And with
this she raised her empty sleeve and struck him.

It seemed to him that it was from her that this strange
effulgence emanated. But when the iron rod suddenly
pierced his side he felt a stab of frightful pain and woke
up in the dark.

Anthime was perhaps a quarter of an hour before coming to his senses. He felt in his whole body a strange kind
of torpor—of stupefied numbness—and then a tingling
which was almost pleasant, so that he doubted now
whether he had really felt any pain in his side; he could
not make out where his dream had begun or ended, and
whether he was awake now or whether he had dreamt
then. He pinched himself, felt himself all over, put his

arm out and finally struck a match. Veronica was asleep beside him with her face to the wall.

Then, untucking the sheets and flinging aside the blankets, he let the tips of his bare feet slide down, till they rested on his slippers. His crutch was there, leaning beside the bedside table; without taking it, he raised himself by pushing with his hands against the bed; then he thrust his feet well into the leather slippers; then, stood bolt upright on his legs; then, still doubtful, with one arm stretched in front of him and one behind, he took a step— two steps alongside the bed—three steps; then across the room. . . . Holy Virgin! Was he . . . ?

Noiselessly and rapidly he slipped into his trousers, put on his waistcoat, his coat. . . . Stop, my pen! What rashness is yours? What matters the cure of a paralysed body, what matter all its clumsy agitations, in comparison with the flutterings of a newly liberated soul, when first she tries her wings?

When, a quarter of an hour later, Veronica, disturbed by some kind of presentiment, awoke, she became uneasy at feeling that Anthime was not beside her; she became still more uneasy when, having struck a match, she saw his crutch (which of necessity never left him) still standing by the bedside. The match went out between her fingers, for Anthime had taken the candle with him when he left the room; Veronica hastily slipped on a few things as best she could in the dark, and then in her turn leaving the room, she followed the thread of light which shone from beneath the laboratory door.

"Anthime, are you there, my dear?"

No answer. Veronica, listening with all her might and main, heard a singular noise. Then, sick with anxiety, she pushed open the door.   What she saw transfixed her with amazement.

Her Anthime was there, straight in front of her.   He was not sitting; he was not standing; the top of his head was on a level with the table and in the full light of the candle, which he had placed upon it; Anthime, the learned man of science, Anthime the atheist, who for many a long year had bowed neither his stiff knee nor his stubborn will (for it was remarkable how in his case body and soul kept pace with each other)—Anthime was kneeling!

He was on his knees, was Anthime; he was holding in his two hands a little fragment of plaster, which he was bathing with his tears, and covering with frantic kisses. At first he took no notice of her, and Veronica, astounded at this mystery, was afraid either to withdraw or to go forward and was already on the point herself of falling on her knees in the doorway opposite her husband, when, oh, miracle! he rose without an effort, walked towards her with a steady step, and, catching her in his arms:

"Henceforth," he said, as he pressed her to his heart and bent his face towards hers, "henceforth, my dearest, we will pray together."

VII

The conversion of the unbeliever could not long remain a secret.   Julius de Baraglioul did not delay a single day before communicating the news to Cardinal André in France, who spread it abroad amongst the conservative party and the higher clergy; while Veronica announced it to Father Anselm, so that it soon reached the ears of the Vatican.

Doubtless Armand-Dubois had been the object of special mercy. It would perhaps be imprudent to affirm that the Virgin had actually appeared to him, but even if he had seen her only in a dream, his cure was still a matter of fact—incontrovertible, demonstrable and assuredly miraculous. Now if perhaps in Anthime's opinion it was enough that he should have been cured, in the Church's it was not. A public recantation was demanded of him, which was to be accompanied by a ceremony of unusual splendour.

"What!" said Father Anselm to him a few days later, "in the course of your errors you have propagated heresy by all the means in your power, and now you would elude the duty of allowing Heaven to dispose of you for its own high purposes of instruction and example? How many souls have been turned aside from the true Light by the false glimmers of your misguided science? It lies with you now to bring them back to the fold, and you hesitate? It lies with you? Nay! It is your strict duty. I will not insult you by supposing that you do not feel it."

No! Anthime would not elude his duty. But he could not help fearing its consequences. He had heavy pecuniary interests in Egypt which, as we have seen, were in the hands of the freemasons. What could he do without the help of the Lodge? And how could he hope to be assisted by the very institution he was flouting? Formerly he had expected fortune at their hands, and now he saw himself absolutely ruined.

He confided as much to Father Anselm, and Father Anselm, who had not been aware of Anthime's high rank as a freemason, rejoiced at the thought that his recantation would be all the more striking. Two days later Anthime's high rank was no longer a secret for any of the readers of the *Osservatore* and the *Santa Croce*.

"You are ruining me," said Anthime.

"On the contrary, my son," answered Father Anselm, "we are bringing you salvation. As for your material needs, take no thought for them. The Church will provide. I have dwelt at length upon your case to Cardinal Pazzi, who is going to speak to Rampolla about it. I may tell you, moreover, that the Holy Father himself is informed of your recantation. The Church understands what you have sacrificed for her sake, and will undertake that you do not suffer. Don't you think, though, that upon this occasion you have over-estimated" (and he smiled) "the value of the freemasons' influence? Not but what I know well enough that they must be reckoned with only too seriously. Never mind! Have you calculated the amount that their hostility may cost you? Tell it me roughly" (he raised his left forefinger to his nose with good-humoured slyness)" and fear nothing."

Ten days after the celebration of the Jubilee, Anthime's recantation took place in the Gesù, attended by every circumstance of excessive pomp. It is not for me to relate this ceremony, which was described in all the Italian papers of the time. Father T., the Jesuit General's socius, pronounced one of his most remarkable orations on this occasion. "The freemason's sick and tormented soul had doubtless come near to madness and the very extremity of his hatred had foreboded the coming of Love." The preacher recalled Saul of Tarsus and pointed out that Anthime's act of iconoclasm showed a surprising analogy to the stoning of St. Stephen. The reverend father's eloquence swelled and rolled through the aisle, as the thronging surges of the tide roll through the vaults of some sounding cavern, and Anthime thought the while of his niece's childish treble, and in his secret heart he thanked her for having called down upon her infidel uncle's sins the merciful attention of her whom henceforth he would serve alone.

From that day onwards, Anthime, absorbed by more elevated preoccupations, scarcely noticed the noise that was made about his name. Julius de Baraglioul suffered in his stead and never opened a paper without a beating heart. The first enthusiasm of the orthodox press was answered by the vituperation of the liberal organs. An important article in the *Osservatore*—"A New Victory for the Church"—was met by a diatribe in the *Tempo Felice*—"Another Fool." Finally the *Dépeche de Toulouse* headed Anthime's usual page, which he had sent in the day before his cure, with a few gibing introductory remarks. Julius, in his brother-in-law's name, wrote a short, dignified letter in reply, to inform the *Dépeche* that it need no longer consider "the convert" as one of its contributors. The *Zukunft* was beforehand with Anthime and politely thanked him for his services, intimating that there would be no further use for them. He accepted these blows with that serenity of countenance which is the mark of the truly devout soul.

"Fortunately the columns of the *Correspondant* will be open to you," snarled Julius.

"But, my dear fellow, what in the world could I write in them?" objected Anthime benevolently. "None of my former occupations has any further interest for me."

Then silence closed down over the affair. Julius had been obliged to return to Paris.

Anthime, in the meanwhile, pressed by Father Anselm, had obediently quitted Rome. The withdrawal of the Lodge's assistance had been rapidly followed by the ruin of his worldly fortunes; and the applications which Veronica, confident of the Church's support, had urged him to make, merely resulted in wearing out the patience of the influential members of the clergy and finally in setting them against him. He was advised in a friendly way to go to Milan. There he was to await the long-since promised compensation and any scraps which might fall from a celestial bounty that had grown in the mean-time singularly lukewarm.

BOOK II: JULIUS DE BARAGLIOUL

"Puisqu'il ne faut jamais ôter le retour à personne."

—Retz, VIII, p. 93.

I

On March 30th, at twelve o'clock at night, the Baragliouls got back to Paris and went straight to their apartment in the Rue de Verneuil.

While Marguerite was getting ready for the night, Julius, with a small lamp in his hand and slippers on his feet, went to his study—a room to which he never returned without pleasure; it was soberly decorated and furnished; one or two Lépines and a Boudin hung on the walls; in one corner a marble bust of his wife by Chapu, which stood on a revolving pedestal, made a patch of whiteness that was somewhat glaring; in the middle of the room stood an enormous Renaissance table, littered with books, pamphlets and prospectuses which had been accumulating during his absence; in a salver of cloisonné enamel lay a few visiting-cards with their corners turned down, and well in sight, apart from the others and leaning against a bronze Barye, there was a letter addressed in a handwriting which Julius recognised as his old father's. He immediately tore open the envelope and read as follows:

46

"MY DEAR SON,

"I have been growing much weaker lately. It is impossible to misunderstand the nature of the warnings which tell me I must be preparing to depart; and indeed I have not much to gain by delaying longer.

"I know that you are returning to Paris to-night and I count on you for doing me a service without delay. In order to make some arrangements, of which I shall shortly inform you, it is necessary for me to know whether a young man called Lafcadio Wluiki (pronounced *Louki*—the *w* and *i* are hardly sounded) is still living at No. 12 Impasse Claude-Bernard.

"I should be much obliged if you would be so good as to call at this address and ask to see the said young man. (A novelist like you will easily be able to invent some excuse for introducing yourself.) I want to know:

"1. What the young man is doing;

"2. What he intends to do—whether he is ambitious. and, if so, in what way?

"3. Lastly, tell me shortly what seem to you to be his means of existence, his abilities, his inclinations and his tastes. . . .

"Don't try to see me for the present; I am in an unsociable mood. You can give me the information I ask just as well by letter. If I am inclined to talk or if I feel the final departure is at hand, I will let you know.

"Yours affec^ly,

"JUSTE-AGÉNOR DE BARAGLIOUL.

"P.S. Don't let it appear that you come from me. The young man knows nothing of me and must continue to know nothing.

"Lafcadio Wluiki is now nineteen—a Roumanian subject—an orphan.

"I have looked at your last book. If after that you don't get into the Academy, such rubbish is unpardonable."

There was no denying it, Julius's last book had not been well received. In spite of his fatigue, the novelist ran his eye over a bundle of newspaper cuttings, in which he found his name mentioned with scant indulgence. Then he opened a window and breathed for a moment the misty night air. Julius's study windows looked on to the gardens of an Embassy—pools of lustral shadow, where eyes and mind could cleanse themselves from the squalor of the streets and from the meannesses of the world. The pure and thrilling note of a blackbird held him listening a moment or two. . . . Then he went back to the bedroom where Marguerite was already asleep.

As he was afraid of insomnia he took from the chest of drawers a bottle of orange-flower water which he frequently used. Ever careful to observe conjugal courtesy, he had taken the precaution of lowering the wick of the lamp, before placing it where it would be least likely to disturb the sleeper; but a slight tinkling of the glass as he put it down after he had finished drinking, reached Marguerite, where she lay plunged in unconsciousness; she gave an animal grunt and turned to the wall. Julius, glad of an excuse for considering her awake, drew near the bed and asked as he began to undress:

"Would you like to hear what my father says about my book?"

"Oh, my dear, your poor father has no feeling for literature. You've told me so a hundred times," murmured Marguerite whose one desire was to go on sleeping. But Julius's heart was too full.

"He says it's unpardonable rubbish."

There was a long silence, during which Marguerite sank once more into the depths of slumber. Julius was already resigning himself to uncompanioned solitude, when, making a desperate effort for his sake, she rose again to the surface:

"I hope you're not going to be upset about it."

"I am taking it with perfect calm, as you can see,"

answered Julius at once. "But at the same time I really don't think it's my father's place to speak so—especially not my father's—and especially not about that book, which in reality is nothing from first to last but a monument in his honour."

Had not Julius, indeed, retraced in this book the old diplomat's truly representative career? As a companion picture to the turbulent follies of romanticism, had he not glorified the dignified, the ordered, the classic calm of Juste-Agénor's existence in its twofold aspect, political and domestic?

"Fortunately, you didn't write it to please him."

"He insinuates that I wrote *On the Heights* in order to get into the Academy."

"Well! and if you did! Even if you did get into the Academy by writing a fine book! What then?" And she added with contemptuous pity: "Let's hope, at any rate, that the reviews will set him right."

Julius exploded.

"The reviews! Good God! The reviews!" he exclaimed, and then turning furiously upon Marguerite as if it were her fault, added with a bitter laugh:

"They do nothing but abuse me."

At last Marguerite was effectually awakened.

"Is there a great deal of criticism?" she asked with solicitude.

"Yes, and a great deal of crocodile praise too."

"Oh, how right you are to despise all those wretched journalists! Think of what M. de Vogué wrote to you the day before yesterday: 'A pen like yours defends France like a sword!'"

"'Threatened as France is with barbarism, a pen like

yours defends her better than a sword!'" corrected
Julius.

"And when Cardinal André promised you his vote the
other day, he declared that you had the whole Church
behind you."

"A precious lot of good *that*'ll do me!"

"Oh, my dear Julius!"

"We've just seen in Anthime's case what the protection
of the clergy is worth."

"Julius, you're getting bitter. . You've often told me
you didn't work for the hope of reward—nor for the
sake of other people's approval—that your own was
enough. You've even written some splendid things to
that effect."

"I know, I know," said Julius impatiently.

With such a rankling pain at his heart, this soothing
syrup was of no avail. He went back to his dressing-
room.

Why did he let himself go in this lamentable fashion
before his wife? His was not the kind of trouble which
could be comforted by the coddling of a wife; pride—
shame—should make him hide it in his heart. "Rubbish!" All the time he was brushing his teeth, the
word throbbed in his temples and played havoc amongst
his noblest thoughts. After all, what did his last book
matter? He forgot his father's phrase—or at any rate
he forgot it was his father's. For the first time in his
life awful questionings beset him. He, who up to that
time had never met with anything but approval and
smiles, felt rising within him a doubt as to the sincerity
of those smiles, as to the value of that approval, as to
the value of his works, as to the reality of his thought,

as to the genuineness of his life. He returned to the bedroom, absent-mindedly holding his tooth-glass in one
hand and his tooth-brush in the other; he placed the glass,
which was half full of rose-coloured water, on the chest
of drawers, and put the brush in the glass; then he sat
down at a little satin-wood escritoire, where Marguerite
did her writing. He seized his wife's pen-holder and,
taking a sheet of paper, which was tinted mauve and
delicately perfumed, began:

"MY DEAR FATHER,
    "I found your note awaiting me on my return home this eve-
ning. Your errand shall be punctually performed to-morrow
morning. I hope to be able to manage the matter to your satisfaction, and by so doing to give you a proof of my devoted attachment."

For Julius was one of those noble natures whose true
greatness flowers amid the thorns of humiliation. Then,
leaning back in his chair, he remained a few moments,
pen in hand, trying to turn his sentence:

    "It is a matter of grief to me that you, of all people in the
world, should be the one to suspect my disinterestedness,
which . . ."

    No! Perhaps:

    "Do you think that literary honesty is less dear to me
than . . ."

The sentence wouldn't come. Julius, who was in his
night things, felt that he was catching cold; he crumpled
up the paper, took up his tooth-glass and went back with
it to his dressing-room, at the same time throwing the
crumpled letter into the slop-pail.

Just as he was getting into bed, he touched his wife upon the shoulder:

"And what do *you* think of my book?" he asked.

Marguerite half opened a glazed and lifeless eye. Julius was obliged to repeat his question. Turning partly round, Marguerite looked at him. His eyebrows raised under a network of wrinkles, his lips contracted, Julius was a pitiable object.

"What's the matter, dear? Do you really think your last book isn't as good as the others?"

That was no sort of answer. Marguerite was eluding the point.

"I think the others are no better than this. So there!"

"Oh, well then! . . ."

And Marguerite, losing heart in the face of these monstrosities, and feeling that all her tender arguments were wasted, turned round towards the dark and once more slept.

II

Notwithstanding a certain amount of professional curiosity and the flattering illusion that nothing human was alien to him, Julius had rarely derogated from the customs of his class and he had very few dealings except with persons of his own *milieu*. This was from lack of opportunity rather than of taste. As he was preparing next morning to start for his visit, Julius realised that his get-up was not exactly what it should have been. His overcoat, his spread tie, even his Cronstadt hat had something or other proper, staid, respectable about them. . . . But, after all, it was perhaps better that his dress should not encourage the young man to too prompt a familiarity. It would be more suitable to engage his confidence by way of conversation. And as he bent his steps towards the Impasse Claude-Bernard, Julius turned over in his mind the manner in which he should introduce himself and pursue his enquiries, running through all the precautions and pretexts that would be necessary.

What in the world could Count Juste-Agénor de Baraglioul have to do with this young man Lafcadio? The question buzzed importunate in Julius's mind. He was certainly not going to allow himself any curiosity on the subject of his father's life just at the very moment he had finished writing it. He did not wish to know any more than his father chose to tell him. During the last few years the Count had grown taciturn, but he had never practised concealment. As Julius was crossing the Luxembourg Gardens he was overtaken by a shower.

In front of the door of No. 12 Impasse Claude-Bernard a *fiacre* was drawn up, in which Julius as he passed caught sight of a lady whose hat was a trifle large and whose dress was a trifle loud.

His heart beat as he gave his name to the porter of the lodging-house; it seemed to the novelist that he was plunging into an unknown sea of adventure; but as he went upstairs the place looked so common, everything in it was so second-rate, that he was filled with disgust; there was nothing here to kindle his curiosity, which flickered out and was succeeded by repugnance.

On the fourth floor an uncarpeted passage, which was lighted only by the staircase, turned at right angles a few steps from the landing; there were shut doors on each side of this passage; the door at the end was ajar and a small shaft of light came from it. Julius knocked; there was no answer; he timidly pushed the door open a little further; there was no one in the room. Julius went downstairs again.

"If he isn't there, he won't be long," the porter had said.

The rain was falling in torrents. In the hall, opposite the staircase, was a waiting-room, into which Julius made a half-hearted attempt to enter; but its rancid smell and God-forsaken appearance drove him out and made him reflect that he might just as well have opened the door upstairs more decidedly and, without more ado, have waited for the young man in his own room. Julius went up again.

As he turned down the passage for the second time, a woman came out of the room that was next-door to the end one. Julius collided with her and apologised.

"You are looking for . . . ?"

"Monsieur Wluiki lives here, doesn't he?"

"He's gone out."

"Oh!" said Julius in a tone of such annoyance that the woman asked:

"Is it very urgent?"

Julius had prepared himself solely for an encounter with the unknown Lafcadio and he was taken aback; yet here was a fine opportunity; this woman was perhaps in a position to give him a great deal of information about the young man; if only he could get her to talk. . . .

"There was something I wanted to ask him about."

"On whose behalf, may I ask?"

"Does she suspect I come from the police?" thought Julius.

"My name is Vicomte Julius de Baraglioul," said he, rather pompously and slightly raising his hat.

"Oh, Monsieur le Comte, I really must beg you to excuse me for not having . . . The passage is so very dark! Please, be so good as to come in." (She pushed open the door of the end room.) "Lafcadio's certain to be back in a moment. He was only going as far as the . . . Oh! excuse me!"

And as Julius was going in, she brushed in front of him and darted towards a pair of ladies' drawers, which were very indiscreetly spread out to view on a chair, and which, after an attempt at concealment had proved ineffectual, she endeavoured to make at any rate less conspicuous.

"I'm afraid the place is very untidy. . . .

"Never mind! Never mind!" said Julius indulgently. "I'm quite accustomed to . . ."

Carola Venitequa was a rather large-sized, not to say plump young person; but her figure was good and she was wholesome-looking; her features were ordinary but not vulgar and not unattractive; she had gentle eyes like an animal's and a voice that bleated. She was dressed for going out and had on a little soft felt hat, a shirt blouse, a sailor tie and a man's collar and white cuffs.

"Have you known M. Wluiki long?"

"I might perhaps give him a message," she remarked without answering.

"Well, I wanted to know whether he was very busy."

"It depends."

"Because if he had any free time, I thought of asking him to do a small job for me."

"What sort of job?"

"Well, that's just it, you see. . . . To begin with, I should have liked to know the kind of pursuits he's engaged in."

The question lacked subtlety. But Carola's appearance was not of the sort to invite subtlety. In the meantime the Comte de Baraglioul had recovered his self-possession; he was seated in the chair which Carola had cleared, and Carola was leaning on the table close to him, just beginning to speak, when a loud disturbance was heard in the passage; the door opened noisily and the woman Julius had noticed in the carriage made her appearance.

"I was sure of it," she said, "when I saw him going upstairs."

Carola drew away a little from Julius and answered quickly:

"Nothing of the kind, my dear—we were just talking. My friend, Bertha Grand-Marnier—Monsieur le Comte . . . there now! I'm so sorry! I've forgotten your name."

"It's of no consequence," said Julius, rather stiffly, as he pressed the gloved hand which Bertha offered him.

"Now, introduce *me*," said Carola. . . .

"Look here, dearie, we're an hour late already," went on the other, after having introduced her friend. "If you want to talk to the gentleman, let him come with us; I've got a carriage."

"He hasn't come to see me."

"Oh, all right! Come along then! Won't you dine with us to-night?"

"I'm exceedingly sorry, but . . ."

Carola blushed. She was anxious now to take her friend off as quickly as possible.

"Will you please excuse me, Sir?" she said. "Lafcadio will be back in a moment."

The two women as they went out left the door open behind them. Every sound in the uncarpeted passage was audible; a person coming from the stairs would not be seen because of the turning, but he would certainly be heard.

"After all," thought Julius, "I shall find out even more from the room than from the woman." He set quietly to work to examine it.

In these commonplace lodgings there was hardly anything, alas! which could offer a clue to curiosity so unskilled as his.

Not a bookshelf! Not a picture on the walls! Standing on the mantelpiece was a vile edition of Defoe's *Moll Flanders* in English and only two-thirds cut, and a copy of the *Novelle* of Anton Francesco Grazzini, styled the Lasca, in Italian. These two books puzzled Julius. Beside them, and behind a bottle of spirits of peppermint, was a photograph which did more than puzzle him. It showed, grouped upon a sandy beach, a woman, who was no longer very young but strangely beautiful, leaning upon the arm of a man of a pronounced English type, slim and elegant and dressed in a sport suit, and at their feet, sitting on an overturned canoe, a well-knit, slender lad of about fifteen, with a mass of fair, tousled hair, with bold laughing eyes and without a stitch of clothes on him.

Julius took up the photograph and, holding it to the light, saw written in the right-hand corner a few words in faded ink: *Duino, July, 1889.* He was not much the wiser for this, though he remembered that Duino was a small town on the Austrian coast of the Adriatic. With tightened lips and a disapproving shake of his head, he put the photograph back. In the empty fire-place were stowed a box of oatmeal, a bag of lentils and a bag of rice; a little further off was a chess-board leaning against the wall. There was nothing which could give Julius any hint of the kind of studies or occupations which filled the young man's days.

Lafcadio had apparently just finished his breakfast; on the table was a spirit lamp and a small saucepan; in this there was still to be seen one of those little perforated, hollow eggs, which ingenious travellers use for making tea; and there were a few bread crumbs and a dirtied cup. Julius drew near the table; in the table was a drawer and in the drawer a key. . . .

I should be sorry if what follows were to give a wrong impression of Julius's character. Nothing was further from Julius than indiscretion; he was respectful of the cloak with which each man chooses to cover his inner life; he was highly respectful of the decencies. But upon this occasion he was bound to waive his personal preferences in obedience to his father's command. He waited and listened for another moment, then, as he heard nothing —against his inclinations and against his principles, but with the delicate feeling of performing a duty—he pulled open the drawer, the key of which had not been turned.

Inside was a Russia-leather pocket-book; which **Julius**

took and opened. On the first page, in the same writing as that on the photograph, were these words:

> For my trusty comrade Cadio,
> This account book from his old uncle,
>   FABY,

and with hardly any space between came the following words, written in a straight, regular and rather childish hand:

Duino. This morning, July 17th, '89, Lord Fabian joined us here. He brought me a canoe, a rifle and this beautiful pocket-book. ·

Nothing else on the first page.

On the third page, under the date Aug. 29th, was written:

Swimming match with Faby. Gave him four strokes.

And the next day:

Gave him twelve strokes.

Julius gathered that he had got hold of a mere training book. The list of days soon stopped, however, and after a blank page, he read:

Sept. 20th. Left Algiers for the Aures.

Then a few jottings of places and dates and finally this last entry:

Oct. 5th. Return to El Kantara—50 kilometres *on horse-back,** without stopping.

Julius turned over a few blank pages, but, a little further on, the entries began again. At the top of a page,

* In English in the original. (*Translator's note.*)

the following words were written in larger and more carefully formed characters, arranged so as to look like a
fresh title:

QUI INCOMMINCIA IL LIBRO
DELLA NOVA ESIGENZA
E
DELLA SUPREMA VIRTU.

And below this came the motto:

"Tanto quanto se ne taglia."
—BOCCACCIO.

Any expression of moral ideas was quick to arouse the
hunter's instinct in Julius; here was game for him. But
the very next page was a disappointment; it landed him
in another batch of accounts. And yet these accounts
were of a different kind. Without any indication of
dates or places appeared the following entries:

For having beaten Protos at chess.............1 punta.
For having shown that I spoke Italian.........3 punte.
For having answered before Protos............1 p.
For having had the last word.................1 p.
For having cried at hearing of Faby's death....4 p.

Julius, reading hurriedly, took *punta* to be some kind
of foreign coin and assumed that the figures were nothing
but a childish and trifling computation of merits and
rewards. Then the accounts came to an end again.
Julius turned another page and read:

This 4th April, conversation with Protos:
"Do you understand the meaning of the words, 'TO PUSH
ON'?

There the writing stopped.

Julius shrugged his shoulders, pursed up his lips, shook his head and put the book back where he had found it. He took out his watch, got up, walked to the window and looked out; it had stopped raining. He went towards the corner of the room where he had put down his umbrella when he first came in; at that moment he saw, leaning back a little in the opening of the doorway, a handsome, fair young man, who was watching him with a smile on his lips.

III

The youth of the photograph had hardly aged. Juste-Agénor had said nineteen; one would not have taken him for more than sixteen. Lafcadio could certainly have only just arrived; when Julius was putting back the pocket-book a moment before, he had raised his eyes to look at the door and had seen no one; but how was it he had not heard him coming? An instinctive glance at the young man's feet showed Julius that he was wearing goloshes instead of boots.

There was nothing hostile about Lafcadio's smile; he seemed amused, on the contrary—and ironical; he had kept his travelling-cap on his head, but when he met Julius's eyes, he took it off and bowed ceremoniously.

"Monsieur Wluiki?" asked Julius.

The young man bowed again without answering.

"Please excuse my sitting down in your room while I was waiting for you. I really shouldn't have ventured to do so if I hadn't been shown in."

Julius spoke faster and louder than usual to convince

himself that he was at ease. Lafcadio frowned imperceptibly; he went towards Julius's umbrella and without a word put it outside to stream in the passage; then coming back into the room again, he motioned Julius to sit down.

"You are no doubt surprised to see me?"

Lafcadio quietly took a cigarette out of a silver cigarette case and lit it.

"I will explain my reason for calling in a few words. Of course you will understand . . ."

The more he spoke, the more he felt his assurance oozing away.

"Well, then!—But first allow me to introduce myself . . ." and as though he felt embarrassed at having to pronounce his own name, he drew a visiting-card out of his waistcoat pocket and held it out to Lafcadio, who put it down on the table without looking at it.

"I am . . . I have just finished a rather important piece of work; it's a small piece of work which I have no time to copy out myself. Someone mentioned you to me as having an excellent handwriting and I thought that, perhaps . . ." here Julius's glance travelled eloquently over the bareness of the room—"I thought that perhaps you would have no objection . . ."

"There is no one in Paris," interrupted Lafcadio, "no one who could have mentioned my handwriting to you." As he spoke, he directed his eyes towards the drawer, in opening which Julius had unwittingly destroyed a minute and almost invisible seal of soft wax; then turning the key violently in the lock and putting it in his pocket:

"No one, that is, who has any right to"; and as he spoke he watched Julius's face redden.

"On the other hand" (he spoke very slowly—almost stolidly, without any expression at all), "I don't quite grasp so far what reasons Monsieur . . ." (he looked at the card) "what reasons Count Julius de Baraglioul can have for taking a special interest in me. Nevertheless" (and his voice suddenly became smooth and mellifluous in imitation of Julius's), "your proposal deserves to be taken into consideration by a person who, as it has not escaped you, is in need of money." (He got up.) "Kindly allow me to bring you my answer to-morrow morning."

The hint to leave was unmistakable. Julius felt too uncomfortable to insist. He took up his hat, hesitated an instant and then:

"I should have liked a little further talk with you," he said awkwardly. "Let me hope that to-morrow . . . I shall expect you any time after ten o'clock."

Lafcadio bowed.

As soon as Julius had turned the corner of the passage, Lafcadio pushed to the door and bolted it. He ran to the drawer, pulled out the pocket-book, opened it at the last telltale page and just at the place where he had left off several months before, he wrote in pencil in a large hand, sloping defiantly backwards and very unlike the former:

For having let Olibrius poke his dirty nose into this book . . . 1 punta."

He took a penknife out of his pocket; its blade had been sharpened away until nothing was left of it but a short point like a stiletto, which he passed over the flame of a match and then thrust through his trouser pocket, straight into his thigh. In spite of himself he made a grimace. But he was still not satisfied. Leaning upon the table, without sitting down, he again wrote just below the last sentence:

"And for having shown him that I knew it.....2 punte."

This time he hesitated; unfastened his trousers and turned them down on one side. He looked at his thigh in which the little wound he had just made was bleeding; he examined the scars of similar wounds, which were like vaccination marks all round. Then, having once more passed the blade over the flame of a match, he very quickly and twice in succession plunged it into his flesh.

"I usedn't to take so many precautions in the old days," he said, going to the bottle of spirits of peppermint and sprinkling a few drops on each of the wounds.

His anger had cooled a little, when, as he was putting back the bottle, he noticed that the photograph of himself and his mother had been slightly disturbed. Then he seized it, gazed at it for the last time with a kind of anguish, and as the blood rushed to his face, tore it furiously to shreds. He tried to burn the pieces, but he could not get them to light; so, clearing the fire-place of the bags which littered it, he took his only two books and set them in the hearth to serve as fire-dogs, pulled his pocket-book apart, hacked it to pieces, crumpled it up, flung his picture on the top and set fire to the whole.

With his face close to the flames he persuaded himself that it was with unspeakable satisfaction that he watched these keepsakes burning, but when he rose to his feet after nothing was left of them but ashes, his head was swimming. The room was full of smoke. He went to his wash-hand-stand and bathed his face.

He was now able to consider the little visiting-card with a steadier eye.

"Count Julius de Baraglioul," he repeated. *"Dapprima importa sapere chi è."*

He tore off the silk handkerchief which he was wearing instead of a collar and tie, unfastened his shirt and, standing in front of the open window, let the cool air play round his chest and sides. Then suddenly all eagerness to go out, with his boots rapidly drawn on, his cravat swiftly knotted, a respectable grey felt hat on his head—appeased and civilised as far as in him lay—Lafcadio shut the door of his room behind him and made his way to the Place St. Sulpice. There, in the big lending-library opposite the town hall, he would be certain to find all the information he wanted.

IV

As he passed under the arcades of the Odéon, Julius's novel, which was on sale in the book shops, caught his eye; it was a yellow paper book, the mere sight of which on any other occasion would have made him yawn. He felt in his pocket and flung a five-franc piece on the counter.

"A fine fire for this evening," thought he, as he carried off the book and the change.

In the lending-library a "Who's Who" gave a short account of Julius's invertebrate career, mentioned the titles of his works and praised them in terms so conventional as effectually to quench any desire to read them.

"Ugh!" said Lafcadio. . . . He was just going to shut up the book when three or four words in the preceding paragraph caught his eye and made him start.

A few lines above *Julius de Baraglioul (Vmte.)* Lafcadio saw under the heading *Juste-Agénor*: "Minister at Bucharest in 1873." What was there in these simple words to make his heart beat so fast?

Lafcadio, whose mother had given him five uncles, had never known his father; he was content to regard him as dead and had always refrained from asking questions. As for his uncles (all of them of different nationalities and three of them in the diplomatic service), he had pretty soon perceived that they had no other relationship with him than that which the fair Wanda chose to give them. Now Lafcadio was just nineteen. He had been born in Bucharest in 1874, exactly at the end of the second year which the Comte de Baraglioul had spent there in his official capacity.

Now that he had been put on the alert by Julius's mysterious visit, how was it possible to look upon this as merely a fortuitous coincidence? He made a great effort to read Juste-Agénor's biography, but the lines danced before his eyes; he just managed to make out that Julius's father, the Comte de Baraglioul, was a man of considerable importance.

The explosion of insolent joy in his heart was so riotous that he thought the outside world must hear it. But no! this covering of flesh was unquestionably solid and impervious. He furtively examined his neighbours—old habitués of the reading-room, all engrossed in their dreary occupations. . . . He began to calculate: "If he was born in 1821, the Count must be seventy-two by now.

Ma chi sa se vive ancora? . . ." He put the dictionary back and went out.

The azure sky was clearing itself of a few light clouds which a fresh breeze had sent scudding. *"Importa di domesticare questo nuovo proposito,"* said Lafcadio to himself, who prized above all things the free possession of his soul; and hopeless of reducing so turbulent a thought to order, he resolved to banish it for a moment from his mind. He took Julius's novel out of his pocket and made a great effort to distract himself with it; but the book had no allurement in it of indirectness or mystery, and nothing could have helped him less to escape from a too urgent self.

"And yet it is to the author of *that* that I am going to-morrow to play at being secretary!" he couldn't refrain from repeating.

He bought a newspaper at a kiosk and went into the Luxembourg. The benches were sopping; he opened the book, sat down on it and unfolded the paper to look at the various items of the day. Suddenly, and as though he had been expecting to find it there, his eye fell upon the following announcement:

"It is hoped that Count Juste-Agénor de Baraglioul, whose health has lately given grave cause for anxiety, is now recovering. His condition, however, still remains too precarious to admit of his receiving any but a few intimate friends."

Lafcadio sprang from the bench. In a moment he had made up his mind. Forgetting his book, he hurried off to a stationer's shop in the Rue de Médicis, where he remembered having seen in the window a notice that visiting-cards were printed "while you wait at three francs the hundred." He smiled as he went, amused by the boldness of his idea and possessed by the spirit of adventure.

"How long will it take to print a hundred cards?" he asked the shopkeeper.

"You can have them before nightfall."

"I'll pay you double if you let me have them by two o'clock this afternoon."

The shopkeeper made a pretence of consulting his order-book.

"Very well . . . to oblige you. You can call for them at two o'clock. What name?"

Then, without a tremor or a blush, but with a heart that beat a little unsteadily, he signed:

Lafcadio de Baraglioul.

"The rascal doesn't believe me," said he to himself as he left, for he was piqued that the shopkeeper's bow had not been lower. Then, as he looked at his reflection in a shop window, "I must admit I don't look very like a Baraglioul," he thought. "We must see whether we can't improve the resemblance before this afternoon."

It was not yet twelve o'clock. Lafcadio, who was in a state of madcap exhilaration, had not begun to feel hungry.

"First, let's take a little walk, or I shall fly into the air," thought he. "And I must keep in the middle of the road. If I go too near the passers-by, they will notice that I'm a head and shoulders taller than any of them. Another superiority to conceal. One has never done putting the finishing touches to one's education."

He went into a post office.

"Place Malesherbes . . . this afternoon!" he said to himself, as he copied out Count Juste-Agénor's address from the directory. "But what's to prevent me from going this morning to prospect Rue de Verneuil?" (This was the address on Julius's card.)

Lafcadio knew and loved this part of Paris; leaving the more frequented thoroughfares, he took a roundabout way by Rue Vaneau; in that quiet street the young freshness of his joy would have space to breathe more freely. As he turned into the Rue de Babylone he saw people running; near the Impasse Oudinot a crowd was collecting in front of a two-storied house from which was pouring an evil-looking smoke. He forced himself not to hurry his pace, though he was naturally a quick walker. . . .

Lafcadio, my friend, here you require the pen of a newspaper reporter—mine abandons you! My readers must not expect me to relate the incoherent comments of the onlookers, the broken exclamations, the . . .

Wriggling through the crowd like an eel, Lafcadio made his way to the front. There a poor woman was sobbing on her knees.

"My children! My little children!" she wept. She was being supported by a young girl, whose simple elegance of dress showed she was no relation; she was very pale and so lovely that Lafcadio was instantly drawn to her. She answered his questions.

"No, I don't know her. I have just made out that her two little children are in that room on the second floor which the flames are just going to reach—they have caught the staircase already; the fire brigade has been sent for, but by the time they come the children will have

been smothered by the smoke. Oh! wouldn't it be possible to get up to the balcony by climbing that wall—
look!—and helping oneself up by that waterpipe? Some
of these people say that thieves did it a little while ago—
thieves did it to steal money, but no one dares do it to
save two children. I've offered my purse, but it's no
good. Oh! if only I were a man!"

Lafcadio listened no longer. Dropping his stick and
hat at the young lady's feet, he darted forward. With
a bound he caught hold of the top of the wall unaided;
a pull of his arms raised him on to it; in a moment he
was standing upright and walking along the narrow edge,
regardless of the broken pieces of glass with which it
bristled.

But the amazement of the crowd redoubled when, seizing hold of the vertical pipe, he swarmed up it, hardly
resting his feet here and there for a second on the clamps
which fixed it to the wall. There he is—at the balcony
now—now he has vaulted the railings; the admiring
crowd no longer trembles—it can only admire, for, indeed,
he moves with consummate ease. One push of his
shoulder shivers the window-pane; he has disappeared
into the room. Agonising moment of unspeakable suspense! Here he comes again, holding a crying infant in
his arms. Out of a sheet torn in two and knotted together end to end, he hastily contrives a rope—ties the
child to it—lowers it gently to the arms of the distracted
mother. The second child is saved in the same way.

When Lafcadio came down in his turn, the crowd
cheered him as a hero.

"They take me for a clown," thought he, as he roughly
and ungraciously repulsed their greetings, exasperated at

feeling himself blush. But when the young lady, whom he again approached, shyly held out to him his hat and stick and with them the purse she had promised, he took it with a smile, emptied it of the sixty francs that it contained, and gave the money to the poor mother, who was smothering her children with kisses.

"May I keep the purse in remembrance of you, Mademoiselle?"

He kissed the little embroidered purse. The two looked at each other for a moment. The young girl was agitated and paler than ever; she seemed desirous of speaking, but Lafcadio abruptly turned on his heel and opened a way through the crowd with his stick. His air was so forbidding that they very soon stopped cheering and following him.

He regained the Luxembourg, made a hasty meal at the restaurant Gambrinus near the Odéon and returned swiftly to his room. There under a board in the floor he kept his store of money; three twenty-franc pieces and one ten-franc piece were extracted from their hiding-place. He reckoned:

    Visiting-cards..................six francs
    A pair of gloves ....five francs
    A tie........................five francs (how shall I get any-
    thing decent at that price?)
    A pair of shoes.............thirty-five francs (I shan't use
    them long.)
    Left over...................nineteen francs for emergencies.

(Lafcadio had a horror of owing anything to anyone and always paid ready money.)

He went to a wardrobe and pulled out a suit made of soft dark tweed, perfectly cut and still fresh.

"Unfortunately," he said to himself, "I've grown since . . ." His thoughts went back to that dazzling time, not so long ago, when he used to dance gaily off with the Marquis de Gesvres (the last of his uncles) to the tailor's, the hatter's, the shirtmaker's.

Ill-fitting clothes were as shocking to Lafcadio as lying to a Calvinist.

"The most urgent first. My uncle de Gesvres used always to say you could judge a man by his foot-wear."

And out of respect for the shoes he was going to try on, he began by changing his socks.

V

Comte Juste-Agénor de Baraglioul had not left the luxurious apartment which he occupied in the Place Malesherbes, for the last five years. It was there that he set about preparing for death; this was his care as he wandered pensively among the rare objects with which his great salons were crowded, or oftener still as he sat shut up in his bedroom, seeking to ease the pain of his aching arms and shoulders with hot cloths and soothing compresses. An enormous madeira-coloured silk handkerchief was wrapped round his fine head like a turban, one end of which fell loose and hung down upon his lace collar and upon his thick brown knitted waistcoat, over which his beard flowed like a silvery waterfall. His feet, shod in soft white leather slippers, rested on a hot water bottle. Beside him, and heated by a spirit lamp, was a bath of hot sand into which he plunged first one and then the other of his pale emaciated hands. A grey shawl was spread over his knees. Incontestably he was like Julius; but he was still more like a portrait by Titian; and Julius's features were only a vapid replica of his father's, just as Julius's novel was a bowdlerised and namby-pamby version of his life.

Juste-Agénor was drinking a cup of tisane and listening to a homily from his confessor, Father April, whom he had fallen into the habit of frequently consulting; at this moment there was a knock at the door and the faithful Hector, who for the last twenty years had acted as the Count's valet and nurse, and on occasion as his confidential adviser, brought in a small envelope on a lacquered salver.

"The gentleman hopes that M. le Comte will be good enough to see him."

Juste-Agénor put down his cup, tore open the envelope and took out Lafcadio's card. He crumpled it nervously in his hand.

"Tell him . . ." Then, controlling himself with an effort: "A gentleman? . . . a young man, you mean? What kind of person is he, Hector?"

"M. le Comte may very well receive him."

"My dear Abbé," said the Count, turning to Father April, "please forgive me if I ask you to put off the rest of our conversation for the present; but mind you come again to-morrow. I shall probably have some news for you; I think you will be pleased."

With his forehead bowed on his hand, he waited until Father April had left the room by the drawing-room door; then at last, raising his head:

"Show him in," he said.

Lafcadio, holding his head high, stepped into the room with a manly and self-confident bearing; as soon as he was in front of the old man, he bowed gravely. As he had made up his mind not to speak before he had had time to count twelve, it was the Count who began.

"In the first place, let me tell you there is no such person as Lafcadio de Baraglioul," said he, tearing up the visiting-card, "and be so good as to inform Monsieur Lafcadio Wluiki, since he is a friend of yours, that if he makes any use of these cards—that if he fails to destroy them all like this" (he tore it up into minute fragments, which he dropped into his empty cup), "I shall give notice to the police and have him arrested for a common swindler. Do you understand? . . . Now, come to the light and let me look at you."

"Lafcadio Wluiki will obey you, Sir." (His voice was very deferential and trembled a little.) "Forgive him for approaching you by such means as these; he had no evil intention. He wishes he could convince you that he is not undeserving of . . . your esteem, at any rate."

"Your figure is good, but your clothes don't fit," went on the Count, who was determined not to hear.

"Then I was not mistaken?" said Lafcadio, venturing upon a smile and submitting himself good-humouredly to the scrutiny.

"Thank God! it's his mother he takes after," muttered the old Count.

"If I don't let it be too apparent, mayn't I be allowed as well to take after . . ."

"I was speaking of your looks. It is too late now for me to know whether your mother is the only person you are like. God will not grant me time."

Just then, the grey shawl slipped off his knees on to the floor.

Lafcadio sprang forward and as he bent down he felt the old man's hand weigh gently on his shoulder.

"Lafcadio Wluiki," went on Juste-Agénor, when he had raised himself, "my days are numbered. I shall not fence with you—it would be too fatiguing. I am willing to grant that you are not stupid; I am glad that you are not ugly. There is a touch of boldness in this venture of yours which is not unbecoming. I thought at first it was impudence, but your voice, your manner reassure me. As to other things, I asked my son Julius to report to me, but I find that I take no great interest in them— it was more important to see you. Now, Lafcadio, listen. There is not a single document of any sort in existence which testifies to your identity. I have been careful to leave you no possibility of making any claims. No, don't protest. It's useless. Don't interrupt me. Your silence up to now is a sign that your mother kept her word not to speak of me to you. Very good. In accordance with the promise I made her, you shall have material proof of my gratitude. In spite of legal difficulties, you will receive at the hands of my son Julius that share of my inheritance which I told your mother should be reserved for you. That is to say, I shall increase my son Julius's legacy by the amount by which the law permits me to reduce that of my other child, the Countess Guy de Saint-Prix— which is actually the exact sum I mean him to pass on to you. It will, I think, come to . . . let us say about forty thousand francs * a year. But I must see my solicitor and go into the exact figures with him. . . . Sit

* Equivalent in pre-war days to £1600. (*Translator's note.*)

down, you will listen more comfortably." (Lafcadio had leant for a breathing-space on the edge of the table.) "Julius may make objections; the law is on his side; but I count on his fairness not to—and I count on yours never to trouble Julius's family, just as your mother never troubled mine. As far as Julius is concerned, the only person who exists is Lafcadio Wluiki. I don't wish you to wear mourning for me. My child, the institution of the family is a closed thing. You will never be anything but a bastard."

Lafcadio, who had been caught by his father's glance in the act of staggering, had nevertheless refused the invitation to be seated. He had already overcome the swimming of his brain and was now leaning on the table on which were placed the cup and the spirit lamp. His attitude remained highly deferential.

"Now, tell me—you saw my son Julius this morning? Did he tell you . . . ?"

"He told me nothing. I guessed."

"Clumsy fellow! . . . Oh! I don't mean *you*. . . . Are you to see him again?"

"He asked me to be his secretary."

"Have you accepted?"

"Do you object?"

"No. But I think it would be better for you not to recognise each other."

"I thought so too. But without recognising him exactly, I should like to get to know him a little."

"I suppose, though, that you don't mean to fill a subordinate position like that for long?"

"Just long enough to look round."

"And after that what do you think of doing, now that you are well off?"

"Why, yesterday I hardly had enough to eat, Sir. Give me time to take the measure of my appetite."

At this moment Hector knocked at the door.

"Monsieur le Vicomte to see you, Sir. Shall I show him in?"

The old man's forehead grew sombre. He kept silent for a moment, but when Lafcadio discreetly rose to take leave:

"Don't go!" cried Juste-Agénor, so violently that the young man's heart went out to him; then turning to Hector:

"It can't be helped. It's his own fault. I told him particularly not to try and see me. . . . Tell him I'm busy, that . . . I'll write to him."

Hector bowed and went out.

The old man remained for a few moments with his eyes closed. He seemed asleep, except that his lips, half-hidden by his beard, could be seen moving. At last he raised his eyelids, held out his hand to Lafcadio, and in a voice that was changed and softened, a voice that seemed broken with fatigue:

"Give me your hand, child," he said. "You must leave me now."

"I must make a confession," said Lafcadio, hesitating. "In order to make myself presentable to come and see you, I exhausted my supplies. If you don't help me, I shall have very little dinner to-night and none at all to-morrow . . . unless your son, M. le Vicomte . . ."

"In the meantime you can have this," said the Count,

taking five hundred francs out of a drawer. "Well, what are you waiting for?"

"I should like to ask you, too . . . whether I mayn't hope to see you again?"

"Upon my word, I'll admit, it would give me pleasure. But the reverend persons who are in charge of my soul, keep me in a frame of mind in which pleasure passes as a secondary consideration. As for my blessing, I'll give it to you at once." And the old man opened his arms to receive him. But Lafcadio, instead of throwing himself into them, knelt down before him and laid his head, sobbing, on the Count's knees; touched in a moment and all subdued to tenderness by the embrace, he felt his heart and all its fierce resolves melt within him.

"My child, my child," stammered the old man, "I have delayed too long."

When Lafcadio got up his face was wet with tears.

At the moment of leaving, as he was putting the note, which he had not immediately taken, into his pocket, Lafcadio came upon his visiting-cards. Holding them out to the Count:

"Here is the whole packet," said he.

"I trust you. Tear them up yourself. Good-bye."

"He would have made the best of uncles," thought Lafcadio, as he was walking back to the Quartier Latin; "and even," he added, with the faintest touch of melancholy, "a little more into the bargain.—Pooh!"

He took the packet of cards, spread them out fan-wise and with a single easy movement tore them in half.

"I never had any confidence in drains," murmured he, as he threw "Lafcadio" down a grating in the street; and it was not till two gratings further on that he threw down "de Baraglioul."

"Never mind! Baraglioul or Wluiki, let's set to work now to settle up our arrears."

There was a jeweller's shop in the Boulevard St. Germain before which Carola used to keep him standing every day. A day or two earlier, she had discovered a curious pair of sleeve-links in the flashy shop window; they were joined together two and two by a little gilt chain and were cut out of a peculiar kind of quartz—a sort of smoky agate, which was not transparent, though it looked as if it were—and made to represent four cats' heads. Venitequa, as I have already said, was in the habit of wearing a tailormade coat and skirt and a man's shirt with stiff cuffs, and as she had a taste for oddities, she coveted these sleeve-links.

They were more queer than attractive; Lafcadio thought them hideous; it would have irritated him to see his mistress wearing them; but now that he was going to leave her . . . He went into the shop and paid a hundred and twenty francs for the links.

"A piece of writing-paper, please." And leaning on the counter, he wrote on a sheet of note-paper which the shopman brought him, these words:

"For Carola Venitequa,
    With thanks for having shown the stranger into my room, and begging her never to set her foot in it again."

He folded the paper and slipped it into the box in which the trinkets were packed.

"No precipitation!" he said to himself as he was on the

point of handing the box to the porter. "I'll pass one
more night under this roof. For this evening let's be
satisfied with locking Miss Carola out."

VI

The moral law which Descartes considered provisional,
but to which he submitted in the meantime, until he had
established the rules that should regulate his life and
conduct hereafter, was the same law—its provisional pow-
ers indefinitely protracted—which governed Julius de
Baraglioul.

But Julius's temperament was not so intractable nor his
intellect so commanding as to have given him hitherto
much trouble in conforming to the proprieties. On the
whole all that he demanded of life was his comfort—part
of which consisted in his being successful as a man of
letters. The failure of his last novel was the first experience of his life which had ever really galled him.

He had been not a little mortified at being refused ad-
mittance to his father; he would have been much more
so if he had known who it was who had forestalled him.
On his way back to the Rue de Verneuil, it was with less
and less conviction that he repelled the importunate sup-
position which had assailed him as he went to visit Lafcadio in the morning. He too had juxtaposed facts and
dates; he too was obliged to recognise in this strange con-
junction something more than a mere coincidence. Lafcadio's youthful grace, moreover, had captivated him, and
though he suspected his father was going to cheat him of
a portion of his patrimony for the sake of this bastard
brother, he felt no ill will towards him; he was even ex-

pecting him this morning with a curiosity that was almost tender in its solicitude.

As for Lafcadio, shy of approach and reticent though he was, this rare opportunity of speaking tempted him—and also the pleasure of making Julius feel a little uncomfortable. For he had never taken even Protos very deeply into his confidence. And how far he had travelled since then! After all he did not dislike Julius—absurd and shadowy though he thought him. It amused him to know that they were brothers.

As he was on his way to Julius's house, the morning after his visit, a somewhat curious adventure befell him.

Whether it was his liking for the roundabout that prompted him, or the inspiration of his guiding genius, or whether he wanted to quell a certain unruliness of body and mind, so as to be master of himself when he arrived at his brother's—for whatever reason, Lafcadio took the longest way round; he had followed the Boulevard des Invalides, passed again by the scene of the fire, and was going down the Rue de Bellechasse.

"Thirty-four Rue de Verneuil," he was saying to himself as he walked along, "four and three, seven—a lucky number."

He was turning out of the Rue St. Dominique where it intersects the Boulevard St. Germain, when, on the other side of the road, he thought he saw and recognised the young girl, who, it must be confessed, had occupied his thoughts not a little since the day before. He immediately quickened his pace. . . . Sure enough, it was she! He caught her up at the end of the short Rue de Villersexel, but, reflecting that it would not be very like a Baraglioul to accost her, he contented himself with smiling, raising his hat a little and bowing discreetly; then, after passing her swiftly, he thought it highly expedient to drop into a tobacconist's shop, while the young lady, who was again in front, turned down the Rue de l'Université.

When Lafcadio came out of the tobacconist's and entered the same street in his turn, he looked right and left: the young girl had vanished.—Lafcadio, my friend, you are verging on the commonplace. If you are going to fall in love, do not count on my pen to paint the disturbance of your heart. . . . But no! the idea of beginning a pursuit was distasteful to him; and besides he did not want to be late for his appointment with Julius, and the roundabout way by which he had come allowed no time for further dawdling. Fortunately the Rue de Verneuil was near at hand, and the house in which Julius lived, at the first corner. Lafcadio tossed the Count's name to the porter and darted upstairs.

In the meantime, Genevieve de Baraglioul, Count Julius's elder daughter—for it was she, on her way back from the Hospital for Sick Children, where she went every morning—had been far more agitated than Lafcadio by this second meeting, and hurrying home as quickly as she could, she had entered the front door just as Lafcadio had turned into the street, and was already nearing the second floor, when the sound of rapid steps behind her made her look round; someone was coming upstairs more quickly than she; she stood aside to let the person pass, but when she recognized Lafcadio, who stopped, petrified, in front of her:

"Is it worthy of you," she said in as angry a tone as she could muster, "to follow me like this?"

"Oh! what can you think of me?" cried Lafcadio. "I'm afraid you'll not believe me when I say that I didn't see you coming into this house—that I'm extremely astonished to meet you here. Isn't this where Count Julius de Baraglioul lives?"

"What?" said Genevieve, blushing; "can you be the new secretary my father is expecting? Monsieur Lafcadio Wlou . . . you have such a peculiar name, I don't know how to pronounce it." And as Lafcadio, blushing in his turn, bowed, she went on:

"Since I've met you, may I ask you as a favour not to speak to my parents about yesterday's adventure, which I don't think would be at all to their taste; and particularly not to say anything about my purse, which I told them I had lost."

"I was going to ask you myself to say nothing about the absurd part you saw me play in the business. I'm like your parents; I don't at all understand it or approve of it. You must have taken me for a Newfoundland. I couldn't restrain myself. Forgive me. I have much to learn. . . . But I shall learn in time, I promise you. . . . Will you give me your hand?"

Genevieve de Baraglioul, who did not own to herself that she thought Lafcadio very handsome, did not own to Lafcadio that, far from thinking him ridiculous, she had set him up as the image of a hero. She held out her hand to him and he raised it impetuously to his lips; then smiling simply, she begged him to go down a few steps and wait till she had gone in and shut the door before ringing in his turn, so that they might not be seen together; and he was to take special care not to show that they had ever met before.

A few minutes later Lafcadio was ushered into the novelist's study.

Julius's welcome was kindly and encouraging; Julius, however, was a blunderer; the young man immediately assumed the defensive.

"I must begin by warning you, M. le Comte, that I can't abide either gratitude or debts; and whatever you may do for me, you will never be able to make me feel that I am under any obligation to you."

Julius in his turn was nettled.

"I am not trying to buy you, Monsieur Wluiki," he began loftily. . . . Then, both realising that to continue in this way would mean burning their boats, they pulled themselves up short. After a moment's silence Lafcadio began in a more conciliatory manner:

"What work was it that you thought of giving me?"

Julius made an evasive answer, excusing himself that his MS. was not quite ready yet; and besides it would be no bad thing for them to begin by getting better acquainted with each other.

"You must admit, M. de Baraglioul," said Lafcadio pleasantly, "that you have lost no time in beginning that without me, and that you did me the honour yesterday of examining a certain pocket-book of mine . . ."

Julius lost countenance and answered in some confusion: "I admit that I did." And then he went on with dignity: "I apologise. If the thing were to occur again . . ."

"It will not occur again. I have burnt the pocket-book."

Julius's features expressed grief.

"Are you very angry?"

"If I were still angry I shouldn't mention it. Forgive my manner when I came in just now," went on Lafcadio, determined to send his thrust home. "All the same I should like very much to know whether you read a scrap of letter as well, that happened to be in the pocket-book?"

Julius had not read any scrap of letter, for the very good reason that he had not found any; but he took the opportunity of protesting his discretion. It amused Lafcadio to show his amusement.

"I partly revenged myself yesterday on your new book."

"It is not at all likely to interest you," Julius hastened to say.

"Oh, I didn't read the whole of it. I must confess I am not very fond of reading. In reality the only book I ever enjoyed was *Robinson Crusoe*. . . . Oh, yes! *Aladdin* too. . . . That must do for me in your opinion."

Julius raised his hand gently.

"I merely pity you. You deprive yourself of great joys."

"I have others."

"Perhaps not of such sterling quality."

"Oh, you may be sure of that!" and Lafcadio's laugh was decidedly impertinent.

"You will suffer for it some day," returned Julius, a little ruffled by this disrespectful gibing.

"When it will be too late," Lafcadio finished the sentence with affected gravity; then he asked abruptly: "Does it really amuse you very much to write?"

Julius drew himself up.

"I don't write for the sake of amusement," he answered

nobly. "The joy that I feel in writing is superior to any
that I might find in living. Moreover, the one is not
incompatible with the other."

"So they say," replied Lafcadio. Then abruptly raising his voice, which he had dropped as though inadvertently: "Do you know what it is I dislike about writing?
—All the scratchings out and touchings up that are
necessary."

"Do you think there are no corrections in life too?"
asked Julius, beginning to prick up his ears.

"You misunderstand me. In life one corrects *oneself*
—one improves *oneself*—so people say; but one can't
correct what one *does*. It's the power of revising that
makes writing such a colourless affair—such a . . ."
(He left his sentence unfinished.) "Yes! that's what
seems to me so fine about life. It's like fresco-painting
—erasures aren't allowed."

"Would there be much to erase in your life?"

"No . . . not much so far. . . . And as one can't . . ."
Lafcadio was silent a moment, and then: "All the
same, it was because I wanted to make an erasure that
I flung my pocket-book into the fire! . . . Too late—
as you see! You must admit, however, that you didn't
understand what it was all about."

No! Julius would never admit that.

"Will you allow me a few questions?" he said, by way
of answer.

Lafcadio rose to his feet so abruptly that Julius thought
he was going to make off on the spot; but he only went
up to the window and, raising the muslin curtain:

"Is this garden yours?" he asked.

"No," said Julius.

"M. de Baraglioul, I have hitherto allowed no one to pry in the smallest degree into my life," went on Lafcadio without turning round. Then, as he walked back towards Julius, who had begun to take him for nothing more than a schoolboy: "But to-day is a red-letter day; for once in my life I will give myself a holiday. Put your questions—I undertake to answer them all. . . . Oh! let me tell you first that I have turned away that young baggage who showed you into my room yesterday."

Julius thought it proper to put on an air of concern. "Because of me! Really . . ."

"Pooh! I had been looking for an excuse to get rid of her for some time past."

"Were you . . . m . . . m . . . living with her?" asked Julius, rather awkwardly.

"Yes; for health's sake. . . . But as little as possible, and in memory of a friend of mine whose mistress she had been."

"Monsieur Protos, perhaps?" ventured Julius, who was now firmly determined to stifle his indignation—his disgust—his reprobation—and to show—on this first occasion—no more of his astonishment than was necessary to make his rejoinders sufficiently lively.

"Yes, Protos," replied Lafcadio, brimming over with laughter. "Would you like to know about Protos?"

"To know something of your friends would be perhaps a step towards knowing you."

"He was an Italian of the name of . . . My word, I've forgotten, and it's of no consequence. The other boys—even the masters—never called him anything but Protos from the day he unexpectedly carried off a first for Greek composition."

"I don't remember ever having been first myself," said Julius, to encourage confidence, "but, like you, I have always wanted to be friends with those who were. So Protos . . . ?"

"Oh! it was because of a bet he made. Before that, though he was among the elder boys, he had always been one of the last of the class—whilst I was one of the youngest—not that I worked any the better for that. Protos showed the greatest contempt for everything the masters taught us; but one day, when one of the fellows who was good at book-learning and whom he detested, said to him: 'It's all very fine to despise what you can't do' (or something to that effect), Protos got his back up, worked hard for a fortnight and to such purpose that at the next Greek composition class he went up over the other fellows' heads and took the first place to the utter amazement of us all—of *them* all, I should say. As for me, I had too high an opinion of Protos to be much astonished. When he said to me: 'I'll show them it's not so difficult as all that,' I believed him."

"If I understand you rightly, Protos influenced you not a little?"

"Perhaps. At any rate he rather overawed me. As a matter of fact, however, I never had but one single intimate conversation with him—but that seemed to me so cogent that the very next day I ran away from school, where I was beginning to droop like a plant in a cellar, and made my way on foot to Baden, where my mother was living at that time with my uncle, the Marquis de Gesvres. . . . But we are beginning by the end. You would certainly question me very badly. Just let me tell you my own story as it comes. You will learn more

in that way than you would ever dream of asking me—
more, very likely, than you will care to learn. . . . No,
thank you, I prefer my own," said he, taking out his case
and throwing away the cigarette which Julius had offered
him when he first came in and which he had allowed to
go out while he was talking.

VII

"I was born at Bucharest in 1874," he began slowly,
"and, as I think you know, I lost my father a few months
after my birth. The first person who stands out in my
recollection at my mother's side, was a German, my
uncle, the Baron Heldenbruck. But as I lost him when
I was twelve years old, I have only a hazy recollection of
him. He was, it seems, a distinguished financier. As
well as his own language, he taught me arithmetic, and
that by such ingenious devices that I found it prodigiously
amusing. He made me what he used laughingly to call
his 'cashier'—that is, he gave into my keeping a whole
fortune of petty cash, and wherever we went together, it
was I who had to do the paying. Whatever he bought—
and he used to buy a great deal—he insisted on my adding up the bill in as short a time as it took me to pull the
notes or coins out of my pocket. Sometimes he used to
puzzle me with foreign money, so that there were
questions of exchange; then of discount, of interest, of
brokerage and finally even of speculation. With such a
training, I very soon became fairly clever at doing multi-
plication—and even division—sums of several figures in
my head. . . . Don't be alarmed" (for he saw Julius's
eyebrows bginning to frown), "it gave me no taste either

for money or reckoning. For instance, if you care to know, I never keep accounts. In reality this early education of mine was merely practical and matter-of-fact. It never touched anything vital in me. . . . Then Heldenbruck was wonderfully understanding about the proper hygiene for children; he persuaded my mother to let me go bare-headed and bare-footed in all weathers, and to keep me out of doors as much as possible; he used even to give me a cold dip himself every day, summer and winter. I enjoyed it immensely. . . . But you don't care about these details."

"Yes, yes!"

"Then he was called away on business to America and I never saw him again.

"My mother's salon in Bucharest was frequented by the most brilliant, and also, as far as I can judge from recollection, by the most mixed society; but her particular intimates at that time were my uncle, Prince Wladimir Bielkowski and Ardengo Baldi, whom for some reason I never called my uncle. They spent three or four years at Bucharest in the service of Russia (I was going to say Poland) and of Italy. I learnt from each of them his own language—Polish, that is, and Italian—as for Russian, I read and understand it pretty well, but I have never spoken it fluently. In the society of the kind of people who frequented my mother's house and who made a great deal of me, not a day passed without my having occasion to practise three or four languages; and at the age of thirteen I could speak them all without any accent and with almost equal ease—and yet French preferably, because it was my father's tongue and my mother had made a point of my learning it first.

"Bielkowski, like everyone else who wanted to please my mother, took considerable notice of me; it always seemed as though *I* were the person to be courted; but in his case I think it was disinterested, for he always followed his bent, however rapidly it led him and in whatever direction. He paid a great deal of attention to me even outside of anything my mother could have knowledge of, and I couldn't help being flattered by the particular attachment he had for me. Our rather humdrum existence was transformed by this singular person, from one day to the next, into a kind of riotous holiday. No! to talk of his *yielding* to his bent is not enough; his bent was a wild and precipitous rush; he flung himself upon his pleasure with a kind of frenzy.

"For three summers he carried us off to a villa, or rather to a castle, on the Hungarian slope of the Carpathians, near Eperjes; we often used to drive there, but we preferred riding and my mother enjoyed nothing better than scouring the country and the forests—which were very beautiful—on horseback and in any direction our fancy led us. The pony which Wladimir gave me was the thing I loved best on earth for a whole year.

"During the second summer, Ardengo Baldi joined us; it was then that he taught me chess. Heldenbruck had broken me in to doing sums in my head and I was pretty soon able to play without looking at the chessboard.

"Baldi got on very well with Bielkowski. Of an evening, in our solitary tower, plunged in the silence of the park and the forest, we all four used to sit up till late into the night, playing game after game of cards; for though I was only a child—thirteen years old—Baldi, who hated dummy, had taught me how to play whist—and how to cheat.

"Juggler, conjurer, mountebank, acrobat, he began to frequent us just at the time when my imagination was emerging from the long fast to which it had been subjected by Heldenbruck. I was hungry for marvels—credulous—of a green and eager curiosity. Later on, Baldi explained his tricks to me, but no familiarity could abolish that first sensation of mystery when, the first evening, I saw him light his cigarette at his little finger-nail, and then, as he had been losing at cards, draw out of my ears and my nose as many roubles as he wanted—which absolutely terrified me, but greatly entertained the company, for he kept saying, still with the same perfect coolness: 'Fortunately this boy here is an inexhaustible mine!'

"On the evenings when he was alone with my mother and me, he was for ever inventing some new game, some surprise, some absurd joke or other; he mimicked all our acquaintance, pulled faces, made himself unrecognisable, imitated all sorts of voices, the cries of animals, the sounds of instruments, produced extraordinary noises from Heaven knows where, sang to the accompaniment of the guzla, danced, pranced, walked on his hands, jumped over the tables and chairs, juggled with his bare feet like a Japanese, twirling the drawing-room screen or the small tea-table on the tip of his big toe; he juggled with his hands still better; at his bidding, a torn and crumpled piece of paper would burst forth into a swarm of white butterflies, which I would blow this way and that, and which the fluttering of his fan would keep hovering in the air. In his neighbourhood, objects lost their weight and reality—their presence even—or else took on some fresh, queer, unexpected significance, totally remote from all utility. 'There are very few things it isn't amusing to juggle with,' he used to say. And with it all he was so funny that I used to grow faint with laughing, and my mother would cry out: 'Stop, Baldi! Cadio will never be able to sleep.' And, indeed, my nerves must have been pretty solid to hold out against such excitements.

"I benefited greatly by this teaching; at the end of a few months I could have given points to Baldi himself in more than one of his tricks, and even . . ."

"It is clear, my dear boy, that you were given a most careful education," interrupted Julius at this moment.

Lafcadio burst out laughing at the novelist's horrified countenance. "Oh! none of it sank very deep; don't be alarmed. But it was high time Uncle Faby appeared on the scene, wasn't it? It was he who became intimate with my mother when Bielkowski and Baldi were called away to other posts."

"Faby? Was it his writing I saw on the first page of your pocket-book?"

"Yes. Fabian Taylor, Lord Gravensdale. He took my mother and me to a villa he had rented near Duino on the Adriatic, where my health and strength greatly improved. The coast at that place forms a rocky peninsula which was entirely occupied by the grounds of the villa. There I ran wild, spending the whole day long under the pines, among the rocks and creeks, or swimming or canoeing in the sea. The photograph you saw belongs to that time. I burnt that too."

"It seems to me," said Julius, "that you might have

made yourself a little more respectable for the occasion."

"That's exactly what I couldn't have done," answered Lafcadio, laughing. "Faby, under pretence of wanting me to get bronzed, kept all my wardrobe under lock and key—even my linen. . . ."

"And what did your mother say?"

"She was very much entertained; she said if her guests were shocked they might go; but as a matter of fact it didn't prevent any single one of our visitors from remaining."

"And during all this time, my poor boy, your education . . . !"

"Yes, I was so quick at learning that my mother rather neglected it; it was not till I was sixteen that she seemed suddenly to become aware of the fact, and after a marvellous journey in Algeria, which I took with Uncle Faby (I think it was the best time of my life), I was sent to Paris and put in charge of a thick-skinned brute of a jailer, who looked after my schooling."

"After such excessive liberty, I readily understand that constraint of that kind must have seemed rather hard to you."

"I should never have borne it without Protos. He was a boarder at the same school as I—in order to learn French, it was said; but he spoke it to perfection and I could never make out the point of his being there—nor of my being there either. I was sick of the whole thing—pining away. I hadn't exactly any feeling of friendship for Protos, but I turned towards him as though I expected him to save me. He was a good deal older than I was and looked even older than he was, without a trace of childhood left in his bearing or tastes. His features were extraordinarily illuminating when he chose, and could express anything and everything; but when he was at rest he used to look like an idiot. One day when I chaffed him about it, he replied that the important thing in this world was never to look like what one was. He was not content merely with being thought humble—he wanted to be thought stupid. It amused him to say that what is fatal to most people is that they prefer parade to drill and won't hide their talents; but he didn't say it to anybody but me. He kept himself aloof from everyone—even from me, though I was the only person in the school he didn't despise. When once I succeeded in getting him to talk he became extraordinarily eloquent, but most of the time he was taciturn and seemed to be brooding over some dark design, which I should have liked to know about. When I asked him—politely, for no one ever treated him with familiarity—what he was doing in such a place, he answered: 'I am getting under way.' He had a theory that in life one could get out of the worst holes by saying to oneself: 'What's the odds!' That's what I repeated to myself so often that I ran away.

"I started with eighteen francs in my pocket and reached Baden by short stages, eating anything, sleeping anywhere. I was rather done up when I arrived, but, on the whole, pleased with myself, for I still had three francs left; it is true that I picked up five or six by the way. I found my mother there with my uncle de Gesvres, who was delighted with my escapade, and made up his mind to take me back to Paris; he was inconsolable, he said, that I should have unpleasant recollections of Paris. And it's a fact that when I went back there with him,

Paris made a much more favourable impression on me.

"The Marquis de Gesvres took a positively frenzied pleasure in spending money; it was a perpetual need— a craving; it seemed as though he were grateful to me for helping him to satisfy it—for increasing his appetite by the addition of my own. It was he who taught me (the contrary of Faby) to like dress. I think I wore my clothes well; he was a good master; his elegance was perfectly natural—like a second sincerity. I got on with him very well. We spent whole mornings together at the shirtmaker's, the shoemaker's, the tailor's; he paid particular attention to shoes, saying that you could tell a man as certainly by his shoes as by the rest of his dress and by his features—and more secretly. . . . He taught me to spend money without keeping accounts and with- out taking thought beforehand as to whether I should have enough to satisfy my fancy, my desire or my hunger. He laid it down as a principle that of these three it was always hunger that should be satisfied last, for (I remem- ber his words) the appeal of fancy or desire is fugitive, while hunger is certain to return and only becomes more imperative the longer it has to wait. He taught me, too, not to enjoy a thing more because it had cost a great deal, nor less if, by chance, it cost nothing at all.

"It was at this point that I lost my mother. A tele- gram called me suddenly back to Bucharest; I arrived in time only to see her dead. There I learnt that after the Marquis's departure she had run so deeply into debt that she had left no more than just enough to clear her es- tate, so that there was no expectation for me of a single copeck, or a single pfennig or a single groschen. Directly after the funeral I returned to Paris, where I thought I

should find my uncle de Gesvres; but he had unexpectedly left for Russia without leaving an address.

"There is no need to tell you my reflections. True,
I had certain accomplishments in my outfit by means of
which one can always manage to pull through; but the
more I was in need of them, the more repugnant I felt
to making use of them. Fortunately one night as I was
walking the pavement rather at a loose end, I came across
Proto's ex-mistress—the Carola Venitequa you saw yesterday—who gave me ·decent house-room. A few days
later I received a rather mysterious communication to
say that a scanty allowance would be paid me on the
first of every month at a certain solicitor's; I have a
horror of getting to the bottom of things and I drew it
without further enquiries. Then you came along . . .
and now you know more or less everything I felt inclined
to tell you."

"It is fortunate," said Julius solemnly, "it is fortunate,
Lafcadio, that a little money is coming your way; with
no profession, with no education, condemned to live by
expedients . . . now that I know you, and such as I
take you for, you were ready for anything."

"On the contrary, ready for nothing," replied Lafcadio,
looking at Julius gravely. "In spite of all I have told
you, I see that you *don't* know me. Nothing hinders me
so effectually as want. I have never yet been tempted
but by the things that could be of no service to me."

"Paradoxes, for instance. And is that what you call
nourishing?"

"It depends on the stomach. You choose to give the
name of paradox to what yours refuses. As for me, I
should let myself die of hunger if I had nothing before

me but such a hash of bare bones as the logic you feed your characters on."

"Allow me . . ."

"The hero of your last book, at any rate. Is it true that it's a portrait of your father? The pains you take to keep him always and everywhere consistent with you and with himself—faithful to his duties and his principles—to your theories, that is—you can imagine how it strikes a person like me! . . . Monsieur de Baraglioul, you may take my word for it—I am a creature of inconsequence. And look, how much I have been talking! when only yesterday I considered myself the most silent, the most secretive, the most retired of beings. But it was a good thing that we should become acquainted without delay—there will be no need to go over the ground again. To-morrow—this evening I shall withdraw again into my privacy."

The novelist, completely thrown off his centre by these remarks, made an effort to recover himself.

"In the first place you may rest assured that there is no such thing as inconsequence—in psychology any more than in physics," he began. "You are a being in process of formation and . . ."

Repeated knocks at the door interrupted him. But as no one appeared, it was Julius who left the room. A confused noise of voices reached Lafcadio through the open door. Then there was a long silence. Lafcadio, after waiting for ten minutes, was preparing to go, when a servant in livery came in to him:

"Monsieur le Comte says that he won't ask you to wait any longer, Sir. He has just had bad news of his father and hopes you will kindly excuse him."

From the tone in which this was said, Lafcadio guessed that the old Count was dead. He mastered his emotion.

"Courage!" said he to himself as he returned homewards. "The moment has come. *It is time to launch the ship*.* From whatever quarter the wind blows now it will be the right one. Since I cannot live really near the old man, I might as well prepare to leave him altogether."

As he passed by the hotel porter's lodge, he gave him the small box which he had been carrying about with him ever since the day before.

"Please give this parcel to Mlle. Venitequa when she comes in this evening, and kindly prepare my bill."

An hour later his box was packed and he sent for a cab. He went off without leaving an address. His solicitor's was enough.

* In English in the original. (*Translator's note.*)

BOOK III: AMÉDÉE FLEURISSOIRE

I

The Countess Guy de Saint-Prix, Julius's younger sister, who had been suddenly summoned to Paris by Count Juste-Agénor's death, had not long since returned to Pezac (an elegant country residence, four miles out of Pau, which she had scarcely ever left since her widowhood, and to which she had become more than ever attached now that her children were all married and settled), when she received a singular visit.

She had just come in from her drive (she was in the habit of going out every morning in a light dog-cart which she drove herself), when she was informed that there was a priest in the drawing-room who had been waiting for over an hour to see her. The stranger came with an introduction from Cardinal André, as was shown by the card which was handed to the Countess; the card was in an envelope; under the Cardinal's name, in his fine and almost feminine handwriting, were written the following words:

"Recommends Father J. P. Salus, canon of Virmontal, to the Countess de Saint-Prix's very particular attention."

That was all—and it was enough. The Countess was always glad to receive members of the clergy; Cardinal André, moreover, held the Countess's soul in the hollow of his hand. Without a second's delay, she hurried to the drawing-room and excused herself for having kept the visitor waiting.

The canon of Virmontal was a fine figure of a man. His noble countenance shone with a manly energy which conflicted strangely with the hesitating caution of his voice and gestures; and in like manner his hair, which was almost white, formed a surprising contrast to the bright and youthful freshness of his complexion.

Notwithstanding the Countess's affability, the conversation at the outset was laborious, lagging in conventional phrases, round about the lady's recent bereavement, Cardinal André's health and Julius's renewed failure to enter the Academy. All this while the Abbé's utterance was becoming slower and more muffled and the expression of his countenance more and more harrowing. At last he rose, but instead of taking leave:

"Madame la comtesse," he said, "I should like to speak to you—on behalf of the Cardinal—about an important matter. But our voices sound very loud in this room and the number of doors alarms me; I am afraid of being overheard."

The Countess adored confidences and mysteries; she showed the chanoine into a small boudoir, which could be entered only from the drawing-room, and shut the door.

"We are alone here," she said. "Speak freely."

But instead of speaking, the abbé, who had seated himself on a pouf opposite the Countess, pulled a silk handkerchief out of his pocket and buried his face in it, sobbing convulsively. The Countess, in some perplexity, stretched out her hand for her work basket, which was standing on a small table beside her, took out a bottle of salts, hesitated whether she should offer them to the abbé, and finally solved the difficulty by smelling them herself.

"Forgive me," said the abbé at last, disinterring an apoplectic face from his handkerchief. "I know you are too good a Catholic, Madame la comtesse, not to understand and share my emotion, when you hear . . ."

The Countess could not abide lack of control; her propriety took refuge behind a lorgnette. The abbé quickly recovered himself and, drawing his chair nearer:

"It required the Cardinal's solemn assurance, Madame la comtesse, before I could bring myself to come and see you—his assurance that your faith was something more than worldly conventionality—not a mere cloak for indifference."

"Let's get to the point, Monsieur l'abbé."

"The Cardinal assured me, then, that I might have perfect confidence in your discretion—the discretion of the confessional, if I may say so. . . ."

"Excuse me, Monsieur l'abbé, but if the secret is one with which the Cardinal is acquainted—a secret of such importance—how is it that he has not told me of it himself?"

The abbé's smile alone would have sufficed to show the Countess the futility of her question.

"In a letter! But, my dear Madam, the post nowadays opens all cardinals' letters."

"He might have confided one to you."

"Yes, Madam, but who knows what may happen to a paper, with the surveillance to which we are subjected? More than that—the Cardinal prefers to ignore what I am about to tell you—to have nothing to do with it. . . .

Ah! Madam, at the last moment my courage fails me and I can hardly . . ."

"Monsieur l'abbé, as you are a stranger to me, I cannot feel offended that your confidence in me is no greater," said the Countess very gently, turning her head aside and letting her lorgnette fall. "I have the utmost respect for the secrets which are confided to me. God knows I have never betrayed the smallest. But I have never been a person to solicit confidences."

She made a slight movement as though to rise; the abbé stretched out his hand toward her.

"You will excuse me, Madame la comtesse, when you condescend to reflect that you are the first woman to have been judged worthy by the persons who have entrusted me with the fearful task of enlightening you—the first, I say, worthy to hear and keep this secret. I am alarmed, I confess, when I consider that this revelation is of a nature to weigh heavily—crushingly—on a woman's intelligence."

"There are very mistaken opinions held about the feebleness of women's intelligence," said the Countess almost dryly; then, with her hands slightly raised, she sat concealing her curiosity beneath an air which was a mixture of absent-mindedness, resignation and ecstatic vagueness—an air which she thought would be appropriate for receiving an important and confidential communication from the Church. The abbé drew his chair still nearer.

But the secret which Father Salus prepared to confide to the Countess seems to me even now so disconcertingly peculiar that I cannot venture to relate it without further precautions.

Fiction there is—and history. Certain critics of no
little discernment have considered that fiction is history
which *might* have taken place, and history fiction which
has taken place. We are, indeed, forced to acknowledge
that the novelist's art often compels belief, just as reality
sometimes defies it. Alas! there exists an order of minds
so sceptical that they deny the possibility of any fact as
soon as it diverges from the commonplace. It is not for
them that I write.

Whether the representative of God upon earth was
actually snatched from the Holy See and by the machinations of the Quirinal stolen, so to speak, from the whole
body of Christendom, is an exceedingly thorny problem,
and one which I have not the temerity to raise here. But
it is an *historical* fact that towards the end of the year
1893 a rumour to that effect was in circulation. Certain
newspapers mentioned it timidly; they were silenced. A
pamphlet on the subject appeared at St. Malo * and was
suppressed. For, on the one hand, the freemasons' were
as little anxious that the report of such an abominable
outrage should be spread abroad, as, on the other, the
Catholic leaders were afraid to support—or could not resign themselves to countenance—the extraordinary collections which were immediately started in this connec-
tion. There is no doubt that innumerable pious souls
bled themselves freely (the sums which were collected—or
dispersed—on this occasion are reckoned at close upon
half a million francs), but what remained doubtful was
whether all those who received the funds were really the

---

* *Compte rendu de la Délivrance de Sa Sainteté Léon XIII
emprisonné dans les cachots du Vatican* (Saint-Malo, imprimerie
Y. Billois, rue de l'Orme 4), 1893. (*Author's note.*)

devout persons they pretended to be, or whether some of them were not mere swindlers. At any rate, for the successful accomplishment of this scheme there was necessary, in the absence of religious conviction, an audacity, a skilfulness, a tact, an eloquence, a knowledge of facts and characters, a vigour of constitution, such as fall to the lot of few only in this world—strapping fellows, like Protos, for instance, Lafcadio's old school-mate. I honestly warn the reader that it is he I am now introducing, under the appearance and borrowed name of the canon of Virmontal.

The Countess, firmly determined neither to open her lips nor change her attitude, nor even her expression, before getting to the very roots of the secret, listened imperturbably to the bogus priest, whose assurance was gradually becoming more and more confident. He had risen and begun striding up and down. To make his explanations clearer, he traced the affair back—not exactly to its sources (since the conflict between the Church and the Lodge—inherent in their very essence— may be said to date from all time) but to certain incidents in which their hostility had openly declared itself. He first of all begged the Countess to remember that in December, '92, the Pope had published two letters, addressed, one to the Italian people, and the other more particularly to the bishops, warning Catholics against the machinations of the freemasons; then, as the Countess's memory failed her, he was obliged to go further back and recall the erection of Giordano Bruno's statue, which had been planned and presided over by Crispi, behind whom the Lodge had till then concealed itself. He told of Crispi's fury that the Pope should have repulsed his advances, should have refused to negotiate with him—and in this instance, what could negotiation mean but submission? He traced the history of that tragic day and told how the two camps had taken up their positions: how the freemasons had at last lifted their mask, and—while the whole diplomatic corps accredited to the Holy See were calling at the Vatican and thus showing their contempt for Crispi and their veneration for the Holy Father in his grievous affliction—how the Lodge, flags flying and bands playing, had acclaimed the illustrious blasphemer in the Campo dei Fiori, on the spot where the insulting and idolatrous effigy had been raised.

"In the consistory which followed shortly after, on June 30, 1889," he continued (he was still standing, leaning now across the table, his arms in front of him, his face bent down towards the Countess), "Leo XIII gave vent to his vehement indignation. His protestations were heard by the entire universe, and all Christendom shuddered to hear him speak of leaving Rome! Leaving Rome! Those were my words! . . . All this, Madame la Comtesse, you know already—you grieved for it—you remember it—as well as I."

He again began his pacing to and fro.

"At last Crispi fell from power. Would the Church be able to breathe again? In December, 1892, you remember, the Pope wrote those two letters. Madam . . ."

He sat down again abruptly, drew his arm-chair nearer to the sofa, and, seizing the Countess's arm:

"A month later the Pope was imprisoned!"

As the Countess remained obstinately impassive, the canon let go her arm and continued in a calmer tone:

"I shall not attempt, Madam, to arouse your pity for the sufferings of a captive. Women's hearts are, I know, always moved by misfortune. It is to your intelligence that I appeal, Countess, and I beg you to consider the state of miserable confusion into which the disappearance of our spiritual leader plunged us Christians."

A slight shade passed over the Countess's pale brow.

"No Pope is a frightful thing, but—God save us—a false Pope is more frightful still. For the Lodge, in order to cover up its crime—nay, more, in the hopes of inducing the Church to compromise herself fatally—the Lodge, I say, has installed on the pontifical throne, in the place of Leo XIII, some cat's-paw or other of the Quirinal's, some vile impostor! And it is to him that we must pretend submission so as not to injure the real one—and oh! shame upon shame! it was to him that all Christendom bowed down at the Jubilee!"

At these words the handkerchief he was wringing in his hands tore across.

"The first act of the false Pope was that too famous encyclical—the encyclical to France—at the thought of which the heart of every Frenchman worthy of the name still bleeds. Yes, yes, Madam, I know how your great lady's generous heart must have suffered at hearing Holy Church deny the holy cause of royalty, and the Vatican such is the fact—give its approval to the Republic. Alas! Be comforted, Madam! You were right in your amazement. Be comforted, Madame la Comtesse. But think of the sufferings of the Holy Father in his captivity at hearing the cat's-paw—the impostor proclaim him a Republican!"

Then, flinging himself back with a laugh that was half a sob:

"And what did you think, Comtesse de Saint-Prix, what did you think, when as a corollary to that cruel encyclical our Holy Father granted an audience to the editor of the *Petit Journal!* You realize the impossibility of such a thing. Your generous heart has already cried aloud to you that it is false!"

"But," exclaimed the Countess, no longer able to contain herself, "it must be cried aloud to the whole world!"

"No, Madam! It must be kept silent!" thundered the abbé, towering formidably above her. It must first be kept silent; we must keep silent so as to be able to act."

Then apologetically, with a voice turned suddenly piteous:

"You see I am speaking to you as if you were a man."

"Quite right, Monsieur l'abbé. To act, you said. Quick! What have you decided on?"

"Ah! I knew I should find in you a noble, virile impatience, worthy the blood of the Baragliouls! But, alas! nothing is more dangerous in the present circumstances than untimely zeal. Certain of the elect, it is true, have been apprised of these abominable crimes, but it is indispensable, Madam, that we should be able to count on their absolute discretion, on their total and ungrudging obedience to the instructions which they will in due time receive. To act without us is to act against us. And in addition to the Church's disapproval, which —God save us!—may even go so far as to entail excommunication, all private initiative will be met with the most explicit and categorical denials from our party. This is a crusade, Madame la comtesse, yes! but a secret crusade. Forgive me for insisting on this point, but I am specially commissioned by the Cardinal to impress it on you; it is his firm intention, moreover, to know absolutely nothing of what is going on, and if he is spoken to on the subject he will fail to understand a single word. The Cardinal will not have seen me; and if, later on, circumstances throw us together again, let it be thoroughly understood there too that you and I have never spoken to each other. Our Holy Father will recognise his true servants in good time."

Somewhat disappointed, the Countess asked timidly: "But then . . . ?"

"We are at work, Madame la comtesse, we are at work; have no fear. And I am even authorised to reveal to you a portion of our plan of campaign."

He settled himself squarely in his arm-chair, well opposite the Countess, who was now leaning forward, her hands up to her face, her elbows on her knees, and her chin resting between her palms.

He began by saying that the Pope was probably not confined in the Vatican, but in the Castle of St. Angelo, which, as the Countess certainly knew, communicated with the Vatican by an underground passage; that doubtless it would not be very difficult to rescue him from this prison, were it not for the semi-superstitious fear that all his attendants had of the freemasons, though in their inmost hearts with and of the Church. The kidnapping of the Holy Father was an example which had struck terror into their souls. Not one of the attendants would agree to give his assistance until means had been afforded him to leave the country and live out of the persecutors' reach. Important sums had been contributed for this purpose by a few persons of noteworthy piety and discretion. There remained but one single obstacle to overcome, but it was one which necessitated more than all the others put together. For this obstacle was a prince—Leo XIII's jailer-in-chief.

"You remember, Madame la comtesse, the mystery which still shrouds the double death of the Archduke Rudolph, the Austrian Crown Prince, and of his young bride, Maria Wettsyera, Princess Grazioli's niece, who was found in a dying condition beside him. . . . Suicide, it was said. But the pistol was put there merely as a blind to public opinion; the truth is they were both poisoned. A cousin of the Archduke's—an Archduke himself—who, alas! was madly in love with Maria Wettsyera, had been unable to bear seeing her the bride of another. . . . After this abominable crime, Jean-Salvador de Lorraine, son of Marie-Antoinette, Grand-Duchess of Tuscany, left the court of his cousin, the Emperor Francis Joseph. Knowing that he was discovered at Vienna, he went to Rome to confess his guilt to the Pope—to throw himself at his feet—to implore his pardon. He obtained it. Monaco, however—Cardinal Monaco-la-Valette—alleging the necessity of penance, had him confined in the Castle of St. Angelo, where he has been languishing for the last three years."

The canon delivered the whole of this speech in a voice that was perfectly level; at this point he paused for a moment; then, emphasising his words with a slight tap of his foot:

"This is the man," he cried, "that Monaco has made jailer-in-chief to Leo XIII."

"What, the Cardinal!" exclaimed the Countess. "Can a cardinal be a freemason?"

"Alas!" said the canon pensively, "the Church has suffered sad inroads from the Lodge. You can easily see, Madame la comtesse, that if the Church had defended herself better, none of this would have happened. The Lodge was enabled to seize the person of the Holy Father only through the connivance of a few highly placed accomplices."

"But it's appalling!"

"What more is there to tell you, Madame la comtesse? Jean-Salvador imagined he was the prisoner of the Church, when in reality he was the prisoner of the freemasons. He will not consent to work for the liberation of our Holy Father unless he is at the same time enabled to flee himself. And he can flee only to a very distant country, where there is no extradition. He demands two hundred thousand francs."

Valentine de Saint-Prix had sunk back in her chair and let her arms drop beside her; at these words she flung her head back, uttered a feeble moan and lost consciousness. The canon darted forward.

"Courage, Madame la comtesse"—he patted her hands briskly—"it's not so bad as all that, God save us!"—he put the smelling-salts to her nose. "A hundred and forty of the two hundred thousand have been subscribed already"—and as the Countess opened one eye: "The duchesse de Lectoure has not promised more than fifty; there remain sixty to be found."

"You shall have them," murmured the Countess, almost inaudibly.

"Countess, the Church never doubted you."

He rose very gravely—almost solemnly—paused a moment, and then:

"Comtesse de Saint-Prix, I have the most absolute confidence in your generous promise; but reflect for a moment on the innumerable difficulties which will accompany, hamper, and possibly prevent the handing over of this sum; a sum, which as I told you, it will be your duty to forget ever having given me, which I myself must deny ever having received; for which I am not even permitted to give you a receipt. . . . The only prudent method is for you to hand it over to me personally. We are watched. My presence in your house may have been observed. Can we ever be sure of the servants? Think of the Comte de Baraglioul's election! I must not be seen here again."

But as after these words he stood rooted to the ground without stirring or speaking, the Countess understood.

"But, Monsieur l'abbé, it stands to reason I haven't got such an enormous sum as that about me. And even . . ."

The abbé showed signs of impatience, so that she did not dare to add that she wanted time (for she had great hopes that she would not have to provide the whole sum herself).

"What is to be done?" she murmured.

Then, as the canon's eyebrows grew more and more menacing:

"It's true I have a few jewels upstairs . . ."

"Oh, fie! Madam! Jewels are keepsakes. Can you fancy me as a bagman? And do you suppose I can afford to arouse suspicion by trying to get a good price for them? Why, I should run the risk of compromising you and our undertaking into the bargain."

His deep voice had grown harsh and violent. The Countess trembled slightly.

"Wait a minute, Monsieur le chanoine, I will go and see what I have got upstairs."

She came down again in a moment or two, nervously crumpling a bundle of bank-notes in her hand.

"Fortunately I have just collected my rents. ! can give you six thousand, five hundred francs at once."

The canon shrugged his shoulders:

"What do you suppose I can do with that?"

And with an air of sorrowful contempt he loftily waved the Countess away.

"No, Madam, no! I will not take those notes. I will take them with the others or not at all. Only petty souls can consent to petty dealings. When can you give me the whole amount?"

"How much time can you let me have? . . . a week . . . ?" asked the Countess, who was thinking how she could make a collection.

"Comtesse de Saint-Prix, has the Church been deceived in you? A week! I will say but one word—the Pope is waiting."

Then, raising his arms to Heaven:

"What! the incomparable honour of delivering him lies in your hands and you delay! Have a fear, Madam, have a fear that the Lord in the day of your own deliverance may keep your niggardly soul waiting and languishing in just such a manner outside the gates of Paradise!"

He became menacing—terrible; then, suddenly and swiftly raising the cross of a rosary to his lips, he absented himself in a rapid prayer.

"Surely there's time for me to write to Paris?" moaned the Countess wildly.

"Telegraph! Tell your banker to deposit the sixty thousand francs at the Crédit Foncier in Paris and tell them to telegraph to the Crédit Foncier at Pau to remit the sum immediately. It's rudimentary."

"I have some money on deposit at Pau," she stammered.

Then his indignation knew no bounds.

"Ah, Madam! all this beating about the bush before you tell me so? Is this your eagerness? What would you say now if I were to refuse your assistance? . . ."

Then pacing up and down the room, his hands crossed behind his back, and as though nothing she could say now could placate him:

"This is worse than lukewarmness," and he made little clicks with his tongue to show his disgust, "this is almost duplicity."

"Monsieur l'abbé, I implore you . . ."

For a few moments the abbé, with frowning brows, inflexibly continued his pacing. Then at last:

"You are acquainted, I know, with Father Boudin, with whom I am lunching this very morning—" (he pulled out his watch) "I shall be late. Make out a cheque in his name; he will be able to cash the sixty thousand at once and hand it over to me. When you see him again, just say that it was 'for the expiatory chapel'; he is a man of discretion and tact—he will not insist further. Well! What are you waiting for?"

The Countess, prostrate on the sofa, rose, dragged herself towards a small bureau, which she opened, and took out from it an olive-green cheque-book, a leaf of which she filled in with her long pointed handwriting.

"Excuse me for having been a little severe with you just now, Madame la comtesse," said the abbé in a softened voice as he took the cheque she held out to him, "but such interests are at stake!"

Then, slipping the cheque into an inner pocket:

"It would be impious to thank you, would it not?—even in the name of Him in whose hands I am but an unworthy instrument."

He was overcome by a brief fit of sobbing, which he stifled in his handkerchief; but recovering himself in a moment, with a sharp stamp of his heel on the ground, he rapidly murmured a few words in a foreign language.

"Are you Italian?" asked the Countess.

"Spanish! The sincerity of my emotions betrays me."

"Your accent doesn't. Really your French is so perfect . . ."

"You are very kind, Madame la comtesse. Excuse me for leaving you a little abruptly. Now that we have come to an arrangement, I shall be able to get to Narbonne this very evening; the archbishop is expecting me there impatiently. Good-bye!"

He took both the Countess's hands in his and, with his head thrown back, looked at her fixedly:

"Good-bye, Countess de Saint-Prix!" Then, with a finger on his lips:

"Remember that a word of yours may ruin everything."

He had no sooner left the house than the Countess flew to the bell-pull.

"Amélie, tell Pierre that I shall want the barouche directly after lunch to drive into Pau. Oh, and wait a minute! . . . Tell Germain to get his bicycle at once and take a note to Madame Fleurissoire. I'll write it now."

And leaning on the bureau which she had not shut, she wrote as follows:

"Dear Madame Fleurissoire,
    "I shall be coming to see you this afternoon. Please expect me at about two o'clock. I have something of the greatest importance to tell you. Will you arrange for us to be alone?"

She signed the note, then sealed the envelope and handed it to Amélie.

II

Madame Amédée Fleurissorie, *née* Péterat, the youngest sister of Veronica Armand-Dubois and Marguerite de Baraglioul, answered to the outlandish name of Arnica. Philibert Péterat, a botanist, who had acquired some celebrity under the Second Empire on account of his conjugal misfortunes, had as a young man determined to give the names of flowers to any children he might happen to have. Some of his friends considered the name of Veronica which he gave to his first-born, somewhat peculiar; but when it was followed by the name of Marguerite and people insinuated that he had climbed down —given in to public opinion—conformed to the commonplace, he determined in a cantankerous moment to bestow upon his third product a name so resolutely botanical as to stop the mouths of all back-biters.

Shortly after Arnica's birth, Philibert, whose temper

had become soured, separated from his wife, left the capital and settled at Pau. His wife would linger on in Paris during the winter months, but every spring, at the beginning of the fine weather, she would return to Tarbes, her native town, and invite her two elder daughters to stay with her there in the old family mansion which she occupied.

Veronica and Marguerite divided the year between Tarbes and Pau. As for little Arnica, whom her mother and sisters looked down upon (it is true she was rather foolish and more pathetic than pretty), she spent the whole time, summer as well as winter, with her father.

The child's greatest joy was to go botanising in the country; but the eccentric old man would often give way to his morose temper and leave her in the lurch; he would go off by himself on an inordinately long expedition, come home dog-tired and immediately after the evening meal take to his bed, without giving his daughter the charity of a word or a smile. When he was in a poetical mood he would play the flute and insatiably repeat the same tune over and over again. The rest of his time he spent drawing portraits of flowers in minute detail.

An old servant, nicknamed Réséda, who was both cook and housemaid, looked after the child and taught her what little she knew herself. With this education, Arnica reached the age of ten hardly knowing how to read. Fear of his neighbour's tongues at last brought Philibert to a better sense of his duty. Arnica was sent to a school kept by a Madame Semène, a widow lady who instilled the rudiments of learning into a dozen or so little girls and a very few small boys.

Arnica Péterat—guileless and helpless creature—had
never until that moment suspected that there might be
anything laughable * in her name; on her first day at
school its ridicule came upon her as a sudden revelation;
she bowed her head, like some sluggish water-weed, to the
stream of jeers that flowed over her; she turned red;
she turned pale; she wept; and Madame Semène, by in-
judiciously punishing the whole class for its indecorous
conduct, added a spice of animosity to what had before
been a boisterous but not unkindly merriment.

Long, limp, anæmic and dull-eyed, Arnica stood with
dangling arms, staring stupidly, in the middle of the
little schoolroom, and when Madame Semène pointed out
"the third bench on the left, Mademoiselle Péterat," the
whole class, in spite of reprimands, burst out again
louder than ever.

Poor Arnica! Life seemed nothing but a dreary
avenue stretching interminably before her and bordered
on either side by sniggers and bullyings. Fortunately
for her, Madame Semène was not impervious to the little girl's misery, and she soon found a refuge in the widow's charitable bosom.

When lessons were over, Arnica was glad enough to
stay behind at school, rather than go home to find her
father absent; Madame Semène had a daughter, a girl
who was seven years older than Arnica and slightly hump-
backed, but good-natured; in the hopes of catching a husband for her, Madame Semène used to have Sunday
evening "at homes," and on two Sundays a year she

* There is an insinuation in Mlle. Péterat's name which might
be rendered in English by calling her Miss Fartwell. (*Translator's note.*)

would even get up a little party with recitations and dancing; these parties were attended by some of her old pupils, who came out of gratitude, escorted by their parents, and by a few youths without either means or prospects, who came out of idleness. Arnica was always present—a flower that lacked lustre—so modest as to be almost indistinguishable—but yet destined not to go altogether unperceived.

When, at fourteen, Arnica lost her father, it was Madame Semène who took in the orphan. Her two sisters, who were considerably older than she was, visited her only rarely. It was in the course of one of these visits, however, that Marguerite first met the young man who was to become her husband. Julius de Baraglioul was then aged twenty-eight and was on a visit to his grandfather, who, as we have already said, had settled in the neighbourhood of Pau shortly after the annexation of the Duchy of Parma by France.

Marguerite's brilliant marriage (as a matter of fact, the Misses Péterat were not absolutely without fortune) made her appear more distant than ever to Arnica's dazzled eyes; she had a shrewd suspicion that no Count—no Julius—would ever stoop to breathe her perfume. She envied her sister for having at last succeeded in escaping from the ill-sounding name of Péterat. The name of *Marguerite* was charming. How well it went with *de Baraglioul!* Alas! was there any name wedded to which *Arnica* would cease to seem ridiculous?

Repelled by the world of fact, her soul, in its soreness and immaturity, tried to take refuge in poetry. At sixteen, she wore two drooping ringlets on each side of her sallow face, and her dreamy blue eyes looked out their astonishment beside the blackness of her hair. Her tone-less voice was not ungentle; she read verses and made strenuous efforts to write them. She considered every-thing that helped her to escape from life, poetical.

Two young men, who since their early childhood had been friends and partners in affection, used to frequent Madame Semène's evening parties. One, weedy without being tall, scraggy rather than thin, with hair that was not so much fair as faded, with an aggressive nose and timid eyes, was Amédée Fleurissoire. The other was fat and stumpy, with stiff black hair growing low on his forehead, and the odd habit of holding his head on one side, his mouth open and his right hand stretched out in front of him: such is the portrait of Gaston Blafaphas. Amédée was the son of a stonecutter with a business in tombstones and funeral wreaths; Gaston's father had an important chemist's shop.

(However strange the name of Blafaphas may seem, it is very common in the villages of the lower slopes of the Pyrenees, though it is sometimes spelt in slightly differ-ent ways. Thus, for instance, in the single small town of Sta. . . , where the writer of these lines was once called on some business connected with an examination, he saw a notary Blaphaphas, a hairdresser Blafafaz, and a pork-butcher Blaphaface, who, on being questioned, disclaimed any common origin, while each one of them expressed considerable contempt for the name of the other two and its inelegant orthography.—But these philo-logical remarks will be of interest only to a somewhat restricted class of reader.)

What would Fleurissoire and Blafaphas have been with-out each other? It is hard to imagine such a thing. At school, during their recreation time they were continually together; constantly teased and tormented by the other boys, they gave each other patience, comfort and support. They were nicknamed the Blafafoires. To each of them their friendship seemed the ark of salvation—the single oasis in life's pitiless desert. Neither of them tasted a joy that he did not immediately wish to share with the other—or, to speak more truly, there were no joys for either of them save those which could be tasted together.

Indifferent scholars—in spite of their disarming industry—and fundamentally refractory to any sort of culture, the Blafafoires would always have been at the bottom of their form if it had not been for the assistance of Eudoxe Lévichon, who, in return for a small consideration, corrected and even wrote their exercises for them. This Lévichon was the son of one of the chief jewellers of the town. (Albert Lévy, shortly after his marriage twenty years earlier with the only daughter of the jeweller Cohen, had found his business so prosperous that he had quitted the lower quarters of the town in order to establish himself not far from the Casino, and at the same time he had judged it a favourable opportunity to unite and agglutinate the two names as he had united the two businesses.)

Blafaphas had a wiry constitution, but Fleurissoire was delicate. At the approach of puberty Gaston's superficies had turned dusky—one would have thought that the sap was going to burst forth into hair over the whole of his body; while Amédée's more sensitive epidermis resisted, grew fiery—grew pimply, as if the hair were bashful at making its appearance. Old Monsieur Blafaphas advised the use of detergents and every Monday Gaston used to bring over in his bag a bottle of anti-scorbutic mixture, which he surreptitiously handed to his friend. They used ointments as well.

About this time Amédée caught his first cold—a cold which, notwithstanding the salubrious climate of Pau, lasted all the winter and left behind an unfortunate bronchial delicacy. This gave Gaston the opportunity for renewed attentions; he overwhelmed his friend with liquorice, with jujubes, with cough mixtures and with eucalyptus pectoral lozenges, specially prepared by Monsieur Blafaphas *père* from a receipt which had been given him by an old *curé*. Amédée became subject to constant catarrh and had to resign himself to never going out without a comforter.

The highest flight of Amédée's ambition was to succeed to his father's business. Gaston, however, notwithtanding his indolent appearance, was not without initiative; even at school he amused himself with devising small inventions, chiefly, it must be confessed, of a somewhat trifling nature—a fly-trap, a weighing-machine for marbles, a safety lock for his desk—which, for that matter, had no more secrets in it than his heart. Innocent as these first applications of his industry were, they nevertheless led him on to the more serious labours which afterwards engaged him, and the first result of which was the invention of a "hygienic, fumivorous [or smoke-consuming] pipe for weak-chested and other smokers," which for a long time occupied a prominent place in the chemist's shop window.

Amédée Fleurissoire and Gaston Blafaphas both fell in love with Arnica at the same moment—it was as inev-

itable as fate. The admirable thing was that this budding passion, which each hastened to confess to the other,
instead of dividing them, only welded them together more
closely than ever. And, indeed, Arnica did not at first
give either of them any great cause for jealousy.
Neither the one nor the other, moreover, had declared
himself; and it would never have occurred to Arnica to
imagine their flame, notwithstanding their trembling
voices when, at Madame Semène's Sunday evenings, she
offered them raspberry vinegar, or camomile, or cowslip tea. And both of them, as they went home in
the evening, praised her grace, and the modesty of her
behaviour—grew concerned for her paleness—gathered
boldness.

They agreed to propose together on the same evening
and then submit to her choice. Arnica, young to love,
thanked Heaven in the surprise and simplicity of her
heart. She begged her two admirers to give her time
to reflect.

Truth to tell, she was not more attracted by the one
than the other, and was interested in them only because
they were interested in her, at a time when she had given
up all hopes of interesting anyone. During six whole
weeks, growing the while more and more perplexed,
Arnica relished with a mild intoxication her two suitors'
parallel wooing. And while, during their midnight walks,
the Blafafoires calculated together the rate of their respective progress, describing to each other lengthily and
undisguisedly every word, look and smile *she* had bestowed on them, Arnica, in the seclusion of her bedroom,
spent the time writing on bits of paper (which she afterwards carefully burnt in the flame of the candle) or else

in repeating indefatigably, turn and turn about: Arnica
Blafaphas? . . . Arnica Fleurissoire?—incapable of de-
ciding between the equal horror of these two atrocious
names.

Then, suddenly, on the evening of a little dance, she
had chosen Fleurissoire; had not Amédée just called her
Arnica, putting the accent on the penultimate in a way
that seemed to her Italian? (As a matter of fact, he had
done it without reflection, carried away, no doubt, by
Mademoiselle Semène's piano, with whose rhythm the
atmosphere was throbbing.) And this name of Arnica
—her own name—had there and then seemed to her
fraught with unexpected music—as capable as any other
of expressing poetry and love. . . . They were alone together in a little sitting-room next-door to the drawing-
room, and so close to each other that when Arnica, almost swooning with emotion and gratitude, let fall her
drooping head, it touched Amédée's shoulder; and then,
very gravely, he had taken Arnica's hand and kissed the
tips of her fingers.

When, during their walk home that night, Amédée had
announced his happiness to his friend, Gaston, contrary
to his custom, had said nothing, and as they were passing
a street lamp, Fleurissoire thought he saw him crying.
Could Amédée really have been simple enough to suppose that his friend would share his happiness to this
last degree? Abashed and remorseful, he took Blafaphas
in his arms (the street was empty) and swore that however great his love might be, his friendship was greater
still, that he had no intention of letting his marriage interfere with it, and, finally, that rather than feel that Blafaphas was suffering from jealousy, he was ready to promise

on his honour never to claim his conjugal rights.

Neither Blafaphas nor Fleurissoire possessed a very ardent temperament; Gaston, however, whose manhood troubled him a little more, kept silence and allowed Amédée to promise.

Shortly after Amédée's marriage, Gaston, who, in order to console himself, had plunged over head and ears into work, discovered his Plastic Plaster. The first consequence of this invention, which, to begin with, had seemed of very little importance, was that it brought about the revival of Lévichon's friendship for the Blafafoires—a friendship which for some time past had been allowed to lapse. Eudoxe Lévichon immediately divined the services which this composition would render to religious statuary. With a remarkable eye to contingencies, he at once christened it Roman Plaster.* The firm of Blafaphas, Fleurissoire and Lévichon was founded.

The undertaking was launched with a capital of sixty thousand francs, of which the Blafafoires modestly subscribed ten thousand. Lévichon, unwilling that his two friends should be pressed, generously provided the other fifty thousand. It is true that of these fifty thousand, forty were advanced by Fleurissoire out of Arnica's marriage portion; the sum was repayable in ten years with compound interest at 4½ per cent—which was more than Arnica had ever hoped for—and Amédée's small for-

---

* Roman Plastic Plaster (announced the catalogue) is a special fabrication of comparatively recent invention. This substance, of which Messrs. Blafaphas, Fleurissoire and Lévichon possess the unique secret, is a great advance on Marblette, Stucceen and other similar compositions, whose inferior qualities have been only too well established by use. (Follow the descriptions of the various models.) (*Author's note.*)

tune was thus guaranteed from the risks which such an undertaking must necessarily incur. The Blafafoires, on their side, brought as an asset their family connexions and those of the Baragliouls, which meant, when once Roman Plaster had proved its reliability, the patronage of several influential members of the clergy; these latter (besides giving one or two important orders themselves) persuaded several small parishes to supply the growing needs of the faithful from the firm of B., F. & L., the increasing improvement of artistic education having created a demand for works of more exquisite finish than those which satisfied the ruder faith of our ancestors. To supply this demand a few artists of acknowledged value in the Church's eyes, were enlisted by the firm of Roman Plaster, and were at last placed in the position of seeing their works accepted by the jury of the Salon. Leaving the Blafafoires at Pau, Lévichon established himself in Paris, where, with his social facility, the business soon developed considerably.

What could be more natural than that the Countess Valentine de Saint-Prix should endeavour, through Arnica, to interest the firm of Blafaphas & Co. in the secret cause of the Pope's deliverance, and that she should confidently hope that the Fleurissoires' extreme piety would reimburse her a portion of what she had subscribed? Unfortunately, the Blafafoires, owing to the minuteness of the amount which they had originally invested in the business, got very little out of it—two-twelfths of the disclosed profits and none at all of the others. The Countess could not be aware of this, for Arnica, like Amédée, was modestly shy of talking about their money matters.

III

"Dear Madame de Saint-Prix, what is the matter? Your letter frightened me."

The Countess dropped into the arm-chair which Arnica pushed towards her.

"Oh, Madame Fleurissoire! . . . Oh! mayn't I call you Arnica? . . . this trouble—it is yours as well as mine—will draw us together. Oh! if you only knew! . . ."

"Speak! Speak! don't leave me in suspense!"

"I've only just heard it myself. I'll tell you directly, but mind, it must be a secret between you and me."

"I have never betrayed anyone's confidence," said Arnica, plaintively—not that anyone had ever confided in her.

"You'll not believe it."

"Yes, yes," wailed Arnica.

"Ah!" wailed the Countess. "Oh, would you be kind enough to get me a cup of . . . anything . . . it doesn't matter what. . . . I feel as if I were fainting."

"What would you like? Cowslip? Lime-flower? Camomile?"

"It doesn't matter. . . . Tea, I think. . . . I wouldn't believe it myself at first."

"There's some boiling water in the kitchen. It won't take a minute."

While Arnica busied herself about the tea, the Countess appraised the drawing-room and its contents with a calculating eye. They were depressingly modest. A few green rep chairs; one red velvet arm-chair; one other arm-chair (in which she was seated) in common tapestry;

one table; one mahogany console; in front of the fire-place, a woolwork rug; on the chimney-piece, on each side of the alabaster clock (which was in a glass case), two large vases in alabaster fretwork, also in glass cases; on the table, a photograph album for the family photo-graphs; on the console, a figure of Our Lady of Lourdes in her grotto, in Roman Plaster (a small-sized model)—there was not a thing in the room that was not discour-aging, and the Countess felt her heart sink within her.

But after all they were perhaps only shamming pov-erty—perhaps they were merely miserly. . . .

Arnica came back with the tea-pot, the sugar and a cup on a tray.

"I'm afraid I'm giving you a great deal of trouble."

"Oh, not at all! . . . I'd rather do it now—before; af-terwards, I mightn't be able to."

"Well, then, listen!" began Valentine, after Arnica had sat down. "The Pope——"

"No, no, don't tell me! don't tell me!" exclaimed Ma-dame Fleurissoire instantly, stretching out her hand in front of her; then, uttering a faint cry, she fell back with her eyes closed.

"My poor dear! My poor dear!" said the Countess, patting her on the wrist. "I felt sure it would be too much for you."

Arnica at last feebly opened half an eye and murmured sadly:

"Dead?"

Then Valentine, bending towards her, slipped into her ear the single word:

"Imprisoned!"

Sheer stupefaction brought Madame Fleurissoire back

to her senses; and Valentine began her long story, stumbling over the dates, mixing up the names and muddling the chronology; one fact, however, stood out, certain and indisputable—our Holy Father had fallen into the hands of the infidel—a crusade was being secretly organised to deliver him, and in order to conduct it successfully a large sum of money was necessary.

"What will Amédée say?" moaned Arnica in dismay.

He was not expected home before evening, having gone out for a walk with his friend Blafaphas. . . .

"Mind you impress on him the necessity of secrecy," repeated Valentine several times over as she took her leave of Arnica. "Give me a kiss, my dear, and courage!"

Arnica nervously presented her damp forehead to the Countess.

"I will look in to-morrow to hear what you think of doing. Consult Monsieur Fleurissoire, but remember that the Church is at stake! . . . It's agreed, then—only to your husband! You promise, don't you? Not a word! Not a word!"

The Comtesse de Saint-Prix left Arnica in a state of depression bordering on faintness. When Amédée came in from his walk:

"My dear," she said to him at once, "I have just heard something extremely sad. The Holy Father has been imprisoned."

"No, not really?" said Amédée, as if he were saying "pooh!"

Arnica burst into sobs:

"I knew, I knew you wouldn't believe me."

"Come, come, darling," went on Amédée, taking off his

overcoat, without which he never went out for fear of a
sudden change of temperature. "Just think! Everyone
would know if anything had happened to the Holy
Father. It would be in all the papers. And who could
have imprisoned him?"

"Valentine says it's the Lodge."

Amédée looked at Arnica under the impression that she
had taken leave of her senses. He said, however:

"The Lodge? What Lodge?"

"How can I tell? Valentine has promised not to say
anything about it."

"Who told her?"

"She forbade me to say. . . . A canon, who was sent
by a cardinal, with his card——"

Arnica understood nothing of public affairs and Madame de Saint-Prix's story had left but a confused
impression on her. The words "captivity" and "imprison-
ment" conjured up before her eyes dark and semi-
romantic images; the word "crusade" thrilled her unspeakably, and when, at last, Amédée's disbelief wavered
and he talked of setting out at once, she suddenly saw
him on horseback, in a helmet and breastplate. . . . As
for him, he had begun by now to pace up and down the
room.

"In the first place," he said, "it's no use talking about
money—we haven't got any. And do you think I could
be satisfied with merely giving money? Do you think
I should be able to sleep in peace merely because I had
sacrificed a few bank-notes? . . . Why, my dear, if this
is true that you've been telling me, it's an appalling thing
and we mustn't rest till we've done something. Appalling, do you understand me?"

"Yes, yes, I quite understand, appalling! . . . But all the same, do explain why."

"Oh, if now I've got to explain!" and Amédée raised discouraged arms to Heaven.

"No, no," he went on, "this isn't an occasion for giving money; it's oneself that one must give. I'll consult Blafaphas; we'll see what he says."

"Valentine de Saint-Prix made me promise not to tell anyone," put in Arnica, timidly.

"Blafaphas isn't anyone; and we'll impress on him that he must keep it strictly to himself."

Then, turning towards her, he implored pathetically:

"Arnica, my dearest, let me go!"

She was sobbing. It was she now who insisted on Blafaphas coming to the rescue. Amédée was starting to fetch him, when he turned up of his own accord, knocking first at the drawing-room window, as was his habit.

"Well! that's the most singular story I ever heard in my life!" he cried when they had told him all about it. "No, really! Who would ever have thought of such a thing?" And then, before Fleurissoire had said anything of his intentions, he went on abruptly:

"My dear fellow, there's only one thing for us to do— set out at once."

"You see," said Amédée, "it's his first thought."

"Unfortunately I'm kept at home by my poor father's health," was his second.

"After all, it's better that I should go by myself," went on Amédée. "Two of us together would attract attention."

"But will you know how to manage?"

At this, Amédée raised his shoulders and eyebrows, as much as to say: "I can but do my best!"

"Will you know whom to appeal to? . . . where to go? . . . And, as a matter of fact, what exactly do you mean to do when you get there?"

"First of all, find out the facts."

"Supposing, after all, there were no truth in the story?"

"Exactly! I can't rest till I know."

And Gaston immediately exclaimed: "No more can I!"

"Do take a little more time to think it over, dear," protested Arnica feebly.

"I have thought it over. I shall go—secretly—but I shall go."

"When? Nothing is ready."

"This evening. What do I need so much?"

"But you haven't ever travelled. You won't know how to."

"You'll see, my love, you'll see! When I come back, I'll tell you my adventures," said he, with an engaging little chuckle which set his Adam's apple shaking.

"You're certain to catch cold."

"I'll wear your comforter." He stopped in his pacing to raise Arnica's chin with the tip of his forefinger, as one does a baby's, when one wants to make it smile. Gaston's attitude was one of reserve. Amédée went up to him:

"I count upon you to look up my trains. Find me a good train to Marseilles with thirds. Yes, yes, I insist upon travelling third. Anyhow, make me out a time-table in detail and mark the places where I shall have to change—and where I can get refreshments—at any rate, as far as the frontier; after that, when I've got a start, I shall be able to look after myself, and with God's guidance I shall get to Rome. You must write to me there poste restante."

The importance of his mission was exciting his brain dangerously. After Gaston had gone, he continued to pace the room; from time to time he murmured, his heart melting with wonder and gratitude:

"To think that such a thing should be reserved for *me!*" So at last he had his *raison d'être*. Ah! for pity's sake, dear lady, let him go! To how many beings on God's earth is it given to find their function?

All that Arnica obtained was that he should pass this one night with her, Gaston, indeed, having pointed out in the time-table which he brought round in the evening, that the most convenient train was the one that left at 8 A. M.

The next morning it poured with rain. Amédée would not allow Arnica or Gaston to go with him to the station; so that the quaint traveller with his cod-fish eyes, his neck muffled in a dark crimson comforter, holding in his right hand a grey canvas portmanteau, on to which his visiting-card had been nailed, in his left an old umbrella, and on his arm a brown and green check shawl, was carried off by the train to Marseilles, without a farewell glance from anyone.

IV

About this time an important sociological congress summoned Count Julius de Baraglioul back to Rome.

He was not perhaps specially invited (his opinions on such subjects being founded more on conviction than knowledge), but he was glad to have this opportunity of getting into touch with one or two illustrious personages. And as Milan lay conveniently on his road—Milan where, as we know, the Armand-Dubois had gone to live on the advice of Father Anselm—he determined to take advantage of the circumstance in order to see his brother-in-law.

On the same day that Fleurissoire left Pau, Julius knocked at Anthime's door. He was shown into a wretched apartment consisting of three rooms—if the dark closet where Veronica herself cooked the few vegetables which formed their chief diet, may be counted as a room. The little light there was came from a narrow court-yard and shone down dismally from a hideous metal reflector; Julius preferred to keep his hat in his hand rather than set it down on the oval table with its covering of doubtfully clean oilcloth, and remained standing because of the horror with which the horsehair chairs inspired him.

He seized Anthime by the arm and exclaimed:

"My poor fellow, you can't stay here."

"What are you pitying me for?" asked Anthime.

Veronica came hurrying up at the sound of their voices.

"Would you believe it, my dear Julius?—that is the only thing he finds to say in spite of the grossly unjust and unfair way in which we have been treated."

"Who suggested your coming to Milan?"

"Father Anselm; but in any case we couldn't have kept on the Via in Lucina apartment."

"There was no need for us to keep it on," said Anthime.

"That's not the point. Father Anselm promised you compensation. Is he aware of your distress?"

"He pretends not to be," said Veronica.

"You must complain to the Bishop of Tarbes."

"Anthime has done so."

"What did he say?"

"He is a worthy man; he earnestly encouraged me in my faith."

"But since you have been here, haven't you complained to anyone?"

"I just missed seeing Cardinal Pazzi, who had shown some interest in my case and to whom I had written; he did come to Milan, but he sent me word by his footman . . ."

"That a fit of the gout unfortunately kept him to his room."

"But it's abominable! Rampolla must be told!" cried Julius.

"Told what, my dear friend? It is true that I am somewhat reduced—but what need have we of more? In the time of my prosperity I was astray; I was a sinner; I was ill. Now, you see, I am cured. Formerly you had good cause to pity me. And yet you know well enough that worldly goods turn us aside from God."

"Yes, but those worldly goods were yours by rights. It's all very well that the Church should teach you to despise them, but not that she should cheat you of them."

"That's the way to talk," said Veronica. "What a relief it is to hear you, Julius! His resignation makes me boil with rage; it's impossible to get him to defend himself. He has let himself be plucked like a goose and said 'thank you' to everyone who robbed him, as long as they did it in the Lord's name."

"Veronica! it grieves me to hear you talk like that. Whatever is done in the Lord's name is well done."

"If you think it's agreeable to be made a fool of!" said Julius.

"God's fool, dear Julius!"

"Just listen to him! That's what he's like the whole time! Nothing but Scripture texts in his mouth from morning to night! And after I've toiled and slaved and done the marketing and the cooking and the housemaid-ing, my good gentleman quotes the Gospel and says I'm being busy about many things and tells me to look at the lilies of the field."

"I help you to the best of my power, dear," said Anthime in a seraphic voice. "Now that I've got the use of my legs again, I've many a time offered to do the mar-keting or the housework for you."

"That's not a man's business. Content yourself with writing your homilies, only try to get a little better pay for them." And then, her voice getting more and more querulous (hers, who used to be so smiling!): "Isn't it a disgrace?" she exclaimed. "When one thinks of what he used to get for his infidel articles in the *Dépêche!* And now when the *Pilgrim* pays him a miserable two-pence halfpenny for his religious meditations, he some-how or other contrives to give three quarters of it to the poor!"

"Then he's a complete saint!" cried Julius, aghast.

"Oh! how he irritates me with his saintliness! . . . Look here! Do you know what this is?" and she fetched a small wicker cage from a dark corner of the room.

"These are the two rats whose eyes my scientific friend put out in the old days."

"Oh, Veronica, why will you harp on it? You used to feed them yourself when I was experimenting on them —and then I blamed you for it. . . . Yes, Julius, in my unregenerate days I blinded those poor creatures, out of vain scientific curiosity; it's only natural I should look after them now."

"I wish the Church thought it equally natural to do for you what you do for these rats—after having blinded you in the same way."

"Blinded, do you say! Such words from *you?* Illumined, my dear brother, illumined!"

"My words were plain matter-of-fact. It seems to me inadmissible that you should be abandoned in such a state as this. The Church entered into an engagement with you; she must keep it—for her own honour—for our faith's sake." Then, turning to Veronica: "If you have obtained nothing so far, you must appeal higher still—and still higher. Rampolla, did I say? It's to the Pope himself that I shall present a petition—to the Pope. He is acquainted with your story. He ought to be informed of such a miscarriage of justice. I am returning to Rome to-morrow."

"You'll stop to dinner, won't you?" asked Veronica, somewhat apprehensively.

"Please excuse me—but really my digestion is so poor . . ." (and Julius, whose nails were very carefully kept, glanced at Anthime's large, stumpy, square-tipped fingers). "On my way back from Rome I shall be able to stop longer, and then I want to tell you about the new book I'm now at work on, my dear Anthime."

"I have just been re-reading *On the Heights* and it seems to me better than I thought it at first."

"I am sorry for you! It's a failure. I'll explain why when you're in a fit state to listen and to appreciate the strange preoccupations which beset me now. But there's too much to say. Mum's the word for the present!"

He bade the Armand-Dubois keep up their spirits, and left them.

BOOK IV: THE MILLIPEDE

"Et je ne puis approuver que ceux qui cher-
chent en gémissant."

—Pascal, 3421.

I

Amédée Fleurissoire had left Pau with five hundred francs in his pocket. This, he thought, would certainly suffice him for his journey, notwithstanding the extra expenses, to which the Lodge's wickedness would no doubt put him. And if, after all, this amount proved insufficient—if he found himself obliged to prolong his stay, he would have recourse to Blafaphas, who was keeping a small sum in reserve for him.

As no one at Pau was to know where he was going, he had not taken his ticket further than Marseilles. From Marseilles to Rome a third-class ticket cost only thirty-eight francs, forty centimes, and left him free to break his journey if he chose—an option of which he took advantage, to satisfy, not his curiosity for foreign parts, which had never been lively, but his desire for sleep, which was inordinately strong. There was nothing he feared so much as insomnia, and as it was important to the Church that he should arrive at Rome in good trim, he would not consider the two days' delay or the additional expense of the hotel bills. . . . What was that in comparison to spending a night in the train?

139

—a night that would certainly be sleepless, and particularly dangerous to health on account of the other travellers' breaths; and then if one of them wanted to renew the air and took it into his head to open a window, that meant catching a cold for certain. . . . He would therefore spend the first night at Marseilles and the second at Genoa, in one of those hotels that are found in the neighbourhood of the station, and are comfortable without being over-grand.

For the rest he was amused by the journey and at making it by himself—at last! For, at the age of forty-seven, he had never lived but in a state of tutelage, escorted everywhere by his wife and his friend Blafaphas. Tucked up in his corner of the carriage, he sat with a faint goat-like smile on his face, wishing himself Godspeed. All went well as far as Marseilles.

On the second day he made a false start. Absorbed in the perusal of the Baedeker for Central Italy which he had just bought, he got into the wrong train and headed straight for Lyons; it was only at Arles that he noticed his mistake, just as the train was starting, so that he was obliged to go on to Tarascon and come back over the same ground for the second time; then he took an evening train as far as Toulon rather than spend another night at Marseilles, where he had been pestered with bugs.

And yet the room which looked on to the Cannebière had not been uninviting, nor the bed either, for that matter; he had got into it without misgivings, after having folded his clothes, done his accounts and said his prayers. He was dropping with sleep and went off at once.

The manners and customs of bugs are peculiar; they wait till the candle is out, and then, as soon as it is dark, sally forth—not at random; they make straight for the neck, the place of their predilection; sometimes they select the wrists; a few rare ones prefer the ankles. It is not exactly known for what reason they inject into the sleeper's skin an exquisitely irritating oily substance, the virulence of which is intensified by the slightest rubbing. . . .

The irritation which awoke Fleurissoire was so violent that he lit his candle again and hurried to the looking-glass to gaze at his lower jaw, where there appeared an irregular patch of red dotted with little white spots; but the smoky dip gave a bad light; the silver of the glass was tarnished and his eyes were blurred with sleep. . . . He went back to bed still rubbing and put out his light; five minutes later he lit it again, for the itching had become intolerable, sprang to the wash-hand-stand, wetted his handkerchief in his water jug and applied it to the inflamed zone, which had greatly extended and now reached as far as his collar-bone. Amédée thought he was going to be ill and offered up a prayer; then he put out his candle once more. The respite which the cool compress had granted him lasted too short a time to permit the sufferer to go to sleep; and there was added now to the agony of the itching, the discomfort of having the collar of his night-shirt drenched with water; he drenched it, too, with his tears. And suddenly he started with horror—bugs! it was bugs! . . . He was surprised that he had not thought of them sooner; but he knew the insect only by name, and how was it possible to imagine that a definite bite could result in this indefinable

burning? He shot out of his bed and for the third time
lit his candle.

Being of a nervous and theoretical disposition, his
ideas about bugs, like many other people's, were all
wrong; cold with disgust, he began by searching for
them on himself—found ne'er a one—thought he had
made a mistake—again believed that he must be falling
ill. There was nothing on his sheets either; but nevertheless, before getting into bed again, it occurred to him
to lift up his bolster. He then saw three tiny blackish
pastilles, which tucked themselves nimbly away into a
fold of the sheet. It was they, sure enough!

Setting his candle on the bed, he tracked them down,
opened out the fold and discovered five of them. Not
daring to squash them with his finger-nail, he flung them
in disgust into his chamber-pot and watered them copi-
ously. He watched them struggling for a few moments
—pleased and ferocious. It soothed his feelings. Then
he got back into bed and blew out his candle.

The bites began again almost immediately with redoubled violence. There were new ones now on the back
of his neck. He lighted his candle once more in a rage
and took his night-shirt right off this time so as to examine the collar at his leisure. At last he perceived
four or five minute light red specks running along the
edge of the seam; he crushed them on the linen, where
they left a stain of blood—horrid little creatures, so tiny
that he could hardly believe that they were bugs already;
but a little later, on raising his bolster again, he un-
earthed an enormous one—their mother for certain; at
that, encouraged, excited, amused almost, he took off the
bolster, undid the sheets and began a methodical search.

He fancied now that he saw them everywhere, but as a matter of fact caught only four; he went back to bed and enjoyed an hour's peace.

Then the burning and itching began again. Once more he started the hunt; then, worn out at last with disgust and fatigue, gave it up, and noticed that if he did not scratch, the itching subsided pretty quickly. At dawn the last of the creatures, presumably gorged, let him be. He was sleeping heavily when the waiter called him in time for his train.

At Toulon it was fleas.

He picked them up in the train, no doubt. All night long he scratched himself, turning from side to side without sleeping. He felt them creeping up and down his legs, tickling the small of his back, inoculating him with fever. As he had a sensitive skin, their bites rose in exuberant swellings, which he inflamed with unrestrained scratching. He lit his candle over and over again; he got up, took off his night-shirt and put it on again, without being able to kill a single one. He hardly caught a fleeting glimpse of them; they continually escaped him, and even when he succeeded in catching them, when he thought they were flattened dead beneath his finger-nail, they suddenly and instantaneously blew themselves out again and hopped away as safe and lively as ever. He was driven to regretting the bugs. His fury and the exasperation of the useless chase effectually wrecked every possibility of sleep.

All next day the bites of the previous night itched horribly, while fresh creepings and ticklings showed him that he was still infested. The excessive heat consid-

erably increased his discomfort. The carriage was packed
to overflowing with workmen, who drank, smoked, spat,
belched and ate such high-smelling victuals that more
than once Fleurissoire thought he was going to be sick.
And yet he did not dare leave the carriage before reaching the frontier, for fear that the workmen might see him
get into another and imagine they were incommoding
him; in the compartment into which he next got, there
was a voluminous wet-nurse, who was changing her baby's
napkins. He tried nevertheless to sleep; but then his
hat got in his way. It was one of those shallow, white
straw hats with a black ribbon round it, of the kind commonly known as "sailor." When Fleurissoire left it in
its usual position, its stiff brim prevented him from leaning his head back against the partition of the carriage;
if, in order to do this, he raised his hat a little, the partition bumped it forwards; when, on the contrary, he
pressed his hat down behind, the brim was caught between the partition and the back of his neck, and the
sailor rose up over his forehead like the lid of a valve.
He decided at last to take it right off and to cover his
head with his comforter, which he arranged to fall over
his eyes so as to keep out the light. At any rate, he
had taken precautions against the night; at Toulon that
morning he had bought a box of insecticide and, even if
he had to pay dear for it, he thought to himself that he
would not hesitate to spend the night in one of the best
hotels; for if he had no sleep that night, in what state of
bodily wretchedness would he not be when he arrived at
Rome?—at the mercy of the meanest freemason!

At Genoa he found the omnibuses of the principal
hotels drawn up outside the station; he went straight up

to one of the most comfortable-looking, without letting
himself be intimidated by the haughtiness of the hotel
servant, who seized hold of his miserable portmanteau;
but Amédée refused to be parted from it; he would not
allow it to be put on the roof of the carriage, but insisted that it should be placed next him—there—on the
same seat. In the hall of the hotel the porter put him
at his ease by talking French; then he let himself go
and, not content with asking for "a very good room,"
inquired the prices of those that were offered him, determined to find nothing to his liking for less than twelve
francs.

The seventeen-franc room which he settled on after
looking at several, was vast, clean, and elegant without
ostentation; the bed stood out from the wall—a bright
brass bed, which was certainly uninhabited, and to which
his precautions would have been an insult. The wash-
stand was concealed in a kind of enormous cupboard.
Two large windows opened on to a garden; Amédée leant
out into the night and gazed long at the indistinct mass
of sombre foliage, letting the cool air calm his fever and
invite him to sleep. From above the bed there hung down
a cloudy veil of tulle, which exactly draped three sides
of it, and which was looped up in a graceful festoon on
the fourth by a few little cords, like those that take in
the reefs of a sail. Fleurissoire recognised that this was
what is known as a mosquito net—a device which he
had always disdained to make use of.

After having washed, he stretched himself luxuriously
in the cool sheets. He left the window open—not wide
open, of course, for fear of cold in the head and oph-
thalmia, but with one side fixed in such a way as to pre-

vent the night effluvia from striking him directly; did his
accounts, said his prayers and put out the light. (This
was electric and the current was cut off by turning down
a switch.)

Fleurissoire was just going off to sleep when a faint
humming reminded him that he had failed to take the
precaution of putting out his light before opening his
window; for light attracts mosquitoes. He remembered,
too, that he had somewhere read praises of the Lord, who
has bestowed on this winged insect a special musical instrument, designed to warn the sleeper the moment before he is going to be stung. Then he let down the im-
penetrable muslin barrier all round him. "After all,"
thought he to himself as he was dropping off, "how much
better this is than those little felt cones of dried hay,
which old Blafaphas sells under the quaint name of
'fidibus'; one lights them on a little metal saucer; as
they burn they give out a quantity of narcotic fumes;
but before they stupefy the mosquitoes, they half stifle
the sleeper. Fidibus! What a funny name! Fidibus . . ." He was just going off, when suddenly a sharp
sting on the left side of his nose awoke him. He put
his hand to the place and as he was softly stroking the
raised and burning flesh—another sting on his wrist.
Then right against his ear there sounded the mock of an
impertinent buzzing. . . . Horror! he had shut the enemy
up within the citadel! He reached out to the switch and
turned on the light.

Yes! the mosquito was there, settled high up on the
net. Amédée was long-sighted and made him out dis-
tinctly; a creature that was wisp-like to absurdity, planted

on four legs, with the other pair sticking out insolently behind him, long and curly; Amédée sat up on his bed. But how could he crush the insect against such flimsy, yielding material? No matter! He gave a hit with the palm of his hand, so hard and so quick that he thought he had burst a hole in the net. Not the shadow of a doubt but the mosquito was done for; he glanced down to look for its corpse; there was nothing—but he felt a fresh sting on the calf of his leg.

At that, in order to get as much as possible of his person into shelter, he crept between the sheets and stayed there perhaps a quarter of an hour, without daring to turn out the light; then, all the same, somewhat reassured at catching neither sight nor sound of the enemy, he switched it off. And instantly the music began again.

Then he put out one arm, keeping his hand close to his face, and from time to time when he thought he felt one well settled on his forehead or cheek, he would give himself a huge smack. But the second after, he heard the insect's sing-song once more.

After this it occurred to him to wrap his head round with his comforter, which considerably interfered with the pleasure of his respiratory organs, and did not prevent him from being stung on the chin.

Then the mosquito, gorged, no doubt, lay low; at any rate, Amédée, vanquished by slumber, ceased to hear it; he had taken off his comforter and was tossing in a feverish sleep; he scratched as he slept. The next morning, his nose, which was by nature aquiline, looked like the nose of a drunkard; the spot on the calf of his leg was budding like a boil and the one on his chin had developed an appearance that was volcanic—he recommended

it to the particular solicitude of the barber when, before leaving Genoa, he went to be shaved, so as to be
respectable when he arrived in Rome.

II

At Rome, as he was lingering outside the station, so
tired, so lost, so perplexed that he could not decide what
to do, and had only just strength enough left to repel
the advances of the hotel porters, Fleurissoire was lucky
enough to come upon a facchino who spoke French. Baptistin was a native of Marseilles, a young man with bright
eyes and a chin that was still smooth; he recognised a
fellow-countryman in Fleurissoire, and offered to guide
him and carry his portmanteau.

Fleurissoire had spent the long journey mugging up his
Baedeker. A kind of instinct—a presentiment—an in-
ward warning—turned his pious solicitude aside from
the Vatican to concentrate it on the Castle of St. Angelo
(in ancient days Hadrian's Mausoleum), the celebrated
jail which had sheltered so many illustrious prisoners of
yore, and which, it seems, is connected with the Vatican
by an underground passage.

He gazed upon the map. "That is where I must find
a lodging," he had decided, setting his forefinger on the
Tordinona quay, opposite the Castle of St. Angelo.
And by a providential coincidence, that was the very
place where Baptistin proposed to take him; not, that is,
exactly on the quay, which is in reality nothing but an
embankment, but quite near it—Via dei Vecchierelli (of
the little old men), which is the third street after the
Ponte Umberto, and leads straight on to the river bank;

he knew of a quiet house (from the windows of the third floor, by craning forward a little, one can see the Mausoleum) where there were some very obliging ladies, who talked every language, and one in particular who knew French.

"If the gentleman is tired, we can take a carriage; yes, it's a long way. . . . Yes, the air is cooler this evening; it's been raining; a little walk after a long railway journey does one good. . . . No, the portmanteau is not too heavy; I can easily carry it so far. . . . The gentleman's first visit to Rome? He comes from Toulouse, perhaps? . . . No; from Pau. I ought to have recognised the accent."

Thus chatting, they walked along. They took the Via Viminale; then the Via Agostino Depretis, which runs into the Viminale at the Pincio; then by way of the Via Nazionale they got into the Corso, which they crossed; after this their way lay through a number of little streets without any names. The portmanteau was not so heavy as to prevent the facchino from stepping out briskly; and Fleurissoire could hardly keep up with him. He trotted along beside Baptistin, dropping with fatigue and dripping with heat.

"Here we are!" said Baptistin at last, just as Amédée was going to beg for quarter.

The street, or rather the alley of the Vecchierelli, was dark and narrow—so much so that Fleurissoire hesitated to enter it. Baptistin, in the meantime, had gone into the second house on the right, the door of which was only a few yards from the quay; at the same moment, Fleurissoire saw a *bersagliere* come out; the smart uniform which he had noticed at the frontier, reassured him—for

he had confidence in the army. He advanced a few
steps. A lady appeared on the threshold (the landlady of
the inn apparently) and smiled at him affably. She
wore an apron of black satin, bracelets, and a sky-blue
silk ribbon round her neck; her jet-black hair was piled
in an edifice on the top of her head and sat heavily on
an enormous tortoise-shell comb.

"Your portmanteau has been carried up to the third
floor," said she to Amédée in French, using the intimate
"thou," which he imagined must be an Italian custom,
or must else be set down to want of familiarity with the
language.

"*Grazia!*" he replied, smiling in his turn. "*Grazia!*—
thank you!"—the only Italian word he could say, and
which he considered it polite to put into the feminine
when he was talking to a lady.

He went upstairs, stopping to gather breath and courage
at every landing, for he was worn out with fatigue, and
the sordidness of the staircase contributed to sink his
spirits still lower. The landings succeeded each other
every ten steps; the stairs hesitated, tacked, made three
several attempts before they managed to reach a floor.
From the ceiling of the first landing hung a canary cage
which could be seen from the street. On to the second
landing a mangy cat had dragged a haddock skin, which
she was preparing to bolt. On the third landing the
door of the closet stood wide open and revealed to view
the seat, and beside it a yellow earthenware vase, shaped
like a top-hat, from whose cup protruded the stick of
a small mop; on this landing Amédée refrained from
stopping.

On the first floor a smoky gasolene lamp was hanging

beside a large glass door, on which the word *Salone* was written in frosted letters; but the room was dark, and Amédée could barely make out through the glass panes of the door a mirror in a gold frame hanging on the wall opposite.

He was just reaching the seventh landing, when another soldier—an artillery man this time—who had come out of a room on the second floor, bumped up against him; he was running downstairs very fast and, after setting Amédée on his feet again, passed on, muttering a laughing excuse in Italian, for Fleurissoire was stumbling from fatigue and looked as if he were drunk. The first uniform had reassured him, but the second made him uneasy.

"These soldiers are a noisy lot," thought he. "Fortunately my room is on the third floor. I prefer to have them below me."

He had no sooner passed the second floor than a woman in a gaping dressing-gown, with her hair undone, came running from the other end of the passage and hailed him.

"She takes me for someone else," thought he, and hurried on, turning his eyes away so as not to embarrass her by noticing the scantiness of her attire.

He arrived panting on the third floor, where he found Baptistin; he was talking Italian to a woman of uncertain age, who reminded him extraordinarily—though she was not so fat—of the Blafaphas' cook.

"Your portmanteau is in No. sixteen—the third door. Take care as you pass of the pail which is in the passage."

"I put it outside because it was leaking," explained the woman in French.

The door of No. sixteen was open; outside No. fifteen a tin slop-pail was standing in the middle of a shiny repugnant-looking puddle, which Fleurissoire stepped across. An acrid odour emanated from it. The portmanteau was placed in full view on a chair. As soon as he got inside the stuffy room, Amédée felt his head swim, and flinging his umbrella, his shawl and his hat on to the bed, he sank into an arm-chair. His forehead was streaming; he thought he was going to faint.

"This is Madame Carola, the lady who talks French," said Baptistin.

They had both come into the room.

"Open the window a little," sighed Fleurissoire, who was incapable of movement.

"Goodness! how hot he is!" said Madame Carola, sponging his pallid and perspiring countenance with a little scented handkerchief, which she took out of her bodice.

"Let's push him nearer the window."

Both together lifted the arm-chair, in which Amédée swung helpless and half unconscious, and put it down where he was able to inhale—in exchange for the tainted atmosphere of the passage—the varied stenches of the street. The coolness, however, revived him. Feeling in his waistcoat pocket, he pulled out the screw of five lire which he had prepared for Baptistin:

"Thank you very much. Please leave me now."

The facchino went out.

"You oughtn't to have given him such a lot," said Carola.

She too used the familiar "thou," which Amédée accepted as a custom of the country; his one thought now

was to go to bed; but Carola showed no signs of leaving;
then, carried away by politeness, he began to talk.

"You speak French as well as a Frenchwoman."

"No wonder. I come from Paris. And you?"

"I come from the south."

"I guessed as much. When I saw you, I said to myself, that gentleman comes from the provinces. Is it your
first visit to Italy?"

"My first."

"Have you come on business?"

"Yes."

"It's a lovely place, Rome. There's a lot to be seen."

"Yes . . . but this evening I'm rather tired," he ventured; and as though excusing himself: "I've been
travelling for three days."

"It's a long journey to get here."

"And I haven't slept for three nights."

At those words, Madame Carola, with a sudden Italian
familiarity, which Amédée still couldn't help being astounded at, chucked him under the chin.

"Naughty!" said she.

This gesture brought a little blood back into Amédée's
face, and in his desire to repudiate the unfair insinuation,
he at once began to expatiate on fleas, bugs and mosquitoes.

"You'll have nothing of that kind here, dearie; you
see how clean it is."

"Yes; I hope I shall sleep well."

But still she didn't go. He rose with difficulty from
his arm-chair, raised his hand to the top button of his
waistcoat and said tentatively:

"I think I'll go to bed."

Madame Carola understood Fleurissoire's embarrassment.

"You'd like me to leave you for a bit, I see," said she tactfully.

As soon as she had gone, Fleurissoire turned the key in the lock, took his night-shirt out of his portmanteau and got into bed. But apparently the catch of the lock was not working, for before he had time to blow out his candle, Carola's head reappeared in the half-opened door —behind the bed—close to the bed—smiling. . . .

An hour later, when he came to himself, Carola was lying against him, in his arms, naked.

He disengaged his left arm, in which his blood was beginning to curdle and then drew away. She was asleep. A light from the alley below filled the room with its feeble glimmer, and not a sound was to be heard but the woman's regular breathing. An unwonted languor lay heavy on Amédée's body and soul; he drew out his thin legs from between the sheets; and sitting on the edge of the bed, he wept.

As first his sweat, so now his tears washed his face and mingled with the dust of the railway carriage; they welled up—silently, uninterruptedly, in a slow and steady stream, coming from his inmost depths, as from a hidden spring. He thought of Arnica, of Blafaphas, alas! Ah! if they could see him now! Never again would he dare to take his place beside them. Then he thought of his august mission, for ever compromised; he groaned below his breath:

"It's over! I'm no longer worthy! Oh! it's over! It's all over!"

The strange sounds of his sobbing and sighing had in

the meantime awakened Carola. There he was, kneeling now, at the foot of the bed, hammering on his weakly chest with little blows of his fist; and Carola, lost in amazement, heard him repeat, as his teeth chattered and his sobs shook him:

"Save us! Save us! The Church is crumbling!"

At last, unable to contain herself any longer:

"You poor old dear, what's wrong with you? Have you gone crazy?"

He turned towards her:

"Please, Madame Carola, leave me. I must—I absolutely must be alone. I'll see you to-morrow morning."

Then, as after all it was only himself that he blamed, he kissed her gently on the shoulder:

"Ah! you don't know what a dreadful thing we've done. No, no! You don't know. You can never know."

III

The swindling concern that went under the pompous name of *Crusade for the Deliverance of the Pope,* extended its shady ramifications through more than one of the French departments; Protos, the false chanoine of Virmontal, was not its only agent, nor the Comtesse de Saint-Prix its only victim. All its victims, however, were not equally accommodating, even if all the agents proved equally dexterous. Even Protos, Lafcadio's old school-mate, was obliged, after this exploit of his, to keep the sharpest possible look-out; he lived in continual apprehension that the clergy (the real clergy) would get wind of the affair, and expended as much ingenuity in covering his rear as in pushing his attack; but his versatility was great, and, moreover, he was admirably seconded; from one end to the other of the band (which went by the name of the Millipede) there reigned extraordinary harmony and discipline.

Protos was informed that same evening by Baptistin of the stranger's arrival, and no little alarmed at hearing that he came from Pau, he hurried off at seven o'clock the next morning to see Carola. She was still in bed.

The information which he gathered from her, the confused account that she gave of the events of the previous night, the anguish of the *pilgrim* (this was what she called Amédée), his protestations, his tears, left no further doubt in his mind. Decidedly his Pau preachifying had brought forth fruit—but not precisely the kind of fruit which Protos might have wished for; he would have to keep an eye on this simple-minded crusader, whose clumsy blunderings might give the whole show away. . . .

"Come! let me pass," said he abruptly to Carola.

This expression might seem peculiar, because Carola was lying in bed; but Protos was never one to be stopped by the peculiar. He put one knee on the bed, passed the other over the woman's body and pirouetted so cleverly that, with a slight push of the bed, he found himself between it and the wall. Carola was no doubt accustomed to this performance, for she asked simply:

"What are you going to do?"

"Make up as a *curé*," answered Protos, no less simply.

"Will you come back this way?"

Protos hesitated a moment, and then:

"You're right; it's more natural."

So saying, he stooped and touched the spring of a

secret door, which was concealed in the thickness of the
wall and was so low that the bed hid it completely.
Just as he was passing through the door, Carola seized
him by the shoulder.

"Listen," she said with a kind of gravity, "you're not
to hurt this one. I won't have it."

"I tell you I'm going to make up as a *curé*."

As soon as he had disappeared, Carola got up and began to dress.

I cannot exactly tell what to think of Carola Venitequa.
This exclamation of hers leads me to suppose that her
heart at that time was not altogether fundamentally
corrupt. Thus sometimes, in the very midst of abjec-
tion, the strangest delicacies of feelings suddenly reveal
themselves, just as an azure tinted flower will grow in
the middle of a dung-heap. Essentially submissive and
devoted, Carola, like so many other women, had need of
guidance. When Lafcadio had abandoned her, she had
immediately rushed off to find her old lover, Protos—
out of spite—out of self-assertion—to revenge herself.
She had once more gone through hard times—and Protos
had no sooner recovered her than he had once more made
her his tool. For Protos liked being master.

Another man than Protos might have raised, rehabili-
tated this woman. But first of all, he must have had the
wish to. Protos, on the contrary, seemed bent on de-
grading her. We have seen what shameful services the
ruffian demanded of her; it is true that she apparently
submitted to them without much reluctance; but the
fiıst impulses of a soul in revolt against the ignominy of
its lot, often pass unperceived by that very soul itself.
It is only in the light of love that the secret kicking

against the pricks is revealed. Was Carola falling in
love with Amédée? It would be rash to affirm it; but,
corrupt as she was, she had been touched to emotion by
the contact of his purity, and the exclamation which I
have recorded came indubitably from her heart.

Protos returned. He had not changed his dress. He
carried in his hand a bundle of clothes, which he put
down on a chair.

"Well! and now what?" she asked.

"I've reflected. I must first go round to the post and
look at his letters. I won't change till this afternoon.
Pass me your looking-glass."

He went to the window, and bending towards his reflection in the glass, he fastened to his lip a pair of short
brown moustaches, a trifle lighter than his hair.

"Call Baptistin."

Carola had finished dressing. She went to the door
and pulled a string hanging near it.

"I've already told you I can't bear to see you in those
sleeve-links. They attract attention."

"You know very well who gave them to me."

"Precisely."

"You aren't jealous, are you?"

"Silly fool!"

At this moment Baptistin knocked at the door and came
in.

"Here! Try and get up in the world a peg or two,"
said Protos, pointing to a coat, collar and tie, which were
lying on the chair and which he had brought back with
him from his expedition to the other side of the wall.
"You're to keep your client company in his walks abroad.

I shan't take him off your hands till this evening. Until then, don't lose sight of him."

It was to S. Luigi dei Franceschi that Amédée went to confess, in preference to St. Peter's, whose enormousness overwhelmed him. Baptistin guided him there, and afterwards led him to the post office. As was to be expected, the Millipede had confederates there too. Baptistin had learnt Amédée's name by means of the little visiting-card which was nailed on to the top of his portmanteau, and had informed Protos, who had no difficulty in getting an obliging employé to hand him over a letter of Arnica's —and no scruple in reading it.

"It's curious!" cried Fleurissoire, when an hour later he came in his turn to ask for his letters. "It's curious! The envelope looks as if it had been opened."

"That often happens here," said Baptistin phlegmatically.

Fortunately the prudent Arnica had ventured only on the most discreet of allusions. The letter, besides, was very short; she simply recommended Amédée, on the advice of Father Mure, to go to Naples and see Cardinal San-Felice S.B. "before attempting to do anything." Her expressions were as vague as could well be desired and in consequence as little compromising.

IV

When he found himself in front of the Castle of St. Angelo, Fleurissoire was filled with bitter disappointment. The huge mass of building rose from the middle of an inner court-yard, access to which was forbidden to the public, and into which only such visitors as were provided with cards were allowed to enter. It was even specified that they must be accompanied by one of the guardians.

These excessive precautions, to be sure, confirmed Amédée's suspicions, but they also enabled him to estimate the extravagant difficulty of his task. Fleurissoire then, having at last got rid of Baptistin, was wandering up and down the quay, which was almost deserted at that hour of the evening, and alongside the outer wall which defends the approach to the castle. Backwards and forwards in front of the drawbridge, he passed and repassed, with gloomy and despondent thoughts; then he would retreat once more to the bank of the Tiber and endeavour from there to get a better view of the building over the top of the first enclosure.

He had not hitherto paid any particular attention to a priest (there are so many of them in Rome) who was sitting on a bench not far from there, and who, though apparently plunged in his breviary, had been observing him for some time past. The worthy ecclesiastic had long and abundant locks of silver, and the freshness of his youthful complexion—the sure sign of purity of life —contrasted curiously with that apanage of old age. From the face alone one would have recognised a priest, and from that peculiarly respectable something which distinguishes him—a French priest. As Fleurissoire was about to pass by the bench for the third time, the *abbé* suddenly rose, came towards him, and in a voice which had in it something of a sob:

"What!" he said, "I am not the only one! You too are seeking him!"

So saying, he hid his face in his hands and the sobs which he had been too long controlling burst forth. Then suddenly recovering himself:

"Imprudent! Imprudent that I am! Hide your tears! Stifle your sighs!" . . . Then, seizing Amédée by the arm: "We must not stay here, Sir. We are observed. The emotion I am unable to master has been remarked already."

Amédée by this time was following him in a state of stupefaction.

"But how," he at last managed to ask, "how could you guess what I am here for?"

"Pray Heaven that no one else has been permitted to suspect it! But how could your anxious face, your sorrowful looks, as you examined this spot, escape the notice of one who has haunted it day and night for the last three weeks? Alas! my dear sir, as soon as I saw you, some presentiment, some warning from on high, told me that a sister soul . . . Hush! Someone is coming. For Heaven's sake, pretend complete unconcern."

A man carrying vegetables was coming along the quay from the opposite direction. Immediately, without changing his tone of voice, but speaking in a slightly more animated manner, and as if he were continuing a sentence:

"And that is why Virginia cigars, which some smokers appreciate so highly, can be lighted only at the flame of a candle, after you have removed the thin straw, that goes through the middle of them, and whose object is to keep open a little channel in which the smoke can circulate freely. A Virginia that doesn't draw well is fit for nothing but to be thrown away. I have seen smokers who are particular as to what they smoke, throw away as many as six, my dear sir, before finding one that suits them. . . ."

And as soon as the man had passed them:

"Did you see how he looked at us? It was essential to put him off the scent."

"What!" cried Fleurissoire, flabbergasted, "is it possible that a common market gardener can be one of the persons of whom we must beware?"

"I cannot certify that it is so, sir, but I imagine it. The neighbourhood of this castle is watched with particular care; agents of a special police are continually patrolling it. In order not to arouse suspicion, they assume the most varied disguises. The people we have to deal with are so clever—so clever! and we so credulous, so naturally confiding! But if I were to tell you, sir, that I was within an ace of ruining everything simply because I gave my modest luggage to an ordinary-looking facchino to carry from the station to the lodging where I am staying! He spoke French, and though I have spoken Italian fluently ever since I was a child . . . you yourself, I am persuaded, would have felt the same emotion . . . I couldn't help giving way to it when I heard someone speaking my mother tongue in a foreign land. . . . Well! this facchino . . ."

"Was he one of them?"

"He was one of them. I was able to make practically sure of it. Fortunately I had said very little."

"You fill me with alarm," said Fleurissoire; "the same thing happened to me the evening I arrived—yesterday, that is—I fell in with a guide to whom I entrusted my portmanteau, and who talked French."

"Good heavens!" cried the *curé,* struck with terror; "could his name have been Baptistin?"

"Baptistin! That was it!" wailed Amédée, who felt his knees giving way beneath him.

"Unhappy man! What did you say to him?" The *curé* pressed his arm.

"Nothing that I can remember."

"Think! Think! Try to remember, for Heaven's sake!"

"No, really!" stammered Amédée, terrified; "I don't think I said anything to him."

"What did you let out?"

"No, nothing, I assure you. But you do well to warn me."

"What hotel did he take you to?"

"I'm not in a hotel. I'm in private lodgings."

"God save us! But you must be somewhere."

"Oh, I'm in a little street which you certainly don't know," stuttered Fleurissoire, in great confusion. "It's of no consequence. I won't stay on there."

"Be very careful! If you leave suddenly, it'll look as if you suspected something."

"Yes, perhaps it will. You're right. I had better not leave at once."

"How I thank a merciful Heaven that you arrived in Rome to-day! One day later and I should have missed you! To-morrow—no later than to-morrow—I'm obliged to leave for Naples in order to see a saintly and important personage, who is secretly devoting himself to the cause."

"Could it be the Cardinal San-Felice?" asked Fleurissoire, trembling with emotion.

The *curé* took a step or two back in amazement:

"How did you know?" Then drawing nearer: "But why should I be astonished? He is the only person in Naples who is in the secret."

"Do you . . . know him?"

"Do I know him? Alas! my dear sir, it is to him I owe . . . But no matter! Were you thinking of going to see him?"

"I suppose so; if I must."

"He is the best of men. . . ." With a rapid whisk of his hand, he wiped the corner of his eye. "You know where to find him, of course?"

"I suppose anyone could tell me. Everyone knows him in Naples."

"Naturally! But I don't suppose you are going to inform all Naples of your visit. Surely, you can't have been told of his participation in . . . you know what, and perhaps entrusted with some message for him, without having been instructed at the same time how to gain access to him."

"Pardon me," said Fleurissoire timidly, for Arnica had given him no such instructions.

"What! were you meaning to go and see him straight off—in the archbishop's palace, perhaps!—and speak to him point-blank?"

"I confess that . . ."

"But are you aware, sir," went on the other severely, "are you aware that you run the risk of getting *him* imprisoned too?"

He seemed so deeply vexed that Fleurissoire did not dare to speak.

"So sacred a cause confided to such imprudent hands!"

murmured Protos, and he took the end of a rosary out of his pocket, then put it back again, then crossed himself feverishly; then turning to his companion:

"Pray tell me, sir, who asked you to concern yourself with this matter. Whose instructions are you obeying?"

"Forgive me, Monsieur l'abbé," said Fleurissoire in some confusion, "I was given no instructions by anyone. I am just a poor distraught soul seeking on my own behalf."

These humble words disarmed the *curé;* he held out his hand to Fleurissoire:

"I spoke to you roughly. . . . But such dangers surround us." Then, after a short hesitation:

"Look here! Will you come with me to-morrow? We will go and see my friend together . . ." and raising his eyes to Heaven: "Yes, I dare to call him my friend," he repeated in a heartfelt voice. "Let's sit down for a minute on this bench. I will write him a line which we will both sign, to give him notice of our visit. If it is posted before six o'clock (eighteen o'clock, as they say here), he will get it to-morrow morning in time for him to be ready to receive us by twelve; we might even, I dare say, have lunch with him."

They sat down. Protos took a note-book from his pocket, and under Amédée's haggard eyes began on a virgin sheet as follows:

"Dear old cock . . ."

Then, seeing the other's stupefaction, he smiled very calmly:

"So, it's the Cardinal you'd have addressed if you'd had your way?"

After that he became more amicable and consented to

explain things to Amédée: once a week the Cardinal San-Felice was in the habit of leaving the archbishop's palace in the dress of a simple *abbé;* he became plain chaplain Bardolotti and made his way to a modest villa on the slopes of Mount Vomero, where he received a few intimate friends, and the secret letters which the initiated addressed him under his assumed name. But even in this vulgar disguise, he could feel no security —he could not be sure that his letters were not opened in the post, and begged therefore that nothing of any significance should be said in any letter and that the tone of a letter should in no way suggest his Eminence, or have in it the slightest trace of respect.

Now that he was let into the secret, Amédée smiled in his turn.

" 'Dear old cock' . . . Let me think! What shall we say to the dear old cock?" joked the *abbé,* hesitating with pencil in hand. "Ah! . . . 'I've got a funny old chap in tow!' (Yes, yes! It's all right! I know the kind of style.) 'I'll bring him along, so dig out a bottle or two of Falernian and to-morrow we'll blow it together and have some fun.' . . . Here! you sign too."

"Perhaps I'd better not sign my own name."

"Oh, it doesn't matter about yours," returned Protos, and after the name of Amédée Fleurissoire he wrote the word *Cave.**

"Oh, that's very clever!"

"What! are you astonished at my signing the name *Cave?* Your head is full of nothing but the Vatican *Cave.* You must know, my good Monsieur Fleurissoire,

* *Cave* meaning *cellar* in French, Protos makes a double pun impossible to render in English. (*Translator's note.*)

that *Cave* is a Latin word too, and that it means BEWARE!"

All this was said in so potent and so strange a tone that poor Amédée felt a cold shiver run down his spine. It lasted only a second; Father Cave had already recovered his affability when he handed him the envelope on which he had just inscribed the Cardinal's apocryphal address.

"Will you post it yourself? It's more prudent; *curés'* letters are opened. And now we'd better part; we mustn't be seen together any longer. Let's agree to meet to-morrow morning in the train that leaves for Naples at seven-thirty. Third class of course. I shall not be in this dress, naturally. What an idea! You must look out for just an ordinary Calabrian peasant. (I don't want to have to cut my hair.) Good-bye! Good-bye!"

He went off, making little signs with his hand.

"Thanks be to Heaven that I met that excellent *abbé!*" murmured Fleurissoire as he returned homewards. "What should I have done without him?"

And Protos murmured as he went:

"You shall have a jolly good dose of your Cardinal, my boy! . . . Why, if he had been left to himself, I'm hanged if he wouldn't have gone to see the *real* one."

V

As Fleurissoire complained of great fatigue, Carola had allowed him to sleep that night notwithstanding the interest she took in him and the tender compassion she was thrown into when he confessed his ignorance in the matter of love . . . sleep, that is, as much as he was able for the intolerable itching of the bites—fleas' as well as mosquitoes'—which covered his whole body.

"You oughtn't to scratch like that, dearie," she said to him the next morning, "you only irritate it. Oh, how inflamed this one is!" and she touched the spot on his chin. Then as he was getting ready to go out: "Here! wear these in remembrance of me." And she fastened the grotesque trinkets which Protos had objected to her wearing, into the *pilgrim's* cuffs. Amédée promised to come back the same evening, or at latest the next morning.

"You'll swear that you'll not hurt him?" repeated Carola a moment later to Protos, who had come through the secret door already disguised; and as he was late because he had waited for Fleurissoire to leave before showing himself, he was obliged to take a carriage to the station.

In his new aspect, with his open shirt, his brown breeches, his sandals, laced over his blue stockings, his short pipe and his tan-coloured hat with its small flat brim, it must be admitted that he looked far more like a regular Abruzzi brigand than like a *curé*. Fleurissoire, who was walking up and down the platform waiting for him, hesitated to recognise the individual who, like St. Peter Martyr, with a finger on his lips, passed by him without seeming to see him and disappeared into a carriage at the head of the train. But after a moment he reappeared at the door of the carriage, and looking in Amédée's direction with one eye half shut, he made him a surreptitious sign with his hand to come up; and as Amédée was about to get in:

"Please see whether there's anyone next door," whispered Protos.

No one; and their compartment was the last in the carriage.

"I was following you in the street," went on Protos; "but I wouldn't speak to you for fear that we might be seen together."

"How is it that I didn't see you?" asked Fleurissoire. "I turned round a dozen times to make sure that I wasn't being followed. Your conversation yesterday filled me with such terror that I see nothing but spies everywhere."

"Yes, you show that you do only too clearly. Do you think it's natural to turn round every twenty paces?"

"What? Really? Do I look . . . ?"

"Suspicious. Alas! That's the word—suspicious. It's the most compromising look you can have."

"And yet I didn't even discover that you were following me! On the other hand, I see something disquieting in the appearance of everyone I pass in the street. It alarms me if they look at me, and if they don't look at me they seem as if they were pretending not to see me. I didn't realise till to-day how rarely people's presence in the street is justifiable. There aren't more than four out of twelve whose occupation is obvious. Ah! you have given me food for thought, and no mistake! For a naturally credulous soul like mine suspicion is not easy; it's an apprenticeship. . . ."

"Pooh! You'll get accustomed to it—quickly too; you'll see; in a short time it'll become a habit—a habit, alas! which I've been obliged to adopt myself. . . . The main thing is to look cheerful all the time. Ah! a word to the wise! When you're afraid you're being followed, don't turn round; just merely drop your stick or your umbrella (according to the weather) or your handkerchief, and as you pick it up—whatever it may be—while your head is down, look between your legs behind you, in a natural kind of way. I advise you to practise. But tell me. What do you think of me in this costume? I'm afraid the *curé* may show through in places."

"Don't worry," said Fleurissoire candidly; "no one but I, I'm sure, could see what you are." Then, looking him up and down benevolently, with his head a little on one side: "Evidently, when I examine you carefully, I can see a slight touch of the ecclesiastic behind your disguise—I can distinguish beneath the joviality of your voice the sickening anxiety which is tormenting us both. But what self-control you must have to let it show so little! As for me, I have still a great deal to learn, it's clear. Your advice . . ."

"What curious sleeve-links you have!" interrupted Protos, amused at seeing Carola's links on Fleurissoire.

"They're a present," he said, blushing.

The heat was sweltering. Protos was looking out of the window; "Monte Cassino," he said; "can you see the celebrated convent up there?"

"Yes, I see it," said Fleurissoire absently.

"You don't care much for scenery, then?"

"Yes, yes, I do care for it! But how can I take an interest in anything as long as I'm so uneasy? It's the same at Rome with the sights. I've seen nothing; I've not tried to see anything."

"How well I understand you!" said Protos. "I'm like that too; I told you that ever since I've been in Rome

I've spent the whole of my time between the Vatican and the Castle of St. Angelo."

"It's a pity, but *you* know Rome already."

In this way our travellers chatted.

At Caserta they got down, and went each on his own account to the buffet, to get a sandwich or two and a drink.

"At Naples too," said Protos, "when we get near his villa we will part company, if you please. You must follow me at a distance; I shall want a little time first, especially if he isn't alone, to explain who you are and the object of your visit, so you mustn't come in till a quarter of an hour after me."

"I'll take the opportunity of getting shaved. I hadn't time this morning."

A tram took them as far as the Piazza Dante.

"Let's part here," said Protos. "It's still rather a long way off, but it's better so. Walk about fifty paces behind me; and don't look at me the whole time as if you were afraid of losing me; and don't turn round either; you would get yourself followed. Look cheerful."

He started off in front. Fleurissoire followed with downcast eyes. The street was narrow and steep; the sun blazed; sweating, hustling, effervescing, the crowd clamoured and gesticulated and sang, while Fleurissoire panted bewildered through their midst. A number of half-naked children were dancing in front of a barrel organ; a kind of mountebank was getting up an impromptu lottery at two sous the ticket, for a fat plucked turkey, which he was holding up at the end of a stick; Protos, to seem more natural, took a ticket as he passed, and disappeared into the crowd; Fleurissoire, unable to

advance, thought he had lost him for good; then, after
he had managed to get through the obstruction, he caught
sight of him again, walking briskly up the hill, with the
turkey under his arm.

At last the houses became smaller and further apart,
fewer people were to be seen, and Protos slackened his
pace. He stopped in front of a barber's shop and,
turning to Fleurissoire, winked his eye; then, twenty
paces further on, stopped again in front of a little low
door and rang the bell.

The barber's window was not particularly attractive
but Father Cave doubtless had his reasons for pointing
it out; moreover, Fleurissoire would have had to go a
long way back before finding another, which would no
doubt have been equally uninviting. The door was left
open on account of the excessive heat; a wide-meshed
curtain kept the flies out and let the air in; one had to
raise it to enter; he entered.

Truly, a skilful fellow, this barber! After soaping
Amédée's chin, he cautiously pushed aside the lather with
a corner of his towel and brought to light the fiery
pimple, which his nervous client pointed out to him.
Oh, somnolence! Oh, warmth and drowsiness of the
quiet little shop! Amédée, half lying in the leather
arm-chair, with his head leaning comfortably back, let
himself drift. Ah! just for one short moment to forget! To think no more of the Pope and the mosquitoes
and Carola! To imagine himself back to Pau with Arnica; to imagine himself somewhere—anywhere else—no
longer to know where he was! . . . He shut his eyes,
then half opening them, saw as in a dream on the wall
opposite him, a woman with streaming hair issuing

out of the Bay of Naples, and bringing up from the watery depths, together with a voluptuous sensation of coolness, a glittering bottle of hair-restorer. Above this advertisement were arranged, on a marble slab, more bottles, a stick of cosmetic and a powder puff, a pair of tweezers, a comb, a lancet, a pot of ointment, a glass jar in which a few leeches were indolently floating, a second glass jar which contained the long ribbon of a tapeworm and lastly a third jar which was without a lid, half full of some gelatinous substance, and had pasted on its crystalline surface a label, inscribed by hand, in large fancy capitals, with the word ANTI-SEPTIC.

The barber now, in order to bring his work to perfection, spread afresh an unctuous lather over the already shaven chin, and with the gleaming edge of a second rasor, which he sharpened on the palm of his damp hand, he set about his final polishing. Amédée thought no more of his appointment, thought no more of leaving, began to doze off. . . . It was just at this moment that there came into the shop a loud-voiced Sicilian, rending the peacefulness with his clatter; it was then that the barber, plunging at once into talk, began to shave with a less attentive hand, and with a sudden sweep of his blade—pop! the pimple was beheaded!

Amédée gave a cry and was putting his hand to the cut, from which a drop of blood came oozing:

"Niente! Niente!" said the barber, holding back his arm; then, taking a piece of discoloured cotton-wool from the back of the drawer, he lavishly dipped it into the ANTISEPTIC and applied it to the place.

Without caring now whether the passers-by turned to

look at him, Amédée fled down the hill towards the town—where else but to the first chemist he could find?

He showed his hurt to the man of healing—a mouldy, greenish, unhealthy-looking old fellow, who smiled and, taking a little round of sticking-plaster out of a box, passed his broad tongue over it and . . .

Flinging out of the shop, Fleurissoire spat with disgust, tore off the slimy plaster and, pressing his pimple between two fingers, made it bleed as much as he could. Then, having wetted his handkerchief with saliva—his own this time—he rubbed the place. Then, looking at his watch, he was seized with panic, rushed up the street at a run, and arrived in front of the Cardinal's door, perspiring, panting, bleeding, red in the face, and a quarter of an hour late.

VI

Protos welcomed him with a finger on his lips.

"As long as the servants are there, nothing must be said to arouse suspicion. They all speak French. Not a word—not a sign to betray us! Don't go plastering him with 'Cardinals,' whatever you do. Your host is Ciro Bardolotti, the chaplain. As for me, I'm not 'Father Cave' but plain Cave. Understand?" And abruptly changing his tone and smacking him on the shoulder, he explained in a loud voice: "Here he is, by Jove! It's Amédée! Well, old man, you've been a fine time over your shave! In another moment or two, per *Bacco*, we should have sat down without you. The turkey that turneth on the spit beginneth to glow like

the setting sun!" Then, in a whisper: "Ah, my dear
sir, how painful it is to play a part! My heart is
wrung . . ." Then in a loud voice: "What do I see?
A cut? Thou bleedest, my lad. Run, Dorino, to the
barn and fetch a cobweb—a sovereign remedy for
wounds. . . ."

Thus clowning it, he pushed Fleurissoire across the
lobby, towards a terrace garden, where a table lay spread
under a trellis of vine.

"My dear Bardolotti, allow me to introduce my
cousin, Monsieur de la Fleurissoire. He's a devil of a
fellow, as I told you."

"I bid you welcome, sir guest," said Bardolotti with
a flourish, but without rising from the arm-chair in
which he was sitting; then, pointing to his bare feet,
which were plunged in a tub of clear water:

"These pedal ablutions improve my appetite and draw
the blood from my head."

He was a funny little roundabout man, whose smooth
face gave no indication of age or sex. He was dressed
in alpaca; there was nothing about him to denote a high
dignitary; one would have had to be exceedingly per-
spicacious, or else in the secret—like Fleurissoire—to
have discovered a discreet touch of cardinalesque unction
beneath the joviality of his manners. He was leaning
sideways on the table, fanning himself languidly with a
kind of cocked hat made out of a sheet of newspaper.

"Er . . . er . . . highly flattered . . . er . . . er . . .
what a charming garden!" stuttered Fleurissoire, finding
speech and silence equally embarrassing.

"Soaked enough!" cried the Cardinal. "Hullo, someone! Take away this tub! Assunta!"

A young maidservant came running up, plump and debonair; she took up the tub and emptied it over a flower-bed; her breasts were bursting out of her stays and all a-quiver beneath the muslin of her bodice; she stayed laughing and lingering beside Protos, and the gleam of her bare arms made Fleurissoire uncomfortable. Dorino put the fiaschi down on the table, which had no cloth on it; and the sun, streaming joyously through the wreaths of vine, set its frolic touch of light and shade on the dishes.

"We don't stand upon ceremony here," said Bardolotti, and he put on the paper hat. "You take my meaning, my dear sir?"

In a commanding tone, emphasising the syllables and beating with his fist on the table, Father Cave repeated in his turn:

"We don't stand upon ceremony here!"

Fleurissoire gave a knowing wink. Did he take their meaning? Yes, indeed, and there was no need for reiteration; but he racked his brains in vain for a pregnant sentence that would say nothing and convey everything.

"Speak! Speak!" prompted Protos. "Make a pun or two. They understand French perfectly."

"Come, come, sit down!" said Ciro. "My dear Cave, stick your knife into this *pastecca* and slice it up into Turkish crescents. Are you one of those persons, Monsieur de la Fleurissoire, who prefer the pretentious melons of the north—prescots—cantaloups—whatnots— to our streaming Italian watermelons?"

"Nothing, I'm sure, could come up to this—but please allow me to refrain; I'm feeling a bit squeamish," said Amédée, who was still heaving with repugnance at the recollection of the chemist.

"Well, then, some figs at any rate! Dorino has just picked them."

"No, not any either. Excuse me."

"That's bad! That's bad! Make a pun or two," whispered Protos in his ear. Then aloud: "We must dose that squeamish stomach of yours with a little wine and get it ready for the turkey. Assunta, fill our worthy guest's glass!"

Amédée was obliged to pledge his hosts and drink more than he was accustomed to; this, added to the heat and fatigue of the day, soon fuddled him. He joked with less effort. Protos made him sing; his voice was shrill but it enraptured his audience. Assunta wanted to kiss him. And yet from the depths of his poor battered faith there rose a sickening and undefinable distress; he laughed so as not to cry. He admired Cave's easy naturalness. . . . Who but Fleurissoire and the Cardinal could ever have imagined that he was playing a part? Bardolotti's dissimulation and self-possession were for that matter, no whit inferior to the *abbé's*, and he laughed and applauded and lewdly jostled Dorino, when Cave, upsetting Assunta in his arms, nuzzled her with his face; and then, as Fleurissoire, with a bursting heart, bent towards Cave and murmured: "How you must be suffering!" Cave seized his hand behind Assunta's back and pressed it silently, his head turned aside and his eyes cast up to Heaven.

Then, rising abruptly, Cave clapped his hands:

"Now then, you must leave us! No, you can clear away later. Be off with you! Via! Via!"

He went to make certain that Dorino and Assunta were not eavesdropping, and came back with a face turned suddenly long and grave, while the Cardinal, passing his hand over his countenance, effaced in an instant all its profane and factitious gaiety.

"You see, Monsieur de la Fleurissoire, you see, my son, to what we are reduced! Oh, this acting! this shameful acting!"

"It makes me turn in loathing," added Protos, "from even the most innocent joys—from the purest gaiety."

"God will count it to your credit, my poor dear Father Cave," went on the Cardinal, turning towards Protos; "God will reward you for helping me to drain this cup," and, by way of symbol, he tossed off the wine which remained in his half-emptied glass, while the most agonised disgust was painted on his features.

"What!" cried Fleurissoire, bending forward, "is it possible that even in this retreat and under this borrowed habit, your Eminence . . ."

"My son, call me plain Monsieur."

"Forgive me! I thought in private . . ."

"Even when I am alone I tremble."

"Can you not choose your servants?"

"They are chosen for me; and those two you have seen . . ."

"Ah! if I were to tell him," said Protos, "that they have gone straight off to report our most trifling words to . . ."

"Is it possible that in the palace . . ."

"Hush! No big words! You'll get us hanged. Don't forget that it's to the chaplain Ciro Bardolotti that you're speaking."

"I am at their mercy," wailed Ciro.

And Protos, who was sitting with his arms crossed on the table, leant across it towards Ciro.

"And if I were to tell him," said he, "that you are never left alone, night or day, for a single hour!"

"Yes, whatever disguise I put on," continued the bogus Cardinal, "I can never be sure that some of the secret police aren't at my heels."

"What! Do these people here know who you are?"

"You misunderstand him," said Protos. "You are one of the few persons—and I say it before God—who can pride themselves on establishing any resemblance between Cardinal San-Felice and the modest Bardolotti. But try to understand this—their enemies are not the same! While the Cardinal in his palace has to defend himself against the freemasons, chaplain Bardolotti is threatened by the . . ."

"Jesuits!" interrupted the chaplain wildly.

"That has not yet been explained to him," said Protos.

"Ah! if we've got the Jesuits against us too!" sobbed Fleurissoire. "But who would have thought it? Are you sure?"

"Reflect a little; you will see it is quite natural. You must understand that the Holy See's recent policy, all made up as it is of conciliation and compromise, is just the thing to please them and that the last encyclicals are exactly to their taste. Perhaps they are not aware that the Pope who promulgated them is not the *real* one; but they would be heart-broken if he were changed."

"If I understand you rightly," Fleurissoire took him up, "the Jesuits are allied with the freemasons in this affair."

"How do you make that out?"

"But Monsieur Bardolotti has just revealed . . ."

"Don't make him say absurdities."

"I'm sorry. I know so little about politics."

"That is why you must believe just what you are told and no more: two great parties are facing each other—the Lodge and the Company of Jesus; and as we who are in the secret cannot get support from either of them without discovering ourselves, we have them both against us."

"What do you think of that? Eh?" asked the Cardinal.

Fleurissoire had given up thinking; he was utterly bewildered.

"Yes, they are all against us," went on Protos; "such is always the way when one has truth on one's side."

"Ah! how happy I was when I knew nothing!" wailed Fleurissoire. "Alas! never, never more shall I be able to know nothing!" . . .

"He has not yet told you all," continued Protos, touching him gently on the shoulder. "Prepare for something more terrible still. . . ." Then, leaning forward, he whispered: "In spite of every precaution, the secret has leaked out; a certain number of sharpers are using it to make a house-to-house collection in the departments which have a reputation for piety; they act in the name of the Crusade and rake in money which in reality ought to come to us."

"How frightful!"

"Added to which," said Bardolotti, "they throw discredit and suspicion on us and oblige us more than ever to make use of the greatest cunning and caution."

"Look here! Read this!" said Protos, holding out a copy of the *Croix* to Fleurissoire; "it's the day before yesterday's paper. This short paragraph tells its own story!"

" 'We cannot too earnestly warn devout souls against certain individuals who are going about the country disguised as ecclesiastics, and in particular against a certain pseudo-canon who, under pretext of being entrusted with a secret mission, shamefully abuses the credulity of the public and actually extorts money from them for a so-called CRUSADE FOR THE DELIVERANCE OF THE POPE. The name alone sufficiently proclaims the absurdity of the business.' "

Fleurissoire felt the ground give way beneath his feet.

"Whom can one trust then? Shall I tell you in ϫy turn, gentlemen, that it is perhaps due to this very swindler—this false canon, I mean—that I am with you today?"

Father Cave looked gravely at the Cardinal, then, striking his fist on the table:

"I suspected as much!" he cried.

"Everything contributes to make me fear," continued Fleurissoire, "that the person who informed me of the affair was herself a victim of this rogue's blandishments."

"It would not surprise me," said Protos.

"You see now," went on Bardolotti, "how difficult our position is, between these sharpers on the one hand, who have stepped into our shoes, and the police on the other, who, when they mean to catch *them*, may very well lay hold upon *us* instead."

"What is one to do?" wailed Fleurissoire. "I see danger everywhere."

"Are you surprised now at our excessive prudence?" asked Bardolotti.

"And can you fail to understand that at moments we do not hesitate to clothe ourselves in the livery of sin and feign indulgence towards the most culpable of pleasures?"

"Alas!" stammered Fleurissoire, "you at any rate do no more than feign, and you only simulate sin to hide your virtues. But I .." And as the fumes of wine and the vapours of melancholy, drunken retchings and hiccuping sobs all beset him at once, he began—bent double in Protos's direction—by bringing up his lunch and then went on to tell a muddled story of his evening with Carola and the lamented loss of his virginity. Bardolotti and Father Cave had a hard job to prevent themselves from bursting into laughter.

"But have you been to confession, my son?" asked the Cardinal, full of solicitude.

"I went next morning."

"Did the priest give you absolution?"

"Far too readily That's why I'm so uneasy. But how could I confide to him that I was no ordinary pilgrim . . . reveal what it was that brought me here? . . . No, no! It's all over now. It was a chosen mission that demanded the service of a blameless life. I was the very man. And now it's all over! I have fallen!" Again he was shaken by sobs and as he struck little blows on his breast, he repeated: "I'm no longer worthy! I'm no longer worthy! . . ." Then he went on in a kind of chant: "Ah! you who hear me, you who see my anguish, judge me, condemn me, punish me. . . . Tell me what extraordinary penance will wash away my extraordinary guilt. What chastisement?"

Protos and Bardolotti looked at one another. The latter rose at last and began to pat Amédée on the shoulder:

"Come, come, my son! You mustn't let yourself go

like that. Well, yes! you have sinned, but, hang it all, you are still needed. (You've dirtied yourself; here, take this napkin; rub it off.) But of course I understand your anguish, and since you appeal to us, we will give you the means of redeeming yourself. (You're not doing it properly. Let me help you.)"

"Oh, don't trouble! Thank you! Thank you!" said Fleurissoire as Bardolotti, scrubbing the while, went on:

"At the same time, I understand your scruples; out of respect to them, I will begin by setting you a little task; there's nothing conspicuous about it, but it will give you the opportunity of atoning and be a test of your devotion."

"I ask nothing more."

"Dear Father Cave, have you that little cheque about you?"

Protos pulled a paper out of the inner pocket of his shirt.

"Surrounded on all sides by enemies as we are," went on the Cardinal, "we sometimes find it difficult to cash the offerings which a few generous souls send us in response to our secret solicitations. Watched at the same time by the freemasons and the Jesuits, by the police and by the swindlers, it would not be suitable for us to be seen presenting cheques or money orders at the banks and post offices, where our person might be recognised. The sharpers Father Cave was telling you about just now have thrown such discredit on our collections!" (Protos, in the meantime, was thrumming impatiently on the table.) "In short, here is a modest little cheque for six thousand francs which I beg you, my son, to cash in our stead; it is drawn on the Credito Commerciale of Rome by the Duchess of Ponte Cavallo; though it was addressed to the archbishop, the name of the payee has purposely been left a blank, so that it may be cashed by the bearer. Do not scruple to sign it with your own name, which will arouse no suspicions. Take care not to let yourself be robbed of it or of . . . What is the matter, my dear Father Cave? You seem agitated."

"Go on! Go on!"

". . . or of the money which you will bring back to me . . . let me see . . . you return to Rome to-night; you can take the six o'clock express to-morrow evening; you will be at Naples again at ten and you will find me waiting for you at the station. After that we will think of employing you on some worthier errand. . . . No, no, my son, do not kiss my hand. Can you not see there is no ring on it?"

Amédée had half prostrated himself at his feet. The Cardinal touched his forehead, and Protos, taking him by the arm, shook him gently:

"Come, come! another glass before you start. I am very sorry I can't go back to Rome with you; but I'm kept here by all sorts of business—besides, it's better we shouldn't be seen together. Good-bye! Let me embrace you, my dear Fleurissoire. May God keep you! I thank Him for having permitted me to know you."

He accompanied Fleurissoire to the door, and as he was leaving:

"Ah! sir," he said, "what do you think of the Cardinal? Is it not distressing to see the state to which persecution has reduced such a noble intelligence?"

Then, as he went back to the bogus Cardinal:

"You fathead! That was a bright idea of yours, wasn't it, to get your cheque endorsed by a silly ass who hasn't even got a passport, and whom I shall have to shadow?"

But Bardolotti, heavy with sleep, let his head roll upon the table, murmuring:

"We must keep the old 'uns busy."

Protos went indoors to take off his wig and his peasant's costume; he appeared a little later, looking thirty years younger and dressed like a bank clerk or a shop assistant of inferior grade. He had very little time to catch the train he knew Fleurissoire was going to take, and he went off without taking leave of the slumbering Bardolotti.

VII

Fleurissoire got back to Rome and the Via dei Vecchierelli that same evening. He was extremely tired and persuaded Carola to allow him to sleep.

The next morning, as soon as he woke, his spot, to judge by the feel, seemed to him odd; he examined it in the glass and found that a yellowish scab had formed over the part that had been grazed; the whole had a decidedly nasty look. As at that moment he heard Carola outside on the landing, he called her in and begged her to examine the place. She led Fleurissoire up to the window and at first glance assured him:

"It's not what you think."

To tell the truth, Amédée had not thought particularly of *it*, but Carola's attempt to reassure him had the contrary effect of filling him with alarm. For, indeed, directly she asserted that it was not *it*, it meant there was a chance that it might be. After all, was she really certain that it wasn't? It seemed to him quite natural that it should be; for there was no doubt that he had sinned; he deserved that it should be *it*; it must be *it*. A cold shudder went down his spine.

"How did you get it?" she asked.

Ah! what signified the occasional cause—the rasor's cut or the chemist's spittle? The real, the root cause, the one that had earned him this chastisement, could he with decency tell her what it was? Would she understand him if he did? She would laugh, no doubt. . . . As she repeated her question:

"It was a barber," he said.

"You ought to put something on it."

This solicitude swept away his last doubts; what she had said at first was merely to reassure him; he saw himself with his face and body eaten away by boils— an object of disgust to Arnica; his eyes filled with tears.

"Then you think . . ."

"No, no, dearie, you mustn't get into such a state; you look like a funeral. In the first place, it would be impossible to tell it at this stage, even if it *is* that."

"It is! It is! . . . Oh! it serves me right! It serves me right!" he repeated.

She was touched.

"And, besides, it never begins like that. Shall I call Madam in to tell you so? . . . No? Well, then, you'd better go out a little to distract your thoughts. Go and get a glass of Marsala." She kept silent for a moment. At last, unable to restrain herself any longer:

"Listen," she broke out. "I've something serious to tell you. You didn't happen to meet a sort of *curé* yesterday, with white hair, did you?"

"Why?" asked Fleurissoire in amazement.

"Well . . . " she hesitated again; then, looking at him and seeing how pale he was, she went on impulsively: "Well, don't trust him. Take my word for it, you poor lamb; he means to fleece you. I oughtn't to tell you so, but . . . don't you trust him."

Amédée was getting ready to go out, not knowing whether he was on his head or on his heels; he was already on the stairs, when she called him back:

"And mind, if you see him again, don't tell him that I said anything. You'd as good as murder me."

Decidedly, life was becoming too complicated for Amédée. And, what is more, his feet were frozen, his head burning and his ideas topsyturvy. How was he to know where he was, if Father Cave himself turned out to be a humbug? . . . Then, the Cardinal too perhaps? . . . But the cheque then? He took the paper out of his pocket, felt it and was reassured by its reality. No, no! It wasn't possible! Carola was wrong. And then what did she know of the mysterious interests that compelled poor Cave to play double? It was much more likely that the whole thing was some paltry vengeance of Baptistin's, against whom, in fact, the *abbé* had warned him. . . . No matter! he would keep his eyes open wider than ever; he would suspect Cave for the future just as he already suspected Baptistin; and who knows if even Carola . . . ?

"And, indeed," he said to himself, "here we have at

once the consequence and the proof of that initial vice —the collapse of the Holy See; everything comes tottering down with that. Whom can one trust if not the Pope? And once the corner-stone on which the Church was built gives way, nothing else deserves to be true."

Amédée was walking hurriedly in the direction of the post office; he was in great hopes of finding news from home—honest, comfortable news, on which he could at length rest his wearied confidence. The slight mistiness of early morning and that southern profusion of light in which everything seemed melting away into a vaporous haze—seemed losing substance and reality—increased his dizziness; he walked as though in a dream, doubting the solidity of the ground, of the walls— doubting the actual existence of the people he passed— doubting, above all, his own presence in Rome. . . . Then he pinched himself so as to wake from this horrid dream and find himself again in Pau, in his own bed, with Arnica already up and bending over him with the accustomed question on her lips: "Have you slept well, dear?"

At the post office they recognised him and made no difficulty in giving him another letter from his wife.

". . . I have just heard from Valentine de Saint-Prix," wrote Arnica, "that Julius is in Rome, too, where he has been summoned to a congress. I am so glad to think that you will meet him! Unfortunately Valentine was not able to give me his address. She thinks he is at the Grand Hotel, but she isn't sure. She knows, however, that he is going to the Vatican on Thursday morning; he wrote beforehand to Cardinal Pazzi so as to be given an audience. He has just been to Milan, where he saw Anthime, who is in great distress because he can't get what the Church promised him after his conversion; so Julius means to go and ask the Holy Father for justice; for of course he knows nothing about it as yet. He is sure to tell you about his visit and then you will be able to inform him.

"I hope you are being very careful to take precautions against the malaria and that you are not tiring yourself too much. I shall be so glad when you write to say that you are coming home. . . ." Etc.

Then, scribbled in pencil across the fourth page, a few words from Blafaphas:

"If you go to Naples, you should take the opportunity of finding out how they make the hole in the macaroni. I am on the brink of a new discovery."

Joy rang through Amédée's heart like a clarion. But it was accompanied by a certain misgiving. Thursday, the day of the audience, was that very day. He had not dared send his clothes to the wash and he was running short of clean linen—at any rate, he was afraid so. That morning he had put on yesterday's collar; but it suddenly ceased to seem sufficiently clean, now that he knew there was a chance of seeing Julius. The joy that this circumstance would otherwise have caused him was slightly dashed. As to returning to the Via dei Vecchierelli, it was not to be thought of if he intended to catch his brother-in-law on his way out from the audience—and this would be less agitating than looking up at the Grand Hotel. At any rate, he took care to turn his cuffs; as for his collar, he pulled his comforter up to cover it, which had the added advantage of concealing his pimple as well.

But what did such trifles matter? The fact is, Fleurissoire felt unspeakably cheered by his letter; and the prospect of renewing contact with one of his own people, with his own past life, abolished at one sweep the

monsters begotten of his traveller's imagination. Carola,
Father Cave, the Cardinal, all floated before him like a
dream which is suddenly interrupted by the crowing of
the cock. Why had he left Pau? What sense was
there in this absurd fable which had disturbed him in
his happiness? There was a Pope, bless us! and he
would soon be hearing Julius declare that he had seen
him. A Pope—that was enough. Was it possible that
God should have authorised such a monstrous substi-
tution? Fleurissoire would certainly never have believed it if it had not been for his absurd pride in the
part he had to play in the business.

Amédée was walking hurriedly; it was all he could do
to prevent himself from running; at last he was regain-
ing confidence, whilst around him once more everything
recovered weight and size, and natural position and con-
vincing reality. He was holding his straw hat in his
hand; when he arrived in front of the basilica, he was in
such a state of lofty exhilaration that he began to walk
round the fountain on the right-hand side; and as he
passed to the windward of the spray, allowing it to wet
him, he smiled up at the rainbow.

Suddenly he came to an abrupt stop. There, close to
him, sitting on the base of the fourth pillar of the
colonnade, surely that was Julius he caught sight of?
He hesitated to recognise him, for if his attire was
respectable, his attitude was very far from being so;
the Comte de Baraglioul had placed his black straw
Cronstadt beside him on the crook of his walking-stick,
which he had stuck into the ground between two paving-
stones, and all regardless of the solemnity of the spot,
with his right foot cocked up on his left knee (like any

prophet in the Sixtine Chapel), he was propping a note-book on his right knee, while from time to time his pencil, poised in air, swooped down upon the pages, and he began to write; so absorbed was his attention, and the dictates of his inspiration so urgent, that Amédée might have turned a somersault in front of him with-out his noticing it. He was speaking to himself as he wrote; and though the splashing of the fountain drowned his voice, the movement of his lips was plainly visible.

Amédée drew near, going discreetly round by the other side of the pillar. As he was about to touch him on the shoulder:

"In that case, what does it matter?" declaimed Julius, and he consigned these words with a final flourish to his note-book; then, putting his pencil in his pocket and rising abruptly, he came nose to nose with Amédée.

"In Heaven's name, what are *you* doing here?"

Amédée, trembling with emotion, began to stutter with-out being able to reply; he convulsively pressed one of Julius's hands between both his own. Julius, in the meanwhile, was examining him:

"My poor fellow, what a sight you look!"

Providence had dealt unkindly with Julius; of the two brothers in-law who were left to him, one was a church mouse and the other a scarecrow. It was less than three years since he had seen Amédée—but he thought him aged by at least twelve; his cheeks were sunken; his Adam's apple was protuberant; his magenta comforter enhanced the paleness of his face; his chin was quiver-ing; his blear eyes rolled in a way which should have been pathetic, but was merely grotesque; his yesterday's expedition had left him with a mysterious hoarseness, so that his voice seemed to come from a long way off. Full of his preoccupations:

"So you have seen him?" he said.

"Seen whom?" asked Julius.

This "whom" sounded in Amédée's ears like a knell and a blasphemy. He particularised discreetly:

"I thought you had just come from the Vatican."

"So I have. Excuse me, I was thinking of something else. . . . If you only knew what has happened to me!"

His eyes were sparkling; he looked on the verge of jumping out of his skin.

"Oh, please!" entreated Fleurissoire, "talk about that afterwards; tell me first of all about your visit. I'm so impatient to hear. . . ."

"Does it interest you?"

"You'll soon know how much. Go on, go on, I beg you."

"Well, then," began Julius, seizing hold of Fleurissoire by one arm and dragging him away from the neighbourhood of St. Peter's, "perhaps you may have heard in what miserable poverty our poor brother Anthime has been living as a result of his conversion. He is still waiting in vain for what the Church promised to give him in order to make up for the loss inflicted on him by the freemasons. Anthime has been duped; so much must be admitted. I don't know, my dear fellow, how this affair strikes you—as for me, I consider it an absolute farce . . . but it's thanks to it perhaps that I'm more or less clear as to the matter in hand, about which I'm most anxious to talk to you. Well, then—a *creature of inconsequence!* That's going rather far perhaps . . . and no doubt his apparent inconsequence hides what is, in reality, a subtler and more recondite sequence—the important point is that what makes him act should not be a matter of interest, or, as the usual phrase is, that he should not be merely actuated by interested motives."

"I don't follow you very well," said Amédée.

"True, true! I was straying from the subject of my visit. Well, then, I had determined to take Anthime's business in hand. . . . Ah, my dear fellow, if you'd seen the apartment in which he's living in Milan! 'You can't possibly stay on here,' I said to him at once. And when I think of that unfortunate Veronica! But he's going in for asceticism—turning into a regular saint; he won't allow anyone to pity him—and as for blaming the clergy! 'My dear friend,' I said to him, 'I grant you that the higher clergy are not to blame, but it can only be because they know nothing about it. You must let me go and tell them how matters stand.' "

"I thought that Cardinal Pazzi . . ." suggested Fleuris-soire.

"Yes, but it wasn't any good. You see, these high dignitaries are all afraid of compromising themselves. It was necessary for someone who was quite an outsider to take the matter up. Myself, for instance. For just see in what a wonderful way discoveries are made!—I mean, the most important ones; the thing seems like a sudden illumination—but not at all—in reality one hasn't ceased thinking of it. So with me; for a long time past I had been worrying over my characters—their excessive logic, and at the same time their insufficient definition."

"I'm afraid," said Amédée gently, "that you're stray-ing from the point again."

"Nothing of the kind," went on Julius; "it's you who

don't follow my idea. In short, I determined to present the petition to the Holy Father himself, and I went this morning to hand it to him."

"Well? Quick! Did you see him?"

"My dear Amédée, if you keep interrupting all the time . . . Well, you can't imagine how difficult it is to get to see him."

"Can't I?" said Amédée.

"What did you say?"

"I'll tell you by and by."

"First of all, I had entirely to give up any idea of presenting my petition myself; it was a neat roll of paper. But as soon as I got to the second antechamber (or the third, I forget which), a great big fellow, dressed up in black and red, politely removed it."

Amédée began to chuckle like a person with private information who knows there is good reason to laugh.

"In the next antechamber, I was relieved of my hat, which they put on a table. In the fifth or sixth, I waited for a long time in the company of two ladies and three prelates, and then a kind of chamberlain came and ushered me into the next room, where as soon as I was in the presence of the Holy Father (he was perched, as far as I could see, on a throne with a sort of canopy over it) he instructed me to prostrate myself—which I did—so that I saw nothing more."

"But surely you didn't keep your head bowed down so low that . . ."

"My dear Amédée, it's all very well for you to talk; don't you know that one can be struck blind with awe? And not only didn't I dare raise my head, but every time I tried to speak of Anthime, a kind of major-domo, with a species of ruler, gave me a little tap on the back of my neck, which made me bow it again."

"But at any rate, did *he* speak to you?"

"Yes, about my book, which he admitted he hadn't read."

"My dear Julius," said Amédée, after a moment's silence, "what you have just told me is of the highest importance. So you didn't see him! And from your whole account one thing stands out clear—that there's a mysterious difficulty about seeing him. Alas! all my cruellest apprehensions are confirmed. Julius, I must now tell you . . . but come along here—this street is so crowded . . ."

He dragged him into an almost deserted *vicolo*, and Julius, amused rather than otherwise, made no resistance.

"What I am going to confide to you is so grave . . . Whatever you do, don't make any sign. Let's look as if we weren't talking about anything important and make up your mind to hear something terrible.—Julius, my dear friend, the person you saw this morning . . ."

"Whom I didn't see, you mean."

"Exactly . . . is not the *real one.*"

"I beg your pardon?"

"I tell you that you can't have seen the Pope, for the monstrous reason that . . . I have it from a secret and unimpeachable source—the real Pope has been kidnapped."

This astonishing revelation had the most unexpected effect upon Julius. He suddenly let go Amédée's arm, and running on ahead, he called out at the top of his voice right across the *vicolo:*

"Oh, no! no! Not that! Good God! No! Not that!"

Then, drawing near Amédée again:

"What! I succeed—with great difficulty—in clearing my mind of the whole thing; I convince myself that there's nothing to be expected—nothing to be hoped for—nothing to be admitted; that Anthime has been taken in—that the whole thing is quackery—that there's nothing left to do but to laugh at it—when up you come and say: 'Hold hard! There's been a mistake—a miscalculation —we must begin again.' Oh, no! Not a bit of it! Never in the world! I shan't budge. If he isn't the real one, so much the worse."

Fleurissoire was horrified.

"But," said he, "the Church . . ." And he regretted that his hoarseness prevented any flights of eloquence. "But supposing the Church herself is taken in?"

Julius planted himself in front of him, standing crosswise so as almost to block up the way, and in a mocking, cutting voice which was not like him:

"Well! What the dickens does it matter to you?"

Then a doubt fell upon Fleurissoire—a fresh, formless, atrocious doubt which was absorbed in some indefinable way into the thick mass of his discomfort—Julius, Julius himself, this Julius to whom he was talking, this Julius to whom he clung with all the longing of his heart-broken faith—this Julius was not the *real* Julius either.

"What! Can it be you who say such things? You, Julius? On whom I was counting so? The Comte de Baraglioul, whose writings . . ."

"Don't talk to me of my writings, I beg. I've heard

quite enough about them this morning from your Pope
—false or true, whichever he may be.   Thanks to my discovery, the next ones will be better—you may count
upon that.   I'm anxious to talk to you now about serious
matters.   You'll lunch with me, won't you?"

"With pleasure; but I must leave you early.   I'm expected in Naples this evening . . . yes, on some business,
which I'll tell you about.   You're not taking me to the
Grand, I hope?"

"No; we'll go to the Colonna."

Julius, on his side, was not at all anxious to be seen
at the Grand Hotel in company with such a lamentable
object as Fleurissoire; and Fleurissoire, who felt pale and
worn out, was already in a twitter at being seated full
in the light at the restaurant table, directly opposite
his brother-in-law and exposed to his scrutinising glance.
If only that glance had sought his own, it would have
been more tolerable; but no, he felt it already going
straight to the border line of his magenta comforter,
straight to that frightful spot where the suspicious
pimple was budding, hopelessly divulged.   And while the
waiter was bringing the hors-d'œuvre:

"You ought to take sulphur baths," said Baraglioul.

"It's not what you think," protested Fleurissoire.

"I'm glad to hear it," answered Baraglioul, who, for
that matter, hadn't thought anything; "I just offered
the suggestion in passing."   Then, throwing himself back
in his chair, he went on in a professorial manner:

"Now this is how it is, my dear Amédée.   I contend
that ever since the days of La Rochefoucauld we have
all followed in his footsteps like blundering idiots; I

contend that self-advantage is *not* man's guiding principle—that there *are* such things as disinterested actions . . ."

"I should hope so," interrupted Fleurissoire, naïvely.

"Don't be in such a hurry, I beg. By *disinterested* I mean gratuitous. Also that evil actions—what are commonly called evil—may be just as gratuitous as good ones."

"In that case, why commit them?"

"Exactly! Out of sheer wantonness—or from love of sport. My contention is that the most disinterested souls are not necessarily the best—in the Catholic meaning of the word; on the contrary, from the Catholic point of view, the best-trained soul is the one that keeps the strictest accounts."

"The one that ever feels its debt towards God," added Fleurissoire seraphically, in an attempt to keep up to the mark.

Julius was obviously irritated by his brother-in law's interruptions; he thought them ludicrous.

"A contempt for what may serve is no doubt the stamp of a certain aristocracy of nature. . . . So once a man has shaken free from orthodoxy, from self-indulgence and from calculation, we may grant that his soul may keep no accounts at all?"

"No! No! Never! We may not grant it!" exclaimed Fleurissoire vehemently; then suddenly frightened by the sound of his own voice, he bent towards Baraglioul and whispered:

"Let's speak lower; we shall be overheard."

"Pooh! How could anyone be interested in what we are saying?"

"Oh, my dear Julius, I see you have no conception what the people of this country are like. I've spent only four days here, but during those four days the adventures I've had have been endless, and of a kind to teach me caution—pretty forcibly too—though it wasn't in my nature, I swear. I am being tracked!"

"It's your imagination."

"I only wish it were! But what's to be done? When falsehood takes the place of truth, truth must needs dissemble. As for me, with this mission that has been entrusted to me (I'll tell you about it presently), placed as I am between the Lodge and the Society of Jesus, it's all up with me. I am an object of suspicion to everyone; everything is an object of suspicion to me. Suppose I were to confess to you, my dear Julius, that just now when you met my distress with mockery, I actually doubted whether it was really you to whom I was talking —whether you weren't an imitation Julius. . . . Suppose I were to tell you that this morning before I met you, I actually doubted my own reality—doubted whether I was really here in Rome—whether I wasn't just dreaming—and whether I shouldn't wake up presently at Pau, lying peacefully beside Arnica, back again in my everyday life."

"My dear fellow, you've got fever."

Fleurissoire seized his hand and in a voice trembling with emotion:

"Fever!" he cried. "You're right! It's fever I've got —a fever that cannot—that *must* not be cured; a fever which I hoped would take you too when you heard what I had to reveal—which I hoped—yes, I own it—you too would catch from me, my brother, so that we might

burn together in its consuming fires. . . . But no! I
see only too clearly now that the path I follow—the
dark and dangerous path I am called upon to follow—
must needs be solitary too; your own words have proved
it to me. What, Julius? Can it be true? *He* is not
to be seen? No one succeeds in seeing him?"

"My dear fellow," said Julius, disengaging himself
from his clasp and in his turn laying a hand on the
excited Amédée's arm, "my dear fellow, I will now confess something I didn't dare tell you just now. When I
found myself in the Holy Father's presence . . . well, I
was seized with a fit of absent-mindedness . . ."

"Absent-mindedness?" repeated Fleurissoire, aghast.

"Yes. I suddenly caught myself thinking of something else."

"Am I really to believe you?"

"For it was precisely at that very moment that I had
my revelation. 'Well, but,' said I to myself, pursuing
my first idea, 'supposing the evil action—the crime—is
gratuitous, it will be impossible to impute it to its perpe-
trator and impossible, therefore, to convict him.'"

"Oh!" sighed Amédée, "are you at it again?"

"For the motive of the crime is the handle by which
we lay hold of the criminal. And if, as the judge will
point out, *is fecit cui prodest* . . . You've studied law,
haven't you?"

"I beg your pardon?" said Amédée, with the beads of
perspiration standing on his brow.

But at that moment the dialogue was suddenly interrupted; the restaurant page-boy came up to them holding
a plate on which lay an envelope inscribed with Fleuris-

soire's name. Petrified with astonishment, he opened the envelope and found inside it these words:

"You have not a moment to lose. The train for Naples starts at three o'clock. Ask Monsieur de Baraglioul to go with you to the Crédit Industriel, where he is known and where he will be able to testify to your identity."

"There! What did I tell you?" whispered Amédée, to whom this incident was a relief rather than otherwise.

"Yes. I admit it's very odd. How on earth do they know my name and that I have an account at the Crédit Industriel?"

"I tell you they know everything."

"I don't much fancy the tone of the note. The writer might have at any rate apologised for interrupting us."

"What would have been the use? He knows well enough that everything must give way to my mission. I've a cheque to cash . . . No, it's impossible to tell you about it here; you can see for yourself that we are being watched." Then, taking out his watch: "Yes, there's only just time."

He rang for the waiter.

"No, no," said Julius. "You're my guest. The Crédit's not far off; we can take a cab if necessary. Don't be flurried. Oh, I wanted to say that if you're going to Naples this evening you can make use of this circular ticket of mine. It's in my name, but it doesn't matter." (For Julius liked to be obliging.) "I took it in Paris, thinking that I should be going further south; but I'm kept here by this congress. How long do you think of staying?"

"As short a time as possible. I hope to be back to-morrow."

"Then I'll expect you to dinner."

At the Crédit Industriel, thanks to the Comte de Baraglioul's introduction, Fleurissoire had no difficulty in cashing his cheque for six bank-notes, which he slipped into the inner pocket of his coat. In the meantime he had told his brother-in-law, more or less coherently, the tale of the cheque, the Cardinal and the *abbé*. Baraglioul, who went with him to the station, listened with only half an ear.

On their way, Fleurissoire went into a shirtmaker's to buy himself a collar, but he didn't put it on at once, so as not to keep Julius waiting outside the shop.

"Haven't you got a bag?" he asked as Fleurissoire joined him.

Fleurissoire would have been only too glad to go and fetch his shawl and his night things; but own up to the Via dei Vecchierelli before Baraglioul? It couldn't be thought of.

"Oh, only for one night!" he said brightly. "Besides, there isn't time to go round by my hotel."

"Where are you staying?"

"Oh, behind the Coliseum," replied Amédée at a venture.

It was as if he had said: "Oh, under a bridge!"

Julius looked at him again:

"What a funny fellow you are!"

Did he really seem so queer? Fleurissoire mopped his brow. For a few moments they paced backwards and forwards in front of the station in silence.

"Well, we must say good-bye now," said Baraglioul, holding out his hand.

"Couldn't you . . . couldn't you come with me?" stammered Fleurissoire timidly. "I don't exactly know why, but I'm a little nervous about going by myself."

"You came to Rome by yourself. What can happen to you? Excuse me for not going with you on to the platform, but the sight of a train going off always gives me an inexpressible feeling of sadness　Good-bye. Good luck!　And bring back my return ticket to Paris with you when you come to the Grand Hotel to-morrow."

BOOK V: LAFCADIO

"There is only one remedy! One thing alone
can cure us from being ourselves! . . ."
"Yes; strictly speaking, the question is not how
to get cured, but how to live."
— Joseph Conrad,
Lord Jim, p. 225.

I

After Lafcadio, with the solicitor's help—Julius acting as intermediary—had come into the 40,000 francs a year left him by the late Count Juste-Agénor de Baraglioul, his chief concern was to let no signs of it appear.

"Off gold plate perhaps," he had said to himself at the time, "but the same victuals."

What he had not considered—or perhaps what he had not yet learned—was that his victuals for the future would have a different taste. Or, put it like this: since struggling with his hunger gave him as much pleasure as indulging his appetite, his resistance—now that he was no longer pressed by want—began to slacken. To speak plainly, thanks to a naturally aristocratic disposition he had not allowed himself to be forced by necessity into committing a single one of those actions—which he might very well commit now, out of a gambling or a mocking humour, just for the fun of putting his pleasure before his interest.

In obedience to the Count's wishes he had not gone into mourning.

A mortifying experience awaited him when he went to replenish his wardrobe in the shops which had been patronised by his last uncle, the Marquis de Gesvres. On his mentioning this gentleman's name as a recommendation, the tailor pulled out a number of bills which the Marquis had neglected to pay. Lafcadio had a fastidious dislike to swindling; he at once pretended that he had come on purpose to settle the account, and paid ready money for his new clothes. The same misadventure awaited him at the bootmaker's. When it came to the shirtmaker, Lafcadio thought it more prudent to choose another.

"Oh, Uncle de Gesvres, if only I knew your address, it would be a pleasure to send you your receipted bills," thought Lafcadio. "You would despise me for it. No matter! I'm a Baraglioul and from this day forward, you scamp of a marquis, I dismiss you from my heart."

There was nothing to keep him in Paris—or to call him elsewhere; he crossed Italy by short stages, making his way to Brindisi, where he meant to embark on some liner bound for Java.

He was sitting all alone in a compartment of the train which was carrying him away from Rome, and contemplating—not without satisfaction—his hands in their grey doeskin gloves, as they lay on the rich fawn-coloured plaid, which, in spite of the heat, he had spread negligently over his knees. Through the soft woollen material of his travelling-suit he breathed ease and comfort at every pore; his neck was unconfined in its collar which without being low was unstarched, and from beneath which the narrow line of a bronze silk neck-tie ran, slender as a grass-snake, over his pleated shirt. He was at ease in his skin, at ease in his clothes, at ease in his shoes, which were cut out of the same doeskin as his gloves; his foot in its elastic prison could stretch, could bend, could feel itself alive. His beaver hat was pulled down over his eyes and kept out the landscape; he was smoking dried juniper, after the Algerian fashion, in a little clay pipe and letting his thoughts wander at their will. He thought:

"——The old woman with the little white cloud above her head, who pointed to it and said: 'It won't rain to-day!' that poor, shrivelled old woman whose sack I carried on my shoulders" (he had followed his fancy of travelling on foot for four days across the Apennines, between Bologna and Florence, and had slept a night at Covigliajo) "and whom I kissed when we got to the top of the hill . . . one of what the *curé* of Covigliajo would have called my 'good actions.' I could just as easily have throttled her—my hand would have been steady— when I felt her dirty wrinkled skin beneath my fingers. . . . Ah! how caressingly she stroked and dusted my coat collar and said *'figlio mio! carino!'* . . . I wonder what made my joy so intense when afterwards—I was still in a sweat—I lay down on the moss—not smoking though—in the shade of that big chestnut-tree. I felt as though I could have clasped the whole of mankind to my heart in my single embrace—or strangled it, for that matter. Human life! What a paltry thing! And with what alacrity I'd risk mine if only some deed of gallantry would turn up—something really rather pleasantly rash and daring! . . . All the same, I can't turn alpinist or aviator. . . . I wonder what that hidebound old Julius would advise. . . . It's a pity he's such a stick-in-the-mud! I should have liked to have a brother.

"Poor Julius! So many writers and so few readers! It's a fact. People read less and less nowadays . . . to judge by myself, as they say. It'll end by some catastrophe—some stupendous catastrophe, reeking with horror. Printing will be chucked overboard altogether; and it'll be a miracle if the best doesn't sink to the bottom with the worst.

"But the curious thing would be to know what the old woman would have said if I had begun to squeeze. One imagines *what would happen if,* but there's always a little hiatus through which the unexpected creeps in. Nothing ever happens exactly as one thinks it's going to. . . . That's what makes me want to act. . . . One does so little! . . . 'Let all that can be, be!' That's my explanation of the Creation. . . . In love with what might be. If I were the Government I should lock myself up.

"Nothing very exciting about the correspondence of that Monsieur Gaspard Flamand which I claimed as mine at the Poste Restante at Bologna. Nothing that would have been worth the trouble of returning to him.

"Heavens! how few people one meets whose portmanteau one would care to ransack! . . . And yet how few there are from whom one wouldn't get some queer reaction if one knew the right word—the right gesture! . . . A fine lot of puppets; but, by Jove, one sees the strings too plainly. One meets no one in the streets nowadays but jackanapes and blockheads. Is it possible for a decent person—I ask you, Lafcadio—to take such

a farce seriously? No, no! Be off with you! It's high
time! Off to a new world! Print your foot upon
Europe's soil and take a flying leap. If in the depths
of Borneo's forests there still remains a belated anthro-
popithex, go there and reckon the chances of a future
race of mankind. . . .

"I should have liked to see Protos again. No doubt
he's made tracks for America. He used to make out that
the barbarians of Chicago were the only persons he
esteemed. . . . Not voluptuous enough for my taste—a
pack of wolves! I'm feline by nature. . . . Well, enough
of that!

"The *padre* of Covigliajo with his cheery face didn't
look in the least inclined to deprave the little boy he
was talking to. He was certainly in charge of him. I
should have liked to make friends with him—not with
the *curé*, my word!—but with the little boy.

"How beautiful his eyes were when he raised them to
mine! He was as anxious and as afraid to meet my
look as I his—but I looked away at once. He was barely
five years younger than I. Yes, between fourteen and
sixteen—not more. What was I at that age? A
stripling * full of covetousness, whom I should like to meet
now; I think I should take a great fancy to myself. . . .
Faby was quite abashed at first to feel that he had fallen
in love with me; it was a good thing he made a clean
breast of it to my mother; after that he felt lighter-
hearted. But how irritated I was by his self-restraint!
Later on in the Aures, when I told him about it under
the tent, we had a good laugh together. . . . I should

* In English in the original. (*Translator's note.*)

like to see him again; it's a pity he's dead. Well, enough of that!

"The truth is, I hoped the *curé* would dislike me. I tried to think of disagreeable things to say to him—I could hit on nothing that wasn't charming. It's wonderful how hard I find it not to be fascinating. Yet I really can't stain my face with walnut juice, as Carola recommended, or start eating garlic. . . . Ah! don't let me think of that poor creature any more. It's to her I owe the most mediocre of my pleasures. . . . Oh!! What kind of ark can that strange old man have come out of?"

The sliding door into the corridor had just let in Amédée Fleurissoire. Fleurissoire had travelled in an empty compartment as far as Frosinone. At that station a middle-aged Italian had got into his carriage and had begun to stare at him with such glowering eyes that Fleurissoire had made haste to take himself off.

In the next compartment, Lafcadio's youthful grace, on the contrary, attracted him.

"Dear me! What a charming boy!" thought he; "hardly more than a child! On his holidays, no doubt. How beautifully dressed he is! His eyes look so candid! Oh, what a relief it will be to be quit of my suspicions for once! If only he knew French, I should like to talk to him."

He sat down opposite to him in the corner next the door. Lafcadio turned up the brim of his hat and began to consider him with a lifeless and apparently indifferent eye.

"What is there in common between me and that squalid little rat?" reflected he. "He seems to fancy himself too.

What is he smiling at me like that for? Does he imagine
I'm going to embrace him? Is it possible that there exist
women who fondle old men? No doubt he'd be exceedingly astonished to know that I can read writing or print
with perfect fluency, upside down, or in transparency, or
in a looking-glass, or on blotting-paper—a matter of three
months' training and two years' practice—all for the love
of art. Cadio, my dear boy, the problem is this: to
impinge on that fellow's fate . . . but how? . . . Oh!
I'll offer him a cachou. Whether he accepts or not, I
shall at any rate hear in what language."

"Grazio! Grazio!" said Fleurissoire as he refused.

"Nothing doing with the old dromedary. Let's go to
sleep," went on Lafcadio to himself, and pulling the brim
of his hat down over his eyes, he tried to spin a dream out
of one of his youthful memories.

He saw himself back at the time when he used to be
called Cadio, in that remote castle in the Carpathians
where his mother and he spent two summers in company
with Baldi, the Italian, and Prince Wladimir Bielkowski.
His room is at the end of a passage. This is the first year
he has not slept near his mother. . . . The bronze door-
handle is shaped like a lion's head and is held in place
by a big nail. . . . Ah! how clearly he remembers his
sensations! . . . One night he is aroused from a deep
sleep to see Uncle Wladimir—or is it a dream?—standing
by his bedside, looking more gigantic even than usual—
a very nightmare, draped in the fold of a huge rust-
coloured caftan, with his drooping moustache, and an
outrageous night-cap stuck on his head like a Persian
bonnet, so that there seems no end to the length of him.

He is holding in his hand a dark lantern, which he sets down on the table near the bed, beside Cadio's watch, pushing aside a bag of marbles to make room for it. Cadio's first thought is that his mother is dead or ill. He is on the point of asking, when Bielkowski puts his finger on his lips and signs to him to get up. The boy hastily slips on his bathing-wrap, which his uncle takes from the back of a chair and hands to him—all this with knitted brows and the look of a person who is not to be trifled with. But Cadio has such immense faith in Wladi that he hasn't a moment's fear. He pops on his slippers and follows him, full of curiosity at these goings-on and, as usual, all agog for amusement.

They step into the passage; Wladimir advances gravely —mysteriously, carrying the lantern well in front of him; they look as if they are accomplishing a rite or walking in a procession; Cadio is a little unsteady on his feet, for he is still dazed with dreaming; but curiosity soon clears his brains. As they pass his mother's room, they both stop for a moment and listen—not a sound! The whole house is fast asleep. When they reach the landing they hear the snoring of a footman whose room is in the attics. They go downstairs. Wladi's stockinged feet drop on the steps as softly as cotton-wool; at the slightest creak he turns round, looking so furious that Cadio can hardly keep from laughing. He points out one particular step and signs to him not to tread on it, with as much seriousness as if they were really in danger. Cadio takes care not to spoil his pleasure by asking himself whether these precautions are necessary, nor what can be the meaning of it all; he enters into the spirit of the game and slides down the banister, past the step. . . . He is so tremendously entertained by Wladi that he would go through fire and water to follow him.

When they reach the ground floor, they both sit down on the bottom step for a moment's breathing-space; Wladi nods his head and gives vent to a little sigh through his nose, as much as to say: 'My word! we've had a narrow squeak!' They start off again. At the drawing-room door, what redoubled precautions! The lantern, which it is now Cadio's turn to hold, lights up the room so queerly that the boy hardly recognises it; it seems to him fantastically big; a ray of light steals through a chink in the shutters; everything is plunged in a supernatural calm; he is reminded of a pond the moment before the stealthy casting of a net; and he recognises all the familiar objects, each one there in its place—but for the first time he realises their strangeness.

Wladi goes up to the piano, half opens it and lightly touches two or three notes with his finger-tips, so as to draw from them the lightest of sounds. Suddenly the lid slips from his hand and falls with a terrific din. (The mere recollection of it made Lafcadio jump again.) Wladi makes a dash at the lantern, muffles it and then crumples up into an arm-chair; Cadio slips under the table; they stay endless minutes, waiting motionless, listening in the dark . . . but no—nothing stirs in the house; in the distance a dog bays the moon. Then gently, slowly, Wladi uncovers the lantern.

In the dining-room, with what an air he unlocks the sideboard! The boy knows well enough it is nothing but a game, but his uncle seems actually taken in by it himself. He sniffs about as though to scent out where the best things lie hid; pounces on a bottle of Tokay; pours out two small glasses full for them to dip their biscuits in; signs to Cadio to pledge him, with finger on lip; the glasses tinkle faintly as they touch. . . . When the midnight feast is over, Wladi sets to work to put things straight again; he goes with Cadio to rinse the glasses in the pantry sink, wipes them, corks the bottle, shuts up the biscuit box, dusts away the crumbs with scrupulous care and gives one last glance to see that everything is tidy again in the cupboard. . . . Right you are! Not the ghost of a trace!

Wladï accompanies Cadio back to his bedroom door and takes leave of him with a low bow. Cadio picks up his slumbers again where he had left them, and wonders the next day whether the whole thing wasn't a dream.

An odd kind of entertainment for a little boy! What would Julius have thought of it? . . .

Lafcadio, though his eyes were shut, was not asleep; he could not sleep.

"The old boy over there believes I am asleep," thought he; "if I were to take a peep at him through my eyelids, I should see him looking at me. Protos used to make out that it was particularly difficult to pretend to be asleep while one was really watching; he claimed that he could always spot pretended sleep by just that slight quiver of the eyelids . . . I'm repressing now. Protos himself would be taken in. . . ."

The sun meanwhile had set, and Fleurissoire, in sentimental mood, was gazing at the last gleams of its splendour as they gradually faded from the sky. Suddenly the electric light that was set in the rounded ceiling of

the railway carriage, blazed out with a vividness that
contrasted brutally with the twilight's gentle melancholy.
Fleurissoire was afraid, too, that it might disturb his
neighbour's slumbers, and turned the switch; the result
was not total darkness but merely a shifting of the current
from the centre lamp to a dark blue night-light. To
Fleurissoire's thinking, this was still too bright; he turned
the switch again; the night-light went out, but two side
brackets were immediately turned on, whose glare was
even more disagreeable than the centre light's; another
turn, and the night-light came on again; at this he gave
up.

"Will he never have done fiddling with the light?"
thought Lafcadio impatiently. "What's he up to now?
(No! I'll *not* raise my eyelids.) He is standing up.
Can he have taken a fancy to my portmanteau? Bravo!
He has noticed that it isn't locked. It was a bright idea
of mine to have a complicated lock fitted to it at Milan
and then lose the key, so that I had to have it picked
at Bologna! A padlock, at any rate, is easy to replace.
. . . God damn it! Is he taking off his coat? Oh! all
the same, let's have a look!"

Fleurissoire, with no eyes for Lafcadio's portmanteau,
was struggling with his new collar and had taken his
coat off, so as to be able to put the stud in more easily;
but the starched linen was as hard as cardboard and he
struggled in vain.

"He doesn't look happy," went on Lafcadio to himself.
"He must be suffering from a fistula or some unpleasant
complaint of that kind. Shall I go to his help? He'll
never manage it by himself. . . ."

Yes, though! At last the collar yielded to the stud.

Fleurissoire then took up his tie, which he had placed on the seat beside his hat, his coat and his cuffs, and going up to the door of the carriage, looked at himself in the window-pane, endeavouring, like Narcissus in the water, to distinguish his reflection from the surrounding landscape.

"He can't see."

Lafcadio turned on the light. The train at that moment was running alongside a bank, which could be seen through the window, illuminated by the light cast upon it from one after another of the compartments of the train; a procession of brilliant squares was thus formed which danced along beside the railroad and suffered, each one in its turn, the same distortions, according to the irregularities of the ground. In the middle of one of these squares danced Fleurissoire's grotesque shadow; the others were empty.

"Who would see?" thought Lafcadio. "There—just to my hand—under my hand, this double fastening, which I can easily undo; the door would suddenly give way and he would topple out; the slightest push would do it; he would fall into the darkness like a stone; one wouldn't even hear a scream. . . . And off to-morrow to the East! . . . Who would know?"

The tie—a little ready-made sailor knot—was put on by now and Fleurissoire had taken up one of the cuffs and was arranging it upon his right wrist, examining, as he did so, the photograph above his seat, which represented some palace by the sea, and was one of four that adorned the compartment.

"A crime without a motive," went on Lafcadio, "what a puzzle for the police! As to that, however, going along beside this blessed bank, anybody in the next-door compartment might notice the door open and the old blighter's shadow pitch out. The corridor curtains, at any rate, are drawn. . . . It's not so much about events that I'm curious, as about myself. There's many a man thinks he's capable of anything, who draws back when it comes to the point. . . . What a gulf between the imagination and the deed! . . . And no more right to take back one's move than at chess. Pooh! If one could foresee all the risks, there'd be no interest in the game! . . . Between the imagination of a deed and . . . Hullo! the bank's come to an end. Here we are on a bridge, I think; a river . . ."

The window-pane had now turned black and the reflections in it became more distinct. Fleurissoire leant forward to straighten his tie.

"Here, just under my hand the double fastening—now that he's looking away and not paying attention—upon my soul, it's easier to undo than I thought. If I can count up to twelve, without hurrying, before I see a light in the country-side, the dromedary is saved. Here goes! One, two, three, four (slowly! slowly!), five, six, seven, eight, nine . . . a light! . . ."

II

Fleurissoire did not utter a single cry. When he felt Lafcadio's push and found himself facing the gulf which suddenly opened in front of him, he made a great sweep with his arm to save himself; his left hand clutched at the smooth framework of the door, while, as he half turned round, he flung his right well behind him and over Lafcadio's head, sending his second cuff, which he had been in the act of putting on, spinning to the other end of the carriage, where it rolled underneath the seat.

Lafcadio felt a horrible claw descend upon the back of his neck, lowered his head and gave another push, more impatient than the first; this was followed by the sensation of nails scraping through his flesh; and after that, nothing was left for Fleurissoire to catch hold of but the beaver hat, which he snatched at despairingly and carried away with him in his fall.

"Now then, let's keep cool," said Lafcadio to himself. "I mustn't slam the door to; they might hear it in the next carriage."

He drew the door towards him, in the teeth of the wind, and then shut it quietly.

"He has left me his frightful sailor hat; in another minute I should have kicked it after him, but he has taken mine along with him and that's enough. That was an excellent precaution of mine—cutting out my initials. . . . But there's the hatter's name in the crown, and people don't order a beaver hat of that kind every day of the week. . . . It can't be helped, I've played now. . . . Perhaps they'll think it an accident. . . . No, not now that I've shut the door. . . . Stop the train? . . . Come, come, Cadio! no touching up! You've only yourself to thank.

"To prove now that I'm perfectly self-possessed, I shall begin by quite quietly seeing what that photograph is the old chap was examining just now. . . . *Miramar!* No desire at all to go and visit *that*. . . . It's stifling in here."

He opened the window.

"The old brute has scratched me . . . I'm bleeding.

. . . It hurts like everything! I must bathe it a little; the lavatory is at the end of the corridor, on the left. Let's take another handkerchief."

He reached down his portmanteau from the rack above him and opened it on the seat, in the place where he had been sitting.

"If I meet anyone in the corridor I must be calm. . . . No! my heart's quiet again. Now for it! . . . Ah! his coat! I can easily hide it under mine. Papers in the pocket! Something to while away the time for the rest of the journey."

The coat was a poor threadbare affair of a dingy liquorice colour, made of a harsh-textured and obviously cheap material; Lafcadio thought it slightly repulsive; he hung it up on a peg in the small lavatory into which he locked himself; then, bending over the basin, he began to examine himself in the glass.

There were two ugly furrows on his neck; one, a thin red streak, starting from the back of his neck, turned leftwards and came to an end just below the ear; the other and shorter one, was a deep scratch just above the first; it went straight up towards the ear, the lobe of which it had reached and slightly torn. It was bleeding, but less than might have been expected; on the other hand, the pain, which he had hardly felt at first, began to be pretty sharp. He dipped his handkerchief into the basin, staunched the blood and then washed the handkerchief. "Not enough to stain my collar," thought he, as he put himself to rights; "all is well."

He was on the point of going out; just then the engine whistled; a row of lights passed behind the frosted window-pane of the closet. Capua! The station was

so close to the scene of the accident that the idea of jumping out, running back in the dark and getting his beaver
back again, flashed, dazzling, on his mind. He regretted
his hat, so soft and light and silky, at once so warm and
so cool, so uncrushable, so discreetly elegant. But it
was never his way to lend an undivided ear to his desires
—nor to like yielding—even to himself. More than all,
he hated indecision, and for ten years he had kept on him,
like a fetish, one of a pair of cribbage dice, which Baldi
had given him in days gone by; he never parted from it;
it was there, in his waistcoat pocket.

"If I throw six," he said to himself as he took it out,
"I'll get down."

He threw five.

"I shall get down all the same. Quick, the victim's
coat! . . . Now for my portmanteau. . . ."

He hurried to his compartment.

Ah! how futile seem all exclamations in face of the
extravagance of fact! The more surprising the occur-
rence, the more simple shall be my manner of relating it.
I will therefore say in plain words, merely this—when
Lafcadio got back to his compartment, his portmanteau
was gone!

He thought at first that he had made a mistake, and
went out again into the corridor. . . . But no! It was
the right place. There was the view of Miramar. . . .
Well, then? He sprang to the window and could not
believe his eyes. There, on the station platform, and not
very far from his carriage, his portmanteau was calmly
proceeding on its way in company of a strapping fellow
who was carrying it off at a leisurely walk.

Lafcadio's first instinct was to dash after him; as he

put out his hand to open the door, the liquorice coat
dropped on to the floor.

"Tut! tut! in another moment I should have put my
foot in it. . . . All the same, that rascal would go a little
quicker if he thought there was a chance of my coming
after him. Can he have seen . . . ?"

At this moment, as he was leaning his head out of the
carriage window, a drop of blood trickled down his cheek.

"Well! Good-bye to my portmanteau! It can't be
helped! The throw said I wasn't to get out here. It
was right."

He shut the door and sat down again.

"There were no papers in my portmanteau and my
linen isn't marked. What are the risks? . . . No matter,
I'd better sail as soon as possible; it'll be a little less
amusing perhaps, but a good deal wiser."

In the meantime the train started again.

"It's not so much my portmanteau that I regret as my
beaver, which I really should have liked to retrieve.
Well! let's think no more about it."

He filled another pipe, lit it, and then, plunging his
hand into the inside pocket of Fleurissoire's coat, pulled
out: a letter from Arnica, a Cook's ticket and a large
yellow envelope, which he opened.

"Three, four, five, six thousand-franc notes! Of no
interest to honest folk!"

He returned the notes to the envelope and the envelope
to the coat pocket.

But when, a moment later, he examined the Cook's
ticket, Lafcadio's brain whirled. On the first page was
written the name of *Julius de Baraglioul*. "Am I going
mad?" he asked himself. "What can he have had to do

with Julius? . . . A stolen ticket? . . . No, not possible!
. . . a borrowed ticket . . . must be. Lord! Lord!
Perhaps I've made a mess of it. These old gentlemen are
sometimes better connected than one thinks. . . ."

Then, his fingers trembling with eagerness, he opened
Arnica's letter. The circumstances seemed too strange;
he found it difficult to fix his attention; he failed, no
doubt, to make out the exact relationship existing between
Julius and the old gentleman, but, at any rate, he managed to grasp that Julius was in Rome. His mind was
made up at once; an urgent desire to see his brother
possessed him—an unbridled curiosity to find out what
kind of repercussion this affair would set up in that calm
and logical mind.

"That's settled. I shall sleep to-night at Naples, get
out my trunk, and to-morrow morning return by the first
train to Rome. It will certainly be a good deal less
wise, but perhaps a little more amusing."

III

At Naples Lafcadio went to a hotel near the station;
he made a point of taking his trunk with him, because
travellers without luggage are looked at askance, and because he was anxious not to attract attention; then he
went out to buy a few necessary articles of toilette and
another hat instead of the odious straw (beside which, it
was too tight) which Fleurissoire had left him. He
wanted to buy a revolver as well, but was obliged to put
this purchase off, as the shops were already shutting.

The train he took next day started early, arriving in
Rome in time for lunch.

His intention was not to approach Julius until after the newspapers had appeared with an account of the "crime." The *crime!* This word seemed odd to him, to say the very least; and *criminal* as applied to himself totally inappropriate. He preferred *adventurer*—a word as pliable as his beaver and as easily twisted to suit his liking.

The morning papers had not yet mentioned the *adventure.* He awaited the evening ones with impatience, for he was eager to see Julius and to feel for himself that the game had begun; until then the time hung heavy on his hands, as with a child playing at hide-and-seek, who, no doubt, doesn't want to be found, but wants, at any rate, to be sure he is being looked for. The vagueness of this state was one with which he was not as yet familiar; and the people he elbowed in the street seemed to him particularly commonplace, disagreeable and hideous.

When the evening came he bought the *Corriere* from a newspaper-seller in the Corso; then he went into a restaurant, but he laid the paper all folded on the table beside him and forced himself to finish his dinner without looking at it—out of a kind of bravado, and as though he thought in this way to put an edge on his desire; then he went out, and once in the Corso again, he stopped in the light of a shop window, unfolded the paper and on the second page saw the following head-line:

CRIME, SUICIDE . . . OR ACCIDENT

He read the next few paragraphs, which I translate:

Last evening in the railway station at Naples, the company's servants found a man's coat in the rack of a first-class carriage of the train from Rome. In the inside pocket of this coat, which is of a dark brown colour, was an unfastened envelope containing six thousand-franc notes. There were no other papers by which to identify the missing owner. If there has been foul play, it is difficult to account for the fact that such a considerable sum of money should have been left in the victim's coat; it may, at any rate, be inferred that the motive was not robbery.

There were no traces of a struggle to be seen in the compartment; but under one of the seats a man's shirt-cuff was discovered with the link attached; this article was in the shape of two cats' heads, linked together by a small silver-gilt chain, and carved out of a semi-transparent quartz, known as opalescent feldspar, and commonly called moonstone by jewellers.

A thorough investigation of the railway line is being made.

Lafcadio crumpled the paper up in his hand.

"What! Carola's sleeve-links now! The old boy is a regular public meeting-place!"

He turned the page and read in the stop-press news:

RECENTISSIME

DEAD BODY FOUND ON RAILWAY LINE

Without waiting to read further, Lafcadio hurried to the Grand Hotel. He slipped his visiting-card into an envelope after adding the following words underneath his name:

Lafcadio Wluiki

would be glad to know whether Count Julius de Baraglioul is not in need of a secretary.

He sent it up.

A manservant at last came to where he was waiting in the hall, led him along various passages and ushered him in to where Julius was sitting.

His first glance showed Lafcadio a copy of the *Corriere della Sera,* which had been thrown down in a corner of the room. On a table in the middle a large, uncorked bottle of eau-de-Cologne was exhaling its powerful perfume. Julius held out his arms.

"Lafcadio! My dear fellow! . . . How very glad I am to see you!"

His ruffled hair waved in agitated fashion on his temples; he seemed strangely excited; in one hand he held a black spotted handkerchief, with which he fanned himself.

"You are certainly one of the persons I least expected to see, but the one in the world I was most wanting to talk to this evening. . . . Was it Madame Carola who told you I was here?"

"What an odd question!"

"Why! as I've just met her . . . I'm not sure, though, that she saw me."

"Carola! Is she in Rome?"

"Didn't you know?"

"I've just this minute arrived from Sicily and you are the first person I have seen. I've no desire to see her."

"I thought she was looking extremely pretty——"

"You're not hard to please."

"I mean, prettier than she did in Paris."

"Exoticism, no doubt—but if you're feeling randy . . ."

"Lafcadio! Such language from you to me isn't permissible."

Julius tried to look severe, but only succeeded in pulling a face. He went on:

"You find me in a great state of agitation. I'm at a turning-point of my career. My head is burning and I feel, as it were, giddy all over, as if I were going to evaporate. I have come to Rome for a sociological congress, and during the three days I've spent here I've been going from surprise to surprise. Your arrival is the finishing touch. . . . I don't recognise myself any longer."

He was striding about the room; suddenly he stopped beside the table, seized the bottle, poured a stream of scent on to his handkerchief, applied it like a compress to his forehead and left it there.

"My dear young friend—if you'll allow me to call you so . . . My new book! I think I've got the hang of it. The way in which you spoke to me of *On the Heights* in Paris, makes me think that you will not find this one uninteresting."

His feet sketched a kind of pirouette; the handkerchief fell to the ground. Lafcadio hastened to pick it up and, as he was stooping, he felt Julius's hand laid gently on his shoulder, just as once before he had felt Juste-Agénor's. Lafcadio smiled and raised himself.

"I've known you such a short time," said Julius, "and yet this evening I can't help talking to you like a . . ."

He stopped.

"I'm listening like a brother, Monsieur de Baraglioul," Lafcadio was emboldened to take up the words, "—since you allow me to."

"You see, Lafcadio, in the set which I frequent in Paris —smart people, and literary people, and ecclesiastics and academicians—there is really nobody I can speak to— nobody, I mean, to whom I can confide the new preoccupations which beset me. For I must confess to you that, since our last meeting, my point of view has completely changed."

"So much the better," said Lafcadio impertinently.

"You can't imagine, because you aren't in the trade, how an erroneous system of ethics can hamper the free development of one's creative faculties. So nothing is further from my old novels than the one I am planning now. I used to demand logic and consistency from my characters, and in order to make quite sure of getting them, I began by demanding them from myself. It wasn't natural. We prefer to go deformed and distorted all our lives rather than not resemble the portrait of ourselves which we ourselves have first drawn. It's absurd. We run the risk of warping what's best in us."

Lafcadio continued to smile as he waited for what was to come next, amused to recognise, at this remove, the effect of his first remarks.

"How shall I put it, Lafcadio? For the first time I see before me a free field. . . . Can you understand what that means? A free field! . . . I say to myself that it always has been, always will be free, and that up till now the only things to hinder me have been impure considerations—questions of a successful career, of public opinion —the poet's continual vain hope of reward at the hands of ungrateful judges. Henceforth I hope for nothing— except from myself—henceforth I hope for everything from myself—I hope for everything from the man who is sincere—everything and anything! For now I feel in myself the strangest possibilities. And as it's only on paper, I shall boldly let myself go. We shall see! We shall see!"

He took a deep breath, flung himself back sideways with one shoulder-blade raised, almost as if a wing were already beginning to sprout, and as if he were stifling with the weight of fresh perplexities. He went on incoherently in a lower voice:

"And since the gentlemen of the Academy shut the door in my face, I'll give them good cause for it; for they had none—no cause whatever."

His voice suddenly turned shrill as he emphasised the last words; then he went on more calmly:

"Well, then, this is what I have imagined. . . . Are you listening?"

"With my whole soul," said Lafcadio, still laughing.

"And do you follow me?"

"To the devil himself!"

Julius again soused his handkerchief and sat down in an arm-chair; Lafcadio sat himself astride on a chair opposite him.

"The hero is to be a young man whom I wish to make a criminal."

"I see no difficulty in that."

"Hum! hum!" said Julius, who was not to be done out of his difficulty.

"But since you're a novelist, once you set about imagining, what's to prevent you imagining things just as you choose?"

"The stranger the things I imagine, the more necessary it is to find motives and explanations for them."

"It's easy enough to find motives for crime."

"No doubt . . . but that's exactly what I don't want to do. I don't want a motive for the crime—all I want is an explanation of the criminal. Yes! I mean to lead him into committing a crime gratuitously—into wanting to commit a crime without any motive at all."

Lafcadio began to prick up his ears.

"We will take him as a mere youth. I mean him to show the elegance of his nature by this—that he acts almost entirely in play, and as a matter of course prefers his pleasure to his interest."

"Rather unusual, I should say," ventured Lafcadio.

"Yes, isn't it?" said Julius, enchanted. "Then, we must add that he takes pleasure in self-control."

"To the point of dissimulation."

"We'll endow him, then, with the love of risk."

"Bravo!" exclaimed Lafcadio, more and more amused. "If, added to that, he is a fellow who can lend an ear to the demon of curiosity, I think your pupil will be done to a turn."

Progressing in this way by leaps and bounds, each in turn overtaking and overtaken by the other, one would have likened them to two schoolboys playing leap-frog.

Julius. First of all, I imagine him training himself. He is an adept at committing all sorts of petty thefts.

Lafcadio. I've often wondered why more aren't committed. It's true that the opportunity of committing them usually occurs only to people who are free from want and without any particular hankerings.

Julius. Free from want! Yes, I told you so. But the only opportunities that tempt him are the ones that demand some skill—some cunning.

Lafcadio. And which run him, no doubt, into some danger.

Julius. I said that he enjoys risk. But swindling is odious to him; he doesn't want to appropriate things, but finds it amusing to displace them surreptitiously. He's as clever at it as a conjurer.

Lafcadio. And, besides, he's encouraged by impunity.

Julius. Yes, but sometimes vexed by it too. If he isn't caught, it must be because the job he set himself was too easy.

Lafcadio. He eggs himself on to take greater risks.

Julius. I make him reason this way . . .

Lafcadio. Do you really think he reasons?

Julius (continuing). The author of a crime is always found out by the need he had to commit it.

Lafcadio. We said that he was very clever.

Julius. Yes, and all the cleverer because he acts with perfect coolness. Just think! A crime that has no motive either of passion or need! His very reason for committing the crime is just to commit it without any reason.

Lafcadio. You reason about his crime—*he* merely commits it.

Julius. There is no reason that a man who commits a crime without reason should be considered a criminal.

Lafcadio. You're too subtle. You have carried him to such a pitch that you have made him what they call "a free man."

Julius. At the mercy of the first opportunity.

Lafcadio. I'm longing to see him at work. What in the world are you going to offer him?

Julius. Well, I was still hesitating. Yes, up till this very evening I was hesitating, and then, this very evening, the latest edition of the newspaper brought me just exactly the example I was in need of. A providential stroke! Frightful! Only think of it! My brother-in-law has just been murdered!

Lafcadio. What! the old fellow in the railway carriage was . . .

Julius. He was Amédée Fleurissoire. I had just lent him my ticket and seen him off at the station. An hour before starting he had taken six thousand francs out of the bank, and as he was carrying them on his person, he was a little bit anxious as he left me; he had fancies— more or less gloomy fancies—presentiments. Well, in the train . . .

But you've seen the paper?

Lafcadio. Only the head-lines.

Julius. Listen! I'll read it to you. (He unfolded the *Corriere.*) I'll translate as I go along.

"This afternoon, in the course of a thorough investigation of the line between Rome and Naples, the police discovered the body of a man lying in the dry bed of the Volturno, about five kilometers from Capua—no doubt the unfortunate owner of the coat that was found last night in a railway carriage. The body is that of a man of about fifty years of age. [He looked older than he really was.] No papers were on him which could give any clue to his identity. [Thank goodness! That'll give me time to breathe, at any rate.] He had apparently been flung out of the railway carriage with sufficient violence to clear the parapet of the bridge, which is being repaired at this point and has been replaced by a wooden railing. [What a style!] The height of the bridge above the river is about fifteen metres. Death must have been caused by the fall, as the body bears no trace of other injuries. The man was in his shirt-sleeves; on his right wrist was a cuff similar to the one picked up in the railway carriage, but in this case the sleeve-link is missing. [What's the matter?]"

Julius stopped. Lafcadio had not been able to suppress a start, for the idea flashed upon him that the sleeve-link had been removed since the committing of the crime. —Julius went on:

"His left hand was found still clutching a soft felt hat . . ."

"Soft felt indeed! The barbarians!" murmured Lafcadio.

Julius raised his nose from the paper:
"What are you so astonished at?"
"Nothing! Nothing! Go on!"

". . . soft felt hat much too large for his head and which presumably belongs to the aggressor; the maker's name has been carefully removed from the lining, out of which a piece of leather has been cut of the size and shape of a laurel leaf . . ."

Lafcadio got up and went behind Julius's chair so as to read the paper over his shoulder—and perhaps, too, so as to hide his paleness. There could no longer be any doubt about it; his crime had been tampered with; someone else had touched it up; had cut the piece out of the lining—the unknown person, no doubt, who had carried off his portmanteau.

In the meantime Julius went on reading:

". . . which seems to prove the crime was premeditated. [Why this particular crime? My hero had perhaps merely taken general precautions just at random. . . .] As soon as the police had made the necessary notes, the body was removed to Naples for the purposes of identification. [Yes, I know they have the means there—and the habit of preserving dead bodies. . . .]"

"Are you quite sure it was he?" Lafcadio's voice trembled a little.

"Bless my soul! I was expecting him to dinner this evening."

"Have you informed the police?"

"Not yet. First of all, I must get clear in my own mind a little. I'm in mourning already, so from that point of view (as regards the dress question, I mean) there's no need to bother; but you see, as soon as the victim's name is published, I shall have to communicate with the family, send telegrams, write letters, make arrangements for the funeral, go to Naples to fetch the body. . . . Oh! my dear Lafcadio, there's this congress I've got to attend—would you mind—would you consent to fetching the body in my place?"

"We'll see about it."

"That is, of course, if it won't upset you too much. In the meantime I'm sparing my sister-in-law a period of cruel anxiety. She'll never suspect from the vague accounts in the newspapers . . . But to return to my subject. Well, then, when I read this paragraph in the paper, I said to myself: 'This crime, which I can imagine to myself so easily, which I can reconstruct, which I can see—I know, I tell you, I know the reason for which it was committed; I know that if it hadn't been for the inducement of the six thousand francs, it would never have been committed.' "

"But suppose . . ."

"Yes, yes. Let's suppose for a moment that there had been no six thousand francs—or, better still, that the criminal didn't take them—why, he'd have been my hero!"

Lafcadio in the meantime had risen; he picked up the paper which Julius had let fall, and opening it at the second page:

"I see," he said in as cool a voice as he could muster, "I see that you haven't read the latest news. That is exactly what *has* happened. The criminal did *not* take the six thousand francs. Look here! Read this: *'The*

motive of the crime, therefore, does not appear to be
robbery.' "

Julius snatched the sheet that Lafcadio held out to
him, read it eagerly, then passed his hand over his eyes,
then sat down, then got up abruptly, darted towards
Lafcadio, and seizing him with both arms, exclaimed:

"The motive of the crime not robbery!" and he shook
Lafcadio in a kind of transport. "The motive of the
crime not robbery! Why, then"—he pushed Lafcadio
from him, rushed to the other end of the room, fanned
himself, struck his forehead, blew his nose—"Why, then,
I know—good heavens!—I know why the ruffian murdered him. . . . Oh! my unfortunate friend! Oh, poor
Fleurissoire! So it was true what he said! And I who
thought he was out of his mind! Why, then, it's appalling!"

Lafcadio awaited the end of this outburst with astonishment; he was a little irritated; it seemed to him that
Julius had no right to evade him in this manner.

"I thought that was the very thing you . . ."

"Be quiet! You know nothing about it. And here
am I wasting my time with you, spinning these ridiculous fancies! . . . Quick! my stick! my hat!"

"Where are you off to in such a hurry?"

"To inform the police, of course!"

Lafcadio placed himself in front of the door.

"First of all, explain," said he imperatively. "Upon
my soul, anyone would think you had gone mad."

"It was just now that I was mad. . . . Oh, poor
Fleurissoire! Oh, unfortunate friend! Luckless, saintly
victim! His death just comes in time to cut me short

in a career of irreverence—of blasphemy. His sacrifice has brought me to reason. And to think that I laughed at him!"

He had again begun to pace up and down the room; suddenly he stopped and laying his hat and stick beside the scent bottle on the table, he planted himself in front of Lafcadio:

"Do you want to know why the ruffian murdered him?"

"I thought it was without a motive."

"To begin with," exclaimed Julius furiously, "there's no such thing as a crime without a motive. He was got rid of because he was in possession of a secret . . . which he confided to me—an important secret—over-important for him, indeed. They were afraid of him. That's what it was. There! . . . Oh! it's all very well for you to laugh—you understand nothing about matters of faith." Then, very pale and drawing himself up to his full height: "*I* am the inheritor of that secret!"

"Take care! They'll be afraid of you next."

"You see how necessary it is to warn the police at once."

"One more question," said Lafcadio, stopping him again.

"No! Let me go. I'm in a desperate hurry. You may be certain that the continual surveillance under which they kept my poor brother and which terrified him to such a degree, will now be transferred to *me*—has now been transferred to me. You have no idea what a crafty set they are. Those people know everything, I tell you. It's more important than ever that you should go and fetch the body instead of me. Now that I'm being watched as I am, there's no knowing what mightn't happen to me. Lafcadio, my dear fellow"—he clasped his hands imploringly—"I've no head at this moment, but I'll make enquiries at the Questura as to how to get a proper authorisation. Where shall I send it to you?"

"I'll take a room in this hotel. It'll be more convenient. Good-bye, till to-morrow. Make haste! Make haste!"

He let Julius go. There was beginning to rise in him a feeling of profound disgust—a kind of hatred almost, of himself, of Julius, of everything. He shrugged his shoulders, and then took out of his pocket the Cook's ticket, which he had found in Fleurissoire's coat and which had the name of Baraglioul written on the first page; he put it on the table, well in sight, leaning it up against the scent bottle—then turned out the light and left the room.

IV

Notwithstanding all the precautions he had taken, notwithstanding his recommendations to the Questura, Julius de Baraglioul did not succeed in preventing the newspapers from divulging his relationship to the victim —nor, indeed, from mentioning in so many words the name and address of his hotel.

That evening, of a truth, he had gone through some incredibly sickening moments of apprehension, when, on his return from the Questura at midnight, he had found, placed in a conspicuous position in his room, the Cook's ticket which had his name written in it and which he had lent to Fleurissoire. He had immediately rung the bell and, going out into the passage, pale and trembling, had begged the waiter to look under his bed—for he did not dare to look himself. A kind of inquiry, which he had held on the spot, led to no results; but what confidence can be placed in the personnel of big hotels? . . . However, after a good night's sleep, behind a solidly bolted door, Julius had woken up more at ease. He was now under police protection. He wrote a number of letters and telegrams, which he took to the post himself.

On his return, he was told that a lady had asked for him; she had not given her name and was waiting for him in the reading-room. Thither Julius went and was not a little surprised to find Carola.

It was not, however, in the first room that he found her, but in another which was more retired, smaller and not so well lighted. She was sitting sideways, at the corner of a distant table, and was absently turning over the leaves of a photograph album, so as to give herself countenance. When she saw Julius come in, she rose, looking more confused than pleased. Beneath the long black cloak she was wearing could be seen a bodice that was dark, plain and almost in good taste; on the other hand, her tumultuous hat, in spite of its being black, gave her away sadly.

"You'll think me very forward, Monsieur le Comte. I don't know how I found courage enough to come to your hotel and ask for you. But you bowed to me so kindly yesterday. . . . And, besides, what I have to say is so important."

She remained standing on the other side of the table;

it was Julius who drew near; he held out his hand to her over the table, without ceremony.

"To what am I indebted for the pleasure of your visit?"

Carola's head sunk.

"I know you have just lost . . ."

Julius did not at first understand; but as Carola took out her handkerchief and wiped her eyes:

"What! Is it a visit of condolence?"

"I knew Monsieur Fleurissoire," she went on

"Really?"

"Oh, I hadn't known him long, but I was very fond of him. He was such a dear! so kind! . . . In fact, it was I who gave him his sleeve-links; you know, the ones they described in the papers. That's how I knew it was he. But I had no idea he was your brother-in-law. It was a great surprise to me, and you may fancy how pleased I was. . . . Oh! I beg your pardon—that wasn't what I meant to say."

"Never mind, dear Miss Carola. You meant, no doubt, that you are pleased to have an opportunity of meeting me again."

Without answering, Carola buried her face in her handkerchief; her sobs were convulsive and Julius thought it was his duty to take her hand.

"And so am I," he said feelingly, "so am I, my dear young lady. Pray believe . . ."

"That very morning, before he went out, I told him to be careful. But it wasn't his nature. . . . He was too confiding, you know."

"A saint, Mademoiselle, a saint!" said Julius fervently, taking out his handkerchief in his turn.

"Yes, yes, that was just how it struck me," cried Carola. "At night, when he thought I was asleep, he used to get up and kneel at the foot of the bed and . . ."

This unconscious revelation put the finishing touch to Julius's discomposure; he returned the handkerchief to his pocket and, drawing still nearer:

"Do take your hat off, my dear young lady."

"No, thank you; it's not in my way."

"But it *is* in mine. Won't you let me . . ."

But as Carola unmistakably drew back, he pulled himself together.

"Let me ask you whether you had any special reason for uneasiness?"

"Who? I?"

"Yes; when you told my brother-in-law to be careful, I want to know whether you had any reason to suppose . . . Speak openly; no one comes in here in the mornings and we can't be overheard. Do you suspect anyone?"

Carola's head sank.

"It's of particular interest to me, you see," went on Julius with volubility. "Put yourself in my place. Last night, when I came back from the Questura, where I had been giving evidence, I found lying on the table in my room—on the very middle of my table—the railway ticket with which poor Fleurissoire had travelled. It had my name on it; I know those circular tickets are not transferable. Quite so; I did wrong to lend it—but that's not the point. The very fact of bringing the ticket back to my room—seizing the opportunity to flout me cynically when I had gone out for a few minutes—constitutes a challenge—a piece of bravado—an insult almost—which

(I need hardly say) would not disturb me in the least
if I hadn't good reason to suppose that I am threatened
in my turn. I'll tell you why. Your poor friend Fleurissoire was in possession of a secret—an abominable secret
—a most dangerous secret—I didn't question him about
it—I had no desire to hear what it was, but he had the
lamentable imprudence to confide it to me. And now I
ask you again—do you know who the person is who actually went so far as to commit a murder for the purpose
of stifling that secret? Do you know who he is?"

"Don't be alarmed, Monsieur le Comte; I gave his
name to the police last night."

"Mademoiselle Carola, I expected no less of you."

"He had promised me not to hurt him; he had only to
keep his promise and I would have kept mine. It's more
than I can stand! He may do what he likes to me—I
don't care!"

Carola was growing more and more excited; Julius
passed behind the table and, drawing near her again:

"We should perhaps be able to talk more comfortably
in my room."

"Oh, Monsieur le Comte," said Carola, "I've told you
everything I had to say; I mustn't keep you any longer."

As she went on retreating, she completed the tour of
the table and found herself near the door once more.

"We had better part now, Mademoiselle," said Julius
virtuously and with the firm determination of appropriat-
ing the credit of this resistance. "Ah! I just wanted to
add that if you mean to come to the funeral the day after
to-morrow, it would be better not to recognise me."

At this they took leave of each other, without having
once mentioned the name of the unsuspected Lafcadio.

V

Lafcadio was bringing Fleurissoire's mortal remains back from Naples. The funeral van which contained them was coupled to the end of the train, but Lafcadio had not thought it indispensable to travel in it himself. At the same time a sense of propriety had made him take his seat—not actually in the next carriage to it, for this contained only second-class compartments—but at any rate as near the body as was compatible with travelling first. He had left Rome that morning and was due back in the evening of the same day. He was reluctant to admit to himself the new sensation which had taken possession of his soul, for there was nothing he held in greater disdain than ennui—that secret malady from which he had hitherto been preserved by the fine carelessness of his youthful appetites and by the pricks of hard necessity. He left his compartment with a heart empty of hope and joy and prowled up and down the whole length of the corridor, harassed by a kind of ill-defined curiosity and vaguely seeking he knew not what new and absurd enterprise in which to engage. He no longer thought of embarking for the East and acknowledged reluctantly that Borneo did not in the least attract him—nor the rest of Italy either; he could not feel any interest in the consequences of his adventure; it appeared to him, in his present mood, compromising and grotesque. He felt resentment against Fleurissoire for not having defended himself better; his soul protested against the pitiful creature; he would have liked to wipe him from his mind.

On the other hand, he would gladly have met that strapping fellow who had carried off his portmanteau—

a fine rascal that! And at Capua he leant out of the
window and searched the deserted platform with his
eyes, as though he hoped to discover him. But would
he have recognised him? He had done no more than
catch a distant glimpse of his back as he disappeared
into the darkness. In his mind's eye he followed him
through the night, saw him reach the river's bed, find
the hideous corpse, rifle it and, almost as a challenge, cut
out of the hat—Lafcadio's own hat—that little bit of
leather which, as the newspapers had elegantly phrased
it, was "of the size and shape of a laurel leaf." With his
hatter's address inscribed on it, it was a piece of damn-
ing evidence, and after all Lafcadio was extremely
grateful to his bag-snatcher for having prevented it
from falling into the hands of the police. It was, no
doubt, very much to this gentleman's own interest not
to attract attention to himself, and if, notwithstanding,
he thought fit to make use of his bit of leather, upon my
word! a trial of wits with him might not be unamusing.

The night by this time had fallen. A dining-car
waiter made his way through the length of the train to
announce to the first and second-class passengers that
dinner was ready. With no appetite, but at any rate
with the saving prospect of an hour's occupation before
him, Lafcadio followed the procession, keeping some way
behind it. The dining-car was at the head of the train.
The carriages through which Lafcadio passed were
empty; here and there various objects, such as shawls,
pillows, books, papers, were disposed on the seats so as
to mark and reserve the diners' places. A lawyer's
brief-case caught his eye. Sure of being last, he stopped
in front of the compartment and went in. In reality he

was not attracted by the bag; it was simply as a matter of conscience that he searched it. On the inner side of the flap, in unobtrusive gilt letters, was written the name

DEFOUQUEBLIZE

FACULTY OF LAW—BORDEAUX

The bag contained two pamphlets on criminal law and six numbers of the *Lawyers' Journal.*

"More fry for the congress! Bah!" thought Lafcadio, as he put everything back in its place and then hastily joined the little file of passengers on their way to the restaurant.

A delicate-looking little girl and her mother brought up the rear, both in deep mourning. Immediately in front of them was a gentleman in a frock coat, long straight hair and grey whiskers—Monsieur Defouqueblize apparently, the owner of the brief-bag. Their advance was slow and unsteady because of the jolting of the train. At the last turn of the corridor, just as the professor was going to make a dash into the kind of accordion which connects one carriage with another, an exceptionally violent bump toppled him over. As he was trying to regain his balance, a sudden sprawl sent his eye-glasses flying—all their moorings broken—into the corner of the narrow space left by the corridor in front of the lavatory door. As he bent down to search for his eyesight, the lady and little girl passed in front of him. Lafcadio stayed for a moment or two watching the learned gentleman's efforts with some amusement; pitiably at a loss, he was groping vaguely and

anxiously over the floor with both hands; it was as
though he were performing the waddling dance of a
plantigrade or, back once more in the days of his infancy, had suddenly started playing "hunt the slip-
per." . . . Come, come, Lafcadio! Listen to your heart!
It is not an evil one. Now for a generous impulse!
Go to the poor man's rescue! Hand him back the indispensable glasses! He will never find them by himself. His back is turned to them; in another minute
he will smash them. Just then a violent jerk flung the
unhappy man head foremost against the door of the
water-closet; the shock was broken by his top-hat, which
was caved in by the force of the impact and jammed
tightly down over his ears. Monsieur Defouqueblize
moaned; rose to his feet; took off his hat. Lafcadio,
meanwhile, having come to the conclusion that the joke
had lasted long enough, picked up the eye-glasses,
dropped them like an alms into the hat, and then fled so
as to escape being thanked.

Dinner had begun. Lafcadio seated himself at a table
for two, next the glass door on the right-hand side of the
gangway; the place opposite him was empty; on the left
side of the gangway, in the same row as himself, the widow
and her daughter were sitting at a table for four, two
seats of which were unoccupied.

"What mortal dullness exudes from such places as
this!" said Lafcadio to himself, as his listless glance
slipped from one to another of the diners, without finding a face on which to dwell. "Herds of cattle going
through life as if it were a monotonous grind, instead of
the entertainment which it is—or which it might be.

How badly dressed they are! But oh! how much uglier they would be if they were naked! I shall certainly expire before dessert, if I don't order some champagne."

Here the professor entered. He had apparently just been washing his hands, which had been dirtied by his hunt, and was examining his nails. A waiter motioned him to sit down beside Lafcadio. The man with the wine-list was passing from table to table. Lafcadio, without saying a word, pointed out a Montebello Grand Crémant at twenty francs, while Monsieur Defouqueblize ordered a bottle of St. Galmier. He was holding his pincenez between his finger and thumb, breathing gently on the glasses and then wiping them with the corner of his napkin. Lafcadio watched him curiously and wondered at his mole's eyes blinking under their swollen eyelids.

"Fortunately he doesn't know it was I who gave him back his eyesight. If he begins to thank me, I shall take myself off on the spot."

The waiter came back with the St. Galmier and the champagne; he first uncorked the latter and put it down between the two diners. The bottle was no sooner on the table than Defouqueblize seized hold of it without noticing which one it was, poured out a glassful and swallowed it at one gulp. The waiter was going to interfere but Lafcadio stopped him with a laugh.

"Oh! what on earth is this stuff?" cried Defouqueblize with a frightful grimace.

"This gentleman's Montebello," replied the waiter with dignity. "*This* is your St. Galmier! Here!"

He put down the second bottle.

"I'm extremely sorry, Sir. . . . My eyesight is so bad. . . . Really, I'm overcome with . . ."

"You would greatly oblige me, Sir," interrupted Lafcadio, "by not apologising—and even by accepting another glass—if the first was to your taste, that is."

"Alas! my dear sir, I must confess that I thought it was horrible and I can't think how I came to be so absent-minded as to swallow a whole glassful. . . . I was so thirsty . . . Would you mind telling me whether it's very strong wine? . . . because I must confess that . . . I never drink anything but water. . . . The slightest drop invariably goes to my head. . . . Good heavens! Good heavens! What'll happen to me? Perhaps it would be more prudent to go back at once to my compartment. I expect I had better lie down."

He made as though to get up.

"Stop! Stop! my dear sir," said Lafcadio, who was beginning to be amused. "You'd better eat your dinner, on the contrary, and not trouble about the glass of wine. I will take you back myself later on, if you're in need of help; but don't be alarmed; you haven't taken enough to turn the head of a baby."

"I'll take your word for it. But really, I don't know how to . . . May I offer you a little St. Galmier?"

"Thank you very much—will you excuse me if I say I prefer my champagne?"

"Ah! really! So it was champagne, was it? And . . . you are going to drink all that?"

"Just to give you confidence."

"You're exceedingly kind, but in your place I should . . ."

"Suppose you were to eat your dinner," interrupted Lafcadio, who was himself eating and had had enough of

Defouqueblize. His attention was now attracted by the widow.

An Italian certainly. An officer's widow, no doubt. What modesty in her bearing! What tenderness in her eyes! How pure a brow! What intelligent hands! How elegantly dressed and yet how simply! . . . Lafcadio, when your heart fails to re-echo to such a blended concord of harmonies, may that heart have ceased to beat! Her daughter is like her, and even at that early age, what nobility—half serious, half sad even—tempers the child's excessive grace! With what solicitude her mother bends towards her! Ah! the fiend himself would yield to such beings as these; to such beings as these, Lafcadio, who can doubt that you would offer your heart's devotion? . . .

At that moment the waiter passed by to change the plates. Lafcadio allowed his to be carried away before it was half empty, for at that moment he was gazing at a sight that filled him with sudden stupor—the widow—the exquisitely refined widow—had bent down towards the side nearest the gangway, and deftly raising her skirt, with the most natural movement in the world, had revealed a scarlet stocking and a neatly turned calf and ankle.

So incongruous was this fiery note that burst into the calm gravity of the symphony . . . could he be dreaming? In the meantime the waiter was handing round another dish. Lafcadio was on the point of helping himself; his eyes fell upon his plate, and what he saw there finally did for him.

There, right in front of him, plain to his sight, in the very middle of his plate, fallen from God knows where, frightful and unmistakable among a thousand—don't doubt it for an instant, Lafcadio—there lies Carola's sleeve-link! The sleeve-link which had been missing from Fleurissoire's second cuff! The whole thing was becoming a nightmare. . . . But the waiter is bending over him with the dish. With a sweep of his hand, Lafcadio wipes his plate and brushes the horrid trinket on to the table-cloth; he puts his plate back on to the top of it, helps himself abundantly, fills his glass with champagne, empties it at a draught and fills it again. For if a man who hasn't dined is to have drunken visions . . . But no! it was not an hallucination; he hears the squeak of the link against his plate; he raises his plate, seizes the link, slips it into his waistcoat pocket beside his watch, feels it again, makes certain—yes! there it is, safe and sound! But who shall say how it came on his plate? Who put it there? . . . Lafcadio looks at Defouqueblize. The learned gentleman is innocently eating, his nose in his plate. Lafcadio tries to think of something else; he looks once more at the widow; but everything about her demeanour and her attire has become proper again and commonplace; he doesn't think her as pretty as before; he tries to imagine afresh the provocative gesture—the red stocking—but he fails; he tries to imagine afresh the sleeve-link on his plate and if he did not actually feel it in his pockets, there's no question but that he would doubt his senses. . . . But now he comes to reflect, why did he take a sleeve-link which doesn't belong to him? What an admission is implied by this instinctive and absurd action—what a recognition! How he has given himself away to the people—whoever they may be—who are watching him—the police, perhaps! He has walked straight into their booby trap like a fool. He feels him-

self grow livid. He turns sharply round; there, behind
the glass door leading into the corridor . . . No! no one.
. . . But a moment ago there may have been someone who
saw him! He forces himself to go on eating, but his
teeth clench with vexation. Unhappy young man! it is
not his abominable crime that he regrets, but this ill-
starred impulse. . . . What has come over the professor
now? Why is he smiling at him?

Defouqueblize had finished eating. He wiped his lips;
then with both elbows on the table, fiddling nervously
with his napkin, he began to look at Lafcadio; his lips
worked in an odd sort of grin; at last, as though unable to
contain himself any longer:

"Might I venture to ask for just a little more?"

He pushed his glass timidly towards the almost empty
bottle.

Lafcadio, surprised out of his uneasiness and delighted
at the diversion, poured him out the last drops.

"I'm afraid it's impossible to give you much. . . .
But shall I order some more?"

"Oh, well, not more than half a bottle then."

Defouqueblize was obviously elevated and had lost all
sense of the proprieties. Lafcadio, for whom dry champagne had no terrors and who was amused at the other's
ingenuousness, ordered the waiter to uncork another
bottle of Montebello.

"No, no, not too much," said Defouqueblize, as with a
quavering hand he raised the glass which Lafcadio succeeded in filling to the brim. "It's curious—I thought it
so nasty at first. That's the way with a great many
things which one makes mountains of till one knows
more about them. The fact is, I thought I was drinking

St. Galmier, and you see I thought that for St. Galmier it had a very queer taste. If you were given St. Galmier now, when you thought you were drinking champagne, wouldn't you say: 'For champagne, it has a very queer taste'? . . ."

He laughed at his own words, then bending across the table to Lafcadio, who was laughing too, he went on in a low voice:

"I can't think why I'm laughing so; it must be the fault of your wine. I suspect, all the same, it's rather more heady than you make out. Eh! Eh! Eh! But you'll take me back to my carriage? That's agreed, isn't it? If I behave indecently, you'll know why."

"When one's travelling," hazarded Lafcadio, "there's no fear of consequences."

"Oh!" replied the other at once, "all the things one would do in this life if there were no fear of consequences, as you justly remark! If one could only be sure that it wouldn't lead to anything! . . . Why, merely what I'm saying to you just now—which, after all, is nothing but a very natural reflection—do you think I should venture to utter it without more disguise, if we were in Bordeaux, now? I say Bordeaux, because Bordeaux is where I live. I'm known there—respected. Not married, but well-to-do in a quiet little way; I'm in an honourable walk of life—Professor of Law at the Faculty of Bordeaux—yes, comparative criminology, a new chair. . . . You can see for yourself that when I'm there, I'm not allowed, actually not *allowed*, to get tipsy—not even once in a while, by accident. My life must be respectable. Just fancy! Supposing one of my pupils were to meet me in the street drunk! . . . Respectable! yes—and it mustn't look as if it were forced; there's the rub; one mustn't make people think: 'Monsieur Defouqueblize' (my name, sir) 'keeps a tight hand on himself—and a jolly good thing too.' . . . One must not only never *do* anything out of the way, one must persuade other people that one *couldn't* do anything out of the way, even with all the licence in the world—that there's nothing whatever out of the way in one, wanting to come out. Is there just a little more wine left? Only a drop or two, my dear accomplice, only a drop or two. . . . Such an opportunity doesn't come twice in a lifetime. To-morrow, at the congress in Rome, I shall meet a number of my colleagues—grave, sober fellows, as tame, as disciplined, as stiffly self-restrained as I shall become myself, once I get back into harness again. People who are in society, like you and me, owe it to ourselves to go masked."

In the meantime the meal was drawing to a close; a waiter went round collecting the scores and pocketing the tips.

As the car emptied, Defouqueblize's voice became deeper and louder; at moments its bursts of sonority made Lafcadio feel almost uncomfortable. He went on:

"And even if there were no society to restrain us, that little group of relations and friends whom we can't bear to displease, would suffice. They confront our uncivil sincerity with an image of ourselves for which we are only half responsible—an image which has very little resemblance to us, but out of whose contours, I tell you, it is indecent not to confine ourselves. At this moment—it's a fact—I have escaped from my shape—taken flight out of myself. . . . Oh! dizzy adventure! Dangerous rapture! . . . But I'm boring you to death!"

"You interest me singularly."

"I keep on talking . . . talking! It can't be helped! Once a professor, always a professor—even when one's drunk; and it's a subject I have at heart. . . . But if you've finished dinner, perhaps you'll be so kind as to give me your arm back to my carriage, while I can still stand on my legs. I'm afraid if I wait any longer, I mayn't be able to get up."

At these words Defouqueblize made a kind of bound as though in an effort to get out of his chair, but subsided again immediately in a half sprawl over the table, where, with his head and shoulders flung forward in Lafcadio's direction, he went on in a lower, semi-confidential voice:

"This is my thesis: Do you know what is needful to turn an honest man into a rogue? A change of scene—a moment's forgetfulness suffice. Yes, sir, a gap in the memory and sincerity comes out into the open! . . . a cessation of continuity—a simple interruption of the current. Naturally, I don't say this in my lectures . . . but, between ourselves, what an advantage for the bastard! Just think! a being whose very existence is owing to an erratic impulse—to a crook in the straight line! . . ."

The professor's voice had again grown loud; the eyes he now fixed on Lafcadio were peculiar; their glance, which was at times vague and at times piercing, began to alarm him. Lafcadio wondered now whether the man's short sight were not feigned, and that peculiar glance seemed to him almost familiar. At last, more embarrassed than he cared to own, he got up and said abruptly:

"Come, Monsieur Defouqueblize, take my arm. Get up. Enough talk!"

Defouqueblize quitted his chair with a lumbering effort. Together they tottered down the corridor towards the compartment where the professor had left his brief-bag. Defouqueblize went in first. Lafcadio settled him in his corner and took his leave. He had already turned his back to go out, when a great hand fell heavily on his shoulder. He turned swiftly round. Defouqueblize had sprung to his feet—but was it really Defouqueblize?—this individual who, in a voice that was at once mocking, commanding and jubilant, exclaimed:

"You mustn't desert an old friend like this, Mr. Lafcadio What-the-deuceki. No? Really? Trying to make off?"

There remained not a trace of the tipsy, uncanny old professor of a moment ago in this great strapping stalwart fellow in whom Lafcadio no longer hesitated to recognise—Protos—a bigger, taller, stouter Protos who gave an impression of formidable power.

"Ah! it's you, Protos?" said he, simply. "That's better. I didn't recognise you till this minute."

For however terrible the reality might be, Lafcadio preferred it to the grotesque nightmare in which he had been struggling for the last hour.

"Not badly got up, was I? I'd taken special pains for your sake. But all the same, my dear fellow, it's you who ought to take to spectacles. You'll get into trouble if you're not cleverer than that at recognising "the slim.'"

What half-forgotten memories this catchword *the slim* aroused in Cadio's mind! The *slim*, in their slang, at the time Protos and he were schoolboys together, were a genus who, for one reason or another, did not present to all persons and in all places the same appearance. Ac-

cording to the boys' classification, there were many cate-
gories of the "slim," more or less elegant and praise-
worthy; and answering to them and opposed to them, was
the single great family of "the crusted," whose members
strutted and swaggered through every walk of life, high
or low.

Our schoolfellows accepted the following axioms:
1. The slim recognise each other.
2. The crusted do not recognise the slim.

All this came back to Lafcadio; as his nature was to
throw himself into the spirit of the game, whatever it
might be, he smiled.   Protos went on:

"All the same, it was lucky I happened to turn up the
other day, eh? . . . Not altogether by accident, maybe.
I like keeping an eye on young novices: they've got ideas;
they're enterprising; they're smart.   But they're too much
inclined to think they can do without advice.   Your
handiwork the other night, my dear fellow, was sadly in
need of touching up. . . . To wear a tile of that kind on
one's head when one's out on the job!   Was there ever
such a notion?   With the hatter's address in the lining
too!   Why! you'd have been collared before the week was
out.   But when it's a case of old friends I've a feeling
heart—and, what's more, I'll prove it.   Do you know,
I used to be very fond of you, Cadio.   I always thought
something might be made of you.   With a handsome face
like yours, we could have got round all the women, and,
for the matter of that, God forgive me! bled one or two
of the men into the bargain.   You can't think how glad
I was to have news of you at last and to hear you were
coming to Italy.   Upon my soul, I was longing to know
what had become of you since the days we used to go and

see that little wench of ours together. You're not bad-looking even now. Oh! she knew a thing or two, did Carola!"

Lafcadio's irritation was becoming more and more manifest—and likewise his endeavours to hide it; all this amused Protos prodigiously, though he pretended to notice nothing. He had taken a little round of leather out of his waistcoat pocket and was now examining it.

"Neatly cut out, eh?"

Lafcadio could have strangled him; he clenched his fists till his nails dug into his flesh. The other went on with his gibing:

"Damned good of me! Well worth the six thousand francs which—by the way, will you tell me why you didn't pocket?"

Lafcadio made a movement of disgust:

"Do you take me for a thief?"

"Look here, my dear boy," went on Protos quietly, "I'm not very fond of amateurs and I'd better tell you so at once quite frankly. And you know, it's not a bit of use taking up the high and mighty line with me or playing the simpleton. You show promise—granted!—remarkable promise, but . . ."

"Stop your witticisms," interrupted Lafcadio, whose anger was now uncontrollable. "What are you driving at? I committed an act of folly the other day—do you think I need to be told so? Yes! you have a weapon against me. I won't ask whether it would be prudent of you, for your own sake, to use it. You want me to buy back that piece of leather? Very well, then, say so! Stop laughing and looking at me like that. You want money? How much?"

His tone was so determined that Protos fell back for a second, but recovered himself immediately.

"Gently! Gently!" he said. "Have I said anything ill-mannered? We are talking between friends—coolly. There's no need to get excited. My word! Cadio, you're younger than ever!"

But as he began to stroke his arm gently, Lafcadio jerked himself away.

"Let's sit down," went on Protos; "we shall talk more comfortably."

He settled himself in a corner beside the door into the corridor and put his feet up on the opposite seat. Lafcadio thought he meant to bar the exit. Without a doubt Protos was carrying a revolver. He himself was unarmed. He reflected that if it came to a hand-to-hand struggle, he would certainly get the worst of it. But if for a moment he had contemplated flight, curiosity was already getting the upper hand—that passionate curiosity of his against which nothing—not even his personal safety—had ever been able to prevail. He sat down.

"Money? Oh, fie!" said Protos. He took a cigar out of his cigar-case and offered one to Lafcadio, who refused. "Perhaps you mind smoke? . . . Well, then, listen to me." He took two or three puffs at his cigar and then said very calmly:

"No, no, Lafcadio, my friend, no, it isn't money I want—it's obedience. You don't seem, my dear boy (excuse my frankness), you don't seem to realise quite exactly what your situation is. You must force yourself to face it boldly. Let me help you a little.

"A youth, then, wished to escape from the social framework that hems us in; a sympathetic youth—a youth, indeed, entirely after my own heart—ingenuous and charmingly impulsive—for I don't suppose there was much calculation in what he did . . . I remember, Cadio, in the old days, though you were a great dab at figures, you would never consent to keep an account of your own expenses. . . . In short, the crusted scheme of things disgusts you. . . . I leave it to others to be astonished at that. . . . But what astonishes *me* is that a person as intelligent as you, Cadio, should have thought it possible to quit a society as simply as all that, without stepping at the same moment into another; or that you should have thought it possible for any society to exist without laws.

" 'Lawless'—do you remember reading that somewhere? 'Two hawks in the air, two fishes swimming in the sea, not more lawless than we . . .' * A fine thing literature! Lafcadio, my friend, learn the law of the slim!"

"You might get on a little."

"Why hurry? We've plenty of time before us. I'm not getting out till Rome. Lafcadio, my friend, it happens that a crime occasionally escapes the detectives. I'll explain you why it is that we are more clever than they—it's because our lives are at stake. Where the police fail we succeed. Damn it, Lafcadio, you've made your choice; the thing's done and it's impossible now for you to escape. I should much prefer you to be obedient, because I should really be extremely grieved to hand an old friend like you over to the police. But what's to be done? For the future you are in their power—or ours."

"If you hand me over, you hand yourself over at the same time."

* In English in the original. (*Translator's note.*)

"I hoped we were speaking seriously. Try and take this in, Lafcadio. The police collar people who kick up a row; but in Italy they're glad to come to terms with 'the slim.' 'Come to terms'—yes, I think that's the right expression. I work a bit for the police myself. I've a way with me. I help to keep order. I don't act on my own —I cause others to act.

"Come, come, Cadio, stop champing at the bit. There's nothing very dreadful about my law. You exaggerate these things; so ingenuous—so impulsive! Do you think it wasn't out of obedience and just because I willed it, that you picked up Mademoiselle Venitequa's sleeve-link off your plate at dinner? Ah! how thoughtless—how idyllic an action! My poor Lafcadio, how you cursed yourself for that little action, eh? The bloody nuisance is that I wasn't the only one to see it. Pooh! Don't take on so; the waiter and the widow and the little girl are all in it too. Charming people! It lies entirely with you to have them for your friends. Lafcadio, my friend, be sensible. Do you give in?"

Out of excessive embarrassment perhaps, Lafcadio had taken up the line of not speaking. He sat stiff— his lips set, his eyes staring straight in front of him.

Protos went on, with a shrug of his shoulders:

"Rum chap! . . . and in reality so easy-going! . . . But perhaps you would have consented already if I had told you what I expect of you. Lafcadio, my friend, enlighten my perplexity. How is it that you, whom I left in such poverty, refrained from picking up a windfall of six thousand francs dropped at your feet? Does that seem to you natural? Old Monsieur de Baraglïoul, Mademoiselle Venitequa told me, happened to die the day after Count Julius, his worthy son, came to pay you a visit; and the evening of the same day you chucked Mademoiselle Venitequa. Since then your connexion with Count Julius has become . . . well! well! let's say exceedingly intimate; would you mind explaining why? Lafcadio, my friend, in old days you were possessed to my knowledge of numerous uncles; since then your pedigree seems to me to have become slightly embaragliouled! . . . No, no, don't say anything. I'm only joking. But what is one to suppose? . . . unless, indeed, you owe your present fortune to Mr. Julius himself? . . . in which case, allow me to say, that attractive as you are, Lafcadio, the affair seems to me considerably more scandalous still. Whichever way it may be, though, and whatever you let us conjecture, the thing is clear enough, Lafcadio, my friend, and your duty is as plain as a pike-staff—you must blackmail Julius. Come, come, don't make a fuss! Blackmail is a wholesome institution, necessary for the maintenance of morals. What! what! are you going to leave me?"

Lafcadio had risen.

"Let me pass!" he cried, striding over Protos's body. Stretched across the compartment from one seat to the other, the latter made no movement to stop him. Lafcadio, astonished at not finding himself detained, opened the corridor door and, as he went off:

"I'm not running away," he said. "Don't be alarmed. You can keep your eye on me. But anything is better than listening to you any longer. Excuse me if I prefer the police. Go and inform them. I am ready."

VI

On that same day the Anthimes arrived from Milan
by the evening train. As they travelled third it was not
till they reached Rome that they saw the Comtesse de
Baraglioul and her daughter, who had come from Paris
in a sleeping-car of the same train.

A few hours before the arrival of the telegram announcing Fleurissoire's death, the Countess had received a letter
from her husband; the Count had written eloquently of
the immense pleasure his unexpected meeting with Lafcadio had caused him. Doubtless he had not breathed
the faintest word of allusion to that semi-fraternity which,
in Julius's eyes, invested the young man with a per-
fidious charm (Julius, faithful to his father's commands,
had never had any open explanation with his wife, any
more than with Lafcadio himself), but certain hints, certain reticences had been sufficient to enlighten the
Countess; I am not quite sure even that Julius, who had
very little to amuse him in the daily round of his bour-
geois existence, did not find some pleasure in fluttering
about the scandal and singeing the tips of his wings. I
am not sure either that Lafcadio's presence at Rome, the
hope of meeting him again, had not something—had not
a great deal—to do with Genevieve's decision to accompany her mother.

Julius was there to meet them at the station. He hurried them back to the Grand Hotel, without speaking more
than a word or two to the Anthimes, whom he was to meet
next day at the funeral. The latter went to the hotel
in the Via Bocca di Leone, where they had stayed for a
day or two during their first visit to Rome.

Marguerite brought the author good news. Not a single hitch remained in the way of the Academy election; Cardinal André had semi-officially informed her the day before that there was no need even for the candidate to pay any further visits; the Academy was advancing to welcome him with open doors.

"You see!" said Marguerite. "What did I tell you in Paris? *Tout vient à point* . . . One has nothing to do in this world but to wait."

"And not to change," added Julius, with an air of compunction, raising his wife's hand to his lips, and not noticing his daughter's eyes grow big with contempt as they dwelt on him. "Faithful to you, to my opinions, to my principles! Perseverance is the most indispensable of virtues."

The recollection of his recent wild-goose chase had already faded from his mind, as well as every opinion that was other than orthodox, and every intention that was other than proper. Now that he knew the facts, he recovered his balance without an effort. He was filled with admiration for the subtle consistency which his mind had shown in its temporary deviation. It was not *he* who had changed—it was the Pope!

"On the contrary, my opinions have been extraordinarily consistent," he said to himself, "extraordinarily logical. The difficulty is to know where to draw the line. Poor Fleurissoire perished from having gone behind the scenes. The simplest course for the simple-minded is to draw the line at the things they know. It was this hideous secret that killed him. Knowledge never strengthens any but the strong. . . . No matter! I am glad that

Carola was able to warn the police.   It allows me to medi-
tate with greater freedom. . . . All the same, if Armand-
Dubois knew that it was not the real Holy Father who
was responsible for his losses and his exile, what a conso-
lation it would be for him—what an encouragement in his
faith—what a solace and relief!   To-morrow, after the
funeral, I must really speak to him."

The funeral did not attract much of a concourse.   Three
carriages followed the hearse.   It was raining.   In the
first carriage came Arnica, supported by the friendly
presence of Blafaphas (as soon as she was out of mourning, he no doubt married her); they had left Pau together two days earlier (the thought of abandoning the
widow in her grief, of allowing her to take the long
journey all by herself, was intolerable to Blafaphas; and
for what?   Had he not gone into mourning like one of
the family?   Was any relation in the world equal to a
friend like him?), but on account of their unfortunately
missing one of their trains, they arrived in Rome only a
few hours before the ceremony.

In the last carriage were Madame Armand-Dubois with
the Countess and her daughter; in the second, the Count
and Anthime Armand-Dubois.

No allusion was made over Fleurissoire's grave to his
unlucky adventure.   But on the way back from the cemetery, as soon as Julius de Baraglioul was alone with Anthime, he began:

"I promised you I would intercede on your behalf with
his Holiness."

"God is my witness that I never asked you to."

"True! But I was so outraged by the state of destitution in which the Church had abandoned you, that I listened only to my own heart."

"God is my witness that I never complained."

"I know . . . I know . . . I was irritated to death by your resignation! And even—since you insist—I must admit, my dear Anthime, that it seemed to me a proof of pride rather than sanctity, and the last time I saw you at Milan that exaggerated resignation of yours struck me really as savouring more of rebellion than of true piety, and was extremely distasteful to me as a Christian. God didn't demand as much of you as all that! To speak frankly, I was shocked by your attitude."

"And I, my dear brother—perhaps I too may be allowed to say so now—was grieved by yours. Wasn't it you yourself who urged me to rebel and . . ."

Julius, who was getting heated, interrupted him:

"My own experience has sufficiently proved to myself —and to others—during the whole course of my career, that it is perfectly possible to be an excellent Christian, without disdaining the legitimate advantages of the state of life to which it pleases God to call us. The fault that I found with your attitude was precisely that its affectation seemed to give it an appearance of superiority over mine."

"God is my witness that . . ."

"Oh, don't go on calling God to witness!" interrupted Julius again. "God has nothing to do with it. I am merely explaining that when I say that your attitude was almost one of rebellion . . . I mean what would be rebellion for me; and what I find fault with is precisely that while you get credit for submitting to injustice, you leave other people to rebel for you. As for me, I wouldn't accept the Church's being in the wrong; while you with your air of not letting butter melt in your mouth, really *put* her in the wrong. So I made up my mind to complain in your stead. You'll see in a moment how right I was to be indignant."

Julius, on whose forehead the beads of perspiration were beginning to gather, put his top-hat on his knee.

"Wouldn't you like a little air?" asked Anthime, as he obligingly lowered the window on his side.

"So," went on Julius, "as soon as I got to Rome, I solicited an audience. It was granted. This step of mine met with the most singular success . . ."

"Ah!" said Anthime indifferently.

"Yes, my dear Anthime, for though in reality I obtained nothing of what I came to ask, at any rate I brought away from my visit an assurance which . . . effectually cleared our Holy Father from all the injurious suppositions we had been making about him."

"God is my witness that I never made any injurious suppositions about our Holy Father."

"I made them for you. I saw you wronged. I was indignant."

"Come to the point, Julius. Did you see the Pope?"

"Well, no, then! I didn't see the Pope," burst out Julius at last, containing himself no longer, "but I became possessed of a secret—a secret which, though almost incredible at first, received sudden confirmation from our dear Amédée's death—an appalling—a bewildering secret—but one from which your faith, dear Anthime, will be able to draw comfort. You must know, then, that the Pope is innocent of the injustice of which you were the victim . . ."

"Tut! I never for a moment doubted it."

"Listen to me, Anthime—I didn't see the Pope—because he is not to be seen. The person who is actually seated on the pontifical throne, who is obeyed by the Church, who promulgates—the person who spoke to me—the Pope who is to be seen at the Vatican—the Pope whom I saw—*is not the real one.*"

At these words Anthime began to shake all over with a fit of loud laughter.

"Laugh away! Laugh away!" went on Julius, nettled. "I laughed too, to begin with. If I had laughed a little less, Fleurissoire would not have been murdered. Ah! poor dear saint that he was! Poor lamb of a victim! . . ." His voice trailed off into sobs.

"What? What? Do you mean to say that this ridiculous story is really true? Dear me! Dear me! . . ." said Armand-Dubois, who was disturbed by Julius's pathos. "All the same, this must be inquired into . . ."

"It was for inquiring into it that he met his death."

"Because if after all I've sacrificed my fortune, my position, my science—if I've consented to be made a fool of . . ." continued Anthime, who was gradually becoming excited in his turn.

"But I tell you the *real* one is in no way responsible for any of that. The person who made a fool of you is a mere man of straw put up by the Quirinal."

"Am I really to believe what you say?"

"If you don't believe me, you can at any rate believe our poor martyr here."

They both remained silent for a few minutes. It had stopped raining; a ray of sunlight broke through the clouds. The carriage slowly jolted into Rome.

"In that case, I know what remains for me to do," went on Anthime in his most decided voice. "I shall give the whole show away."

Julius started with horror.

"My dear friend, you terrify me. You'll get yourself excommunicated for a certainty."

"By whom? If it's by a sham Pope, I don't care a damn!"

"And I, who thought I should help you to extract some consolatory virtue out of this secret," went on Julius, in dismay.

"You're joking! . . . And who knows but what Fleurissoire, when he gets to heaven, won't find after all that his Almighty isn't the *real* God either?"

"Come, come, my dear Anthime, you're rambling! As if there *could* be two! As if there could be another!"

"It's all very easy for you to talk—you, who have never in your life given up anything for Him—you, who profit by everything—true or false. Oh! I've had enough! I want some fresh air!"

He leant out of the window, touched the driver on the shoulder with his walking-stick and stopped the carriage. Julius prepared to get out with him.

"No! Let me be! I know all that's necessary for my purpose. You can put the rest in a novel. As for me, I shall write to the Grand Master of the Order this very evening, and to-morrow I shall take up my scientific reviewing for the *Dépêche*. Fine fun it'll be!"

"What!" said Julius, surprised to see that he was limping again. "You're lame?"

"Yes, my rheumatism came back a few days ago."

"Oh, I see! So *that's* at the bottom of it!" said Julius, as he sank back into the corner of the carriage, without looking after him.

VII

Did Protos really intend to give Lafcadio up to the police as he had threatened? I cannot tell. The event proved at any rate that the police were not entirely composed of his friends. These gentlemen, who had been advised by Carola the day before, laid their mousetrap in the Vicolo dei Vecchierelli; they had long been acquainted with the house and knew that the upper floor had easy means of communication with the next-door house, whose exits also they watched.

Protos was not afraid of the detectives; nor of any particular accusation that might be brought against him; the machinery of the law inspired him with no terrors; he knew that it would be hard to catch him out; that he was innocent in reality of any crime and guilty only of misdemeanours too trifling to be brought home to him. He was therefore not excessively alarmed when he realised that he was trapped—which he did very quickly, having a particular flair for nosing out these gentry, in no matter what disguise.

Hardly more than slightly perplexed, he shut himself up in Carola's room and waited for her to come in; he had not seen her since Fleurissoire's murder, and was anxious to ask her advice and to leave a few instructions in the very probable event of his being run in.

Carola, in the meantime, in deference to Julius's wishes, had not shown herself in the cemetery. No one knew that, hidden behind a mausoleum and beneath an umbrella, she was assisting at the melancholy ceremony from afar. She waited patiently, humbly, until the approach to the newly dug grave was free; she saw the procession re-form—Julius go off with Anthime and the carriages drive away in the drizzling rain. Then, in her turn, she went up to the grave, took out from beneath her cloak a big bunch of asters, which she put down a little way from the family's wreaths; there she stayed for a long time, looking at nothing, thinking of nothing, and crying instead of praying.

When she returned to the Vicolo dei Vecchierelli, she noticed, indeed, two unfamiliar figures on the threshold, but without realising that the house was being watched. She was anxious to rejoin Protos; she did not for a moment doubt that it was he who had committed the murder, and she hated him. . . .

A few minutes later the police rushed into the house on hearing her screams—too late, alas! Protos, exasperated at learning that she had betrayed him, had already strangled Carola.

This happened about midday. The news came out in the evening papers, and as the piece of leather cut out of the hat-lining was found in his possession, his two-fold guilt did not admit of a doubt in anyone's mind.

Lafcadio, in the meantime, had spent the hours till evening in a state of expectancy—of vague fear. It was not the police with whom Protos had threatened him that he feared, so much as Protos himself, or some nameless thing or other, against which he no longer attempted to defend himself. An incomprehensible torpor lay heavy on him—mere fatigue perhaps; at any rate, he gave up.

The day before, he had seen Julius for barely a moment, when the latter had come to meet the train from Naples and take over the consignment of the corpse; then he had tramped the town for hours, trying to walk down the exasperation that had been left in him by his conversation with Protos and by the feeling of his dependence.

And yet the news of Protos's arrest did not bring Lafcadio the relief that might have been expected. It was almost as though he were disappointed. Queer creature! As he had deliberately rejected all the material profits of the crime, so he was unwilling to part with any of the risks. He could not consent to the game's coming to an end so soon. He would gladly—as in the old days when he used to play chess—have given his adversary a rook; and as though this latest development had made his victory too easy and taken away all his interest in the match, he felt that he should never rest content till he had set Fate at defiance more rashly still.

He dined in a neighbouring *trattoria* so as not to be obliged to dress. Directly he had finished his dinner, he returned to the hotel, and as he was passing the restaurant glass doors he caught sight of Count Julius, who was sitting at table with his wife and daughter. He had not seen Genevieve since his first visit and was struck with her beauty. As he was lingering in the smoking-room, waiting for dinner to be finished, a servant came in to tell him that the Count had gone upstairs to his room and was expecting him.

He went in. Julius de Baraglioul was alone. He had changed into a morning coat.

"So they've caught the murderer," he said at once, putting out his hand.

But Lafcadio did not take it. He remained standing in the embrasure of the door.

"What murderer?" he asked.

"Why, my brother-in-law's, of course!"

"*I* am your brother-in-law's murderer."

He said it without a tremor, without altering or lowering his voice, without making a movement and so naturally that at first Julius did not understand. Lafcadio was obliged to repeat:

"Your brother-in-law's murderer has not been arrested, I tell you, for the good reason that I am your brother-in-law's murderer."

If there had been anything fierce about Lafcadio, Julius might perhaps have taken fright, but he looked a mere child. He seemed younger even than the first time Julius had met him; his eyes were as limpid, his voice as clear. He had shut the door, but remained leaning with his back against it. Julius, standing near the table, sank all of a heap into an arm-chair.

"My poor boy!" was the first thing he said, "speak lower! . . . What can have possessed you? How could you have done such a thing?"

Lafcadio bowed his head. He already regretted having spoken.

"How can I tell? I did it very quickly—just when it came over me."

"What grudge can you have had against Fleurissoire—worthy, virtuous man?"

"I don't know. He didn't look happy. . . . What's the use of wanting me to explain to you what I can't explain to myself?"

The silence between them grew increasingly painful; their words broke it by fits and starts, but each time it closed round them again, heavier, deeper; and through it, from the big hall of the hotel below, there came floating up to them snatches of vulgar Neapolitan music. Julius was picking at a spot of candle grease on the table-cloth with his little finger-nail, which he kept very long and pointed. He suddenly noticed that this exquisite nail of his was broken. There was a tear right across it which spoiled the beautiful pinkness of its polished surface. How could he have done it? And how came he not to have noticed it before? .In any case, the damage was beyond repair. There was nothing left for Julius to do but to cut it. His vexation was extreme, for he took great care of his hands and was particularly attached to this nail, which he had been long cultivating, and which enhanced and at the same time drew attention to the elegance of his finger. The scissors were in his dressing-table drawer and he half rose to get them, but he would have had to pass in front of Lafcadio; with his usual tact he put off the delicate operation till later.

"And what do you mean to do now?" he asked.

"I don't know. Give myself up, perhaps. I shall take the night to think it over."

Julius let his arm drop beside his arm-chair, he gazed at Lafcadio for a moment or two and then in a tone of utter discouragement sighed out:

"And to think that I was beginning to care for you!"

It was said with no unkind intention. Lafcadio could have no doubt of that; but for all their unconsciousness the words were none the less cruel and they struck at his very heart. He raised his head and stiffened himself against the sudden pang of anguish that stabbed him. He looked at Julius. "Did I really feel almost like his brother only yesterday?" thought he. His eyes wandered over the room where such a short time ago he had been able to talk so gaily, in spite of his crime; the scent bottle was still on the table, almost empty. . . .

"Come, Lafcadio," went on Julius, "your situation doesn't seem to me altogether hopeless. The presumed author of the crime . . ."

"Yes, I know; he has been arrested," interrupted Lafcadio dryly. "Are you going to advise me to allow an innocent man to be condemned in my place?"

"Innocent? He has just murdered a woman—you knew her too."

"Very comforting, isn't it?"

"I don't mean that exactly, but . . ."

"You mean he's just the only person who could denounce me."

"There's some hope left still, you see."

Julius got up, walked to the window, straightened the folds of the curtain, came back and then leaning forward with his arms folded on the back of the chair he had just left:

"Lafcadio, I shouldn't like to part from you without a word of advice. It lies entirely with you, I'm convinced, to become an honest man again and to take your place in the world—as far, that is, as your birth permits. . . .

The Church is there to help you. Come, my lad, a little courage; go and confess yourself."

Lafcadio could not suppress a smile.

"I will think over your kind words." He took a step forward and then:

"No doubt you will prefer not to shake hands with a murderer. But I should like to thank you for your . . ."

"Yes, yes," said Julius with a cordial and distant wave of the hand. "Good-bye, my lad. I hardly dare say 'au revoir.' None the less, if later on, you . . ."

"For the present you have nothing further to say to me?"

"Nothing further for the present."

"Good-bye, Monsieur de Baraglioul."

Lafcadio bowed gravely and went out.

He went up to his room on the floor above, half undressed and flung himself on his bed. The end of the day had been very hot and no freshness had come with the night. His window stood wide open but not a breath stirred the air; the electric globes of the Piazza dei Termi, far away on the other side of the garden, shone into his room and filled it with a diffused and bluish light which might have been the moon's. He tried to reflect, but a strange torpor—a despairing numbness—crept over his mind; it was not of his crime that he thought nor of how to escape; the only effort he could make was not to hear those dreadful words of Julius: "I was beginning to care for you." . . . If he himself did not care for Julius, were those words worth his tears? . . . Was that really why he was weeping? . . . The night was so soft that he felt as though he had only to let himself go for death to take him. He reached out for the water bottle by his bed-side, soaked his handkerchief and held it to his heart, which was hurting him

"No drink will ever slake again the thirst of my parched heart," said he, letting the tears course down his face unchecked, so as to taste their bitterness to the full on his lips. A line or two of poetry, read he knew not where and unconsciously remembered, kept singing in his ears:

> "My heart aches and a drowsy numbness pains
> My senses . . ."

He fell into a doze.

Is he dreaming? Or is that a knock at his door? His door, which he always leaves unlocked at night, opens gently and a slender white figure comes in. He hears a faint call:

"Lafcadio! . . . Are you there, Lafcadio?"

And yet, through his half-waking slumber, Lafcadio recognises that voice. Can it be that he doubts the reality of so gracious an apparition? Or does he fear that a word, a movement, may put it to flight? . . . He keeps silent.

Genevieve de Baraglioul, whose room was next-door to her father's, had in spite of herself overheard the whole of the conversation between him and Lafcadio. An intolerable dread had driven her to his room and when her call remained unanswered, fully convinced that Lafcadio had killed himself, she rushed towards the bed and fell sobbing on her knees beside it.

As she knelt there, Lafcadio raised himself and bent over her with his whole being drawn towards her, but not daring as yet to put his lips on the fair forehead he saw gleaming in the darkness. Then Genevieve de Baraglioul felt all her strength dissolve; throwing back her forehead, which Lafcadio's breath was already caressing, and not knowing where to turn for help against him, save to himself alone:

"Dear friend, have pity," she cried.

Lafcadio mastered himself at once; drawing back and at the same time pushing her away:

"Rise, Mademoiselle de Baraglioul," he said. "Leave me! I am not—I cannot be your friend."

Genevieve rose, but she did not move from the side of the bed where Lafcadio, whom she had thought dead, lay half reclining. She tenderly touched his burning forehead, as though to convince herself he was still alive.

"Dear friend," she said, "I overheard everything you said to my father this evening. Don't you understand that that is why I am here?"

Lafcadio half raised himself and looked at her. Her loosened hair fell about her; her whole face was in the shadow so that he could not see her eyes but he felt her look enfold him. As though unable to bear its sweetness, he hid his face in his hands.

"Ah!" he groaned, "why did I meet you so late? What have I done that you should love me? Why do you speak to me so now when I am no longer free and no longer worthy to love you?"

She protested sadly:

"It is to you I have come, Lafcadio—to no one else. To you—a criminal. Lafcadio! How many times have I sighed your name since the first day when you appeared to me like a hero—indeed, you seemed a little overdaring . . . I must tell you now—I made a secret vow to myself that I would be yours, from that very moment when I saw you risk your life so nobly   What has happened since then?   Can you really have killed someone? What have you let yourself become?"

And as Lafcadio shook his head without answering: "Did I not hear my father say that someone else had been arrested—a ruffian, who had just committed a murder? . . . Lafcadio! while there is still time, save yourself! This very night! Go! Go!"

Then Lafcadio:

"Too late!" he murmured.   And as he felt Genevieve's loosened hair on his hands, he caught it, pressed it passionately to his eyes, his lips.   "Flight! Is that really what you counsel me?   But where can I possibly fly? Even if I escaped from the police, I could not escape from myself . . . And, besides, you would despise me for escaping."

"I! Despise you!"

"I lived unconscious; I killed in a dream—a nightmare, in which I have been struggling ever since."

"I will save you from it," she cried.

"What is the use of waking me, if I am to wake a criminal?"   He seized her by the arm: "Can't you understand that the idea of impunity is odious to me? What is there left for me to do—if not to give myself up as soon as it is daybreak?"

"You must give yourself up to God, not to man.   Even if my father had not said it already, I should say so myself now: Lafcadio, the Church is there to prescribe your penance and to help you back to peace through repentance."

Genevieve is right; most certainly the best thing Laf-

cadio can do now is to be conveniently submissive; he
will realise this sooner or later and that every other issue
is closed to him. . . . Vexatious, though, that that milk-
sop of a Julius should have been the first to tell him so.

"Are you repeating that by heart?" said he angrily.
"Can it be you speaking like that?"

He dropped her arm which he had been holding and
pushed it from him; and as Genevieve drew back, there
swelled up in him a blind feeling of resentment against
Julius, a desire to get Genevieve away from her father,
to drag her down, to bring her nearer to himself; as he
lowered his eyes he caught the sight of her bare feet in
their little silk slippers.

"Don't you understand that it's not remorse that I'm
afraid of, but . . ."

He left the bed, turned away from her and went to the
open window; he was stifling; he leant his forehead against
the glass pane and cooled his burning palms on the iron
balustrade; he would have liked to forget that she was
there, that he was near her.

"Mademoiselle de Baraglioul, you have done everything
that a young lady could be expected to do for a criminal
—possibly a little more. I thank you with all my heart.
You had better leave me now. Go back to your father,
your duties, your habits.   .   Good-bye. Who can tell
whether I shall ever see you again? Consider that when
I give myself up to-morrow, it will be to prove myself a
little less unworthy of your affection. Consider that . . .
No, don't come nearer. . . . Do you think that a touch
of your hand would suffice me?"

Genevieve would have braved her father's anger, the

world's opinion and its contempt, but at Lafcadio's icy
tones, her heart fails her. Has he not understood, then,
that to come and speak to him like this at night, to confess her love to him like this, requires courage and resolu-
tion on her part too, and that her love deserves more,
maybe, than a mere "thank you"? . . . But how can she
tell him that she too, up till to-day, has been living and
moving in a dream—a dream from which she escapes
only now and then among her poor children at the hospital, where, binding up their wounds in sober earnest-
ness, she does seem sometimes to be brought into contac'
with a little reality—a petty dream, in which her parents
move beside her, hedged in by all the ludicrous conventions of their world—and that she can never succeed in
taking any of it seriously, either their behaviour or their
opinions, or their ambitions or their principles, or indeed,
their persons themselves? What wonder, then, that Lafcadio had not taken Fleurissoire seriously? Oh! is it
possible that they should part like this? Love drives
her, flings her towards him. Lafcadio seizes her, clasps
her, covers her pale forehead with kisses.

Here begins a new book.
Oh, desire! Oh, palpable and living truth! At your
touch the phantoms of my brain grow dim and vanish.
We will leave our two lovers at cockcrow, at the hour
when colour, warmth and light begin at last to triumph
over night. Lafcadio raises himself from over Genevieve's
sleeping form. But it is not at his love's fair face, nor
her moist brows, nor pearly eyelids, nor warm parted lips,
nor perfect breasts, nor weary limbs—no, it is at none

of all this that he gazes—but through the wide-open window, at the coming of dawn and a tree that rustles in the garden.

It will soon be time for Genevieve to leave him; but still he waits; leaning over her, he listens above her gentle breathing to the vague rumour of the town as it begins to shake off its torpor. From the distant barracks a bugle's call rings out. What! is he going to renounce life? Does he still, for the sake of Genevieve's esteem (and already he esteems her a little less now that she loves him a little more), does he still think of giving himself up?

ALSO BY ANDRÉ GIDE

THE COUNTERFEITERS

Published in 1926, *The Counterfeiters* shocked many with its honest treatment of homosexuality and the collapse of morality in middle-class France. Its three themes—morality, the problems of the literary artist, and the problems of society—are strikingly illuminated as the protagonist, a young artist, pursues a search for knowledge in the relationships of his own adolescent relatives.

Fiction/Literature/0-394-71842-9

IF IT DIE . . .

In this unflinchingly honest autobiography, Gide relays the circumstances of his youth and the birth of his philosophic wandering. Inspired equally by his family's strict Protestant ethic and his passion for the sensual world, Gide fluctuates between acts of indulgence and self-imposed severity. When he finally gratifies his homosexual longings, he neither implores our judgment nor abandons his spiritual love for his young cousin and future wife, Emmanuéle. Gide's exhilarating belief in free thought and his need "to make himself loved" remain irreconcilable in this work of acute insight.

Autobiography/Literature/0-375-72606-3

THE IMMORALIST

First published in 1902 and immediately assailed for its themes of sexual abandon and aestheticism, this groundbreaking work opens the door onto a world of unfettered impulse. Shortly after his wedding, Gide's frail protagonist, Michel, nearly dies of tuberculosis. Nursed back to health by his wife, he is suddenly determined to live unencumbered by God or values. What ensues is a wild flight into the realm of the senses, where Michel's hunger for new experiences bears lethal consequences. *The Immoralist* is a book with the power of an erotic fever dream—lush, prophetic, and eerily seductive.

Fiction/Literature/0-679-74191-7

Printed in the United States
by Baker & Taylor Publisher Services